A WOMAN ALONE
A LON

Not turning he   it
was the same r

   The driver l   e
halfway out the   y
the pickup dri   her lane, crowding her little
car. Her heart pounding, Tory eased up on the
accelerator. But he dropped back with her, keeping
her pinned in the left lane. She couldn't slow down
any more without letting herself be trapped. She tried
edging forward gently, but he stayed right with her,
his front bumper even with hers. Then she heard the
taunting toot-toot-ta-toot of his horn. Really frightened
now, Tory sped up and held the Miata at a steady 70.
The pickup kept pace with her. *Christ, what do I do
now?*

Jove titles by Beverly Hastings

DON'T LOOK BACK
DON'T TALK TO STRANGERS
DON'T WALK HOME ALONE

The massive oak door opened. Framed in it was a plump, comfortable-looking woman who held Melissa's hand in hers. The child looked pale as she clung to the woman, but her eyes lit up when she saw them.

"Tory!" Missy raced out of the house and flung herself into Tory's arms. Gathering her up, Tory buried her face in the little girl's silken hair and then raised her eyes to meet Zack's. With a grave smile, Zack put his arm around Tory's shoulders and the three of them moved toward the house.

DON'T LOOK BACK

BEVERLY HASTINGS

JOVE BOOKS, NEW YORK

To Aldriches × 6 + Nancy Michaelis

DON'T LOOK BACK

A Jove Book / published by arrangement with
the author

PRINTING HISTORY
Jove edition / October 1991

ISBN: 0-515-10685-2

Jove Books are published by The Berkley Publishing Group,
200 Madison Avenue, New York, New York 10016.
The name "JOVE" and the "J" logo
are trademarks belonging to Jove Publications, Inc.

PRINTED IN THE UNITED STATES OF AMERICA

10 9 8 7 6 5 4 3 2 1

Prologue

The man picked up a tiny bud vase that held a stem of miniature roses. He placed it on a tray that was covered with a fancy mat and set with a plate, cup, and saucer. Now he got a butter knife and a spoon out of the drawer and laid them on the tray. Glancing at the stove, he saw that the water hadn't yet boiled. From the refrigerator he took a jar of marmalade and spooned some into a small glass dish.

He dumped four heaping spoonfuls of sugar into the small teapot waiting next to the stove. Then, with a glance over his shoulder, he reached into his pocket and pulled out a small flat metal container. Opening it, he poured the pills into his hand. There were at least twenty of them. These, too, he added to the teapot.

At last the kettle whistled and he poured water into the teapot until it was about half full. Ignoring the steam that rose into his face, he stirred vigorously and then peered into the pot. The sugar and the pills had dissolved.

Now, moving quickly and purposefully, he added tea

to the pot and filled it with water. It held about two cups, which should be plenty. Opening the oven door, he took out a croissant and set it on the plate. He picked up the tray and then put it down again—he'd almost forgotten the napkin. But now everything was ready.

Opening the door of the bedroom, he walked across and set the tray on the bedside table. "Happy birthday, sweetheart," he said.

The young woman in the bed looked up at him. Her tousled hair framed her pretty face, and the man felt an inward sigh of regret. Smiling, she sat up. "What's all this?"

"I let you sleep late," he said. "And I made breakfast in bed for the birthday girl. The tea's extra sweet, just the way you like it."

"Thanks, honey," she said, sounding slightly surprised. "Aren't you having anything?"

He shook his head. "No, but I'll sit with you. Here, let me pour your tea."

Twenty minutes later the teapot was empty, and the man put everything back on the tray. The woman stretched and said, "Oh, it's nice to be so lazy for a change. But I guess I'd better get up and moving."

"No need for that," he told her. "You're always so busy. Why don't you take a morning for yourself and just lounge in bed for a while? I know you wanted to finish that book you're reading."

"Well," she said slowly, and then shrugged. "You talked me into it."

For the first time the man smiled. "Good. I'm not going in to work until later, so I'll be around if you need anything."

He kissed her quickly and handed her the paperback best-seller that lay on the table. Then he picked up the tray. At the door he turned and gazed at her for a moment. She looked very attractive as she leaned back against the pillows, her head bent over the book. It did seem kind of a pity.

In the kitchen he washed all the dishes and put everything away. Then he walked into the living room and sat down at his desk. His watch said 9:30. It would be interesting to see how long it would take.

At 11:30 the man returned to the bedroom. His wife lay slumped against the pillows, her book on the floor. Calmly he reached for her wrist and held it for a moment. Satisfied, he walked into the bathroom. Using his handkerchief, he took an empty plastic pill vial out of the medicine cabinet. At the bedside, he carefully pushed the vial under his wife's pillows. Then he picked up the telephone. Time to call the police.

Chapter 1

Tory strained to hear Tim Phelps's voice over the din of the party around them. Why did all show biz people seem to think that the level of their importance directly correlated with how loud they could yell "darling!" across the room? Finally Tim gave up and grabbed her hand, pulling her through the crowd gathered around one of the tables piled high with food.

Chasen's, of course, was famous for its chili, but there were lots of other foods to choose from. Tim thrust a plate loaded with cracked crab and caviar into Tory's hand and then scooped up a bunch of oysters on the half shell for himself. Stopping a passing waiter, he took a couple of glasses of champagne from the tray and then led Tory toward a small table in the corner.

Tory looked around the glass-enclosed back room that had been added to the famous restaurant a few years before. Chasen's had been a Hollywood legend for more than half a century, and Tory had been thrilled when she'd been taken there for dinner to celebrate the sale of her first film script. But it was definitely beyond her price range except on very special occasions. Popping another pumpernickel round topped with caviar into her mouth, Tory thought of the many other movie industry gatherings this venerable establishment had hosted.

Tonight was certainly no ordinary wrap party. Usually the celebration of wrapping up the shooting of a movie was a jeans-and-sneakers, beer-and-pretzels get-together for the cast and crew who had worked on the film. But this party was a far dressier affair, marking the completion of a well-known director's tenth film, *Midnight Mission*. Tim worked at the agency that represented both the director and the film's leading lady, and he and his fellow agents were here in force.

Surveying the milling crowd, Tory recognized two other famous directors and an elegant older actor whose face was known to millions. Clearly a lot of people had been invited besides cast, crew, and agents, and they all seemed to be having a wonderful time.

A short, wiry guy with glasses materialized out of the crowd in front of them. "Hi, Tim," he said with a grin. "Some kind of party, huh?"

Tim clapped him on the shoulder. "Hey, Jerry, good to see you. Do you know Tory Ryan? Tory, this is Jerry Schwartz."

"Oh, it's great to meet you," Tory said as she shook the hand he offered. "I really loved *Watcher in the Dark*. In fact, I saw it twice."

"Tory's a screenwriter, too," Tim informed Jerry. He slid his arm around Tory's waist and gave her a squeeze. "I keep trying to talk her into signing with me, but so far she's resisted."

"Well, Tim Phelps is the best there is, in my book," Jerry said earnestly. "He's done wonders for my career. And when I think about some of the other agents in this town, I really feel fortunate.''

"Wow, that's some testimonial," Tory said lightly. "And totally unsolicited. Tim, you'd better get that in writing," she teased.

Jerry turned to greet the pretty young blonde who'd sidled up next to him as Tory and Tim moved out into the room. Suddenly Angus McFarland, the producer of *Midnight Mission*, reached out and caught Tim's arm. "Who's the pretty little lady?" He grinned wolfishly at Tory and went on, "You two certainly make a great-looking couple. If you ever get tired of this guy, honey, just give old Angus a call.''

Angus had obviously been celebrating a little too much—his words were slurred, and as he launched into a long dirty joke, his train of thought was difficult to follow. But Tim had a marvelous way of looking totally absorbed. He really was a good agent, Tory thought. At one time she'd seriously considered signing with him. Then she'd realized it was a poor idea. Tim was a pal, and mixing business with friendship often led to problems. Also, she'd wondered lately whether Tim's interest in her was more than just friendly. She hoped not, because she didn't feel the least bit romantic about him. Besides, at the moment she was involved with someone else.

Better to keep things uncomplicated, she thought. Her own "small-time" agents kept her busy enough, and she would never owe them more than the ten percent they earned. She was better off for now, being a big fish in their little pond; they worked hard at finding her writing assignments. She guessed Tim had already figured out the situation for himself, since he had pretty much given up nagging her to leave her agents and sign with him.

Half an hour later the party was still going strong. Tim had introduced Tory to several of his clients and a number of other people in the business. Amazingly, one of them turned out to be the wife of the man who was to interview her the next day. As they left the party, Tim laughed and told Tory, "There really are only five hundred people in the whole world. You just keep running into them over and over."

In the alley behind Tory's run-down Venice beach house, Tim got out of the car and came around to open Tory's door. She stood up and gave him a quick kiss on the cheek. "Thanks, Tim. That was a lot of fun. You're so nice to take me along to these power bashes. What would I do without a friend like you?" Ignoring his resigned look, she checked her watch. "Wow, it's late! I've got to get to sleep or I'll be totally out of it tomorrow for my interview."

Accepting disappointment gracefully, Tim said with a smile, "Well, I wouldn't want that to happen. I'll call you tomorrow and see how it went."

"Great. Thanks again, Tim. Good night." With a wave, Tory turned and walked up the path to her door. This slightly awkward conclusion to an evening with Tim was a scene the two of them had played before. She wondered how long they would be able to play it without rewriting the ending.

As she struggled to get the key in the lock, Tory glanced around a little nervously, then cursed silently as she caught herself doing it. She was the one who had insisted on living in the shabby old two-story house. For the same money she could have rented a shiny modern apartment in Westwood. But she loved being able to walk out her front door barefoot and saunter down the block to the beach whenever she felt like it. She didn't like elevators, and she hated bathrooms with no windows. She couldn't afford any of the higher-priced beach communities, so she had happily settled for this one. Hovering at the edge of a ghetto and suffering under a soaring crime rate, it was expensively seedy, but it was home.

Light crept out from under the shades upstairs. Bill and Marcia, the high school science teacher and his wife who lived on the second floor, were away on a trip and had left a light timer on to ward off burglary attempts. All was quiet up there. And the light in Tory's living room glowed faintly all the way to the back door.

She banged into the house, carefully double-locking the door behind her, and switched on the kitchen light. She turned on the gas under the pot of coffee left over from that morning. Kicking off her shoes and unbuttoning her silk shirt, she headed for the bedroom.

"Hi, beautiful, welcome home." A tall blond man was half lying, half sitting on her bed paging through her latest script.

Tory screamed and clutched her blouse closed. Her heart was pounding, and for a moment she felt she couldn't breathe. Then she registered who he was. "Oh, my God! Michael, you scared me half to death! What are you doing here?"

Without bothering to reply he slowly stood and moved toward her. He leaned over and nibbled at her neck, his hands tugging at the blouse she still held tightly closed. He obviously expected her to melt in his arms, but he'd misjudged her reaction. The fright he'd given her had turned to cold fury. She pushed him aside and strode back into the kitchen.

"The coffee's boiling."

"Tory, I'm sorry I frightened you. I thought you'd be glad to see me. Forget the coffee. Let's go to Ziggy's and get some ham and eggs. I'm starving."

"Well, I'm not."

"Don't tell me Mr. Hollywood Show Biz finally took you someplace where you got something to eat!" Michael tried for a light sarcastic touch, but the underlying bitterness showed through. And Tory was quick to pounce on it.

"At least Mr. Hollywood Show Biz takes me *someplace*. He's not forever fooling around with his rats and pigeons and weirdo experiments, like some people I know."

She saw his impatient expression and knew what he was thinking. He'd explained it to her a million times. Doing experiments was what an experimental psychologist did. And he had to let his subjects set the pace. Rats and especially humans never ran exactly according to schedule. They had to have a certain amount of freedom within the structure of the experiment so he could observe their natural reactions. The purpose of his government grant was to study responses to various kinds of environmental stress. It was important work; he hoped to discover some of the ways in which normal people were pushed into behavior that was labeled crazy.

Michael accepted the cup of coffee she handed him without comment. The silence lengthened, and then she blurted out, "I'm sorry, Michael. I'm tired and I've got a heavy day tomorrow."

He carefully put down the coffee cup and pulled her to him. He kissed her—her mouth, her eyes, her throat. His strong hands slid down her back, pushing the length of her body into him. He whispered in her ear, "I'm sorry, too, sweetheart. You know I think about you all the time."

Oh, Michael, I think about you, too, she thought. But why did he have to spend so much time in that lab, implanting tiny electrodes into pea-sized rat brains? He'd be preoccupied for days on end, leaving her to her own devices, to find her own companionship, and then suddenly show up so warm and tender and wanting.

Tory fought the battle seething within her. She wanted him. But not tonight. No, not tonight. She really did have a rough day coming up, and it was already after midnight. Besides, he had to learn that she wasn't at his beck and call. If he wanted to see her, he'd have to plan ahead; he'd have to give her the same consideration he gave his precious work.

"Michael, it's late." It came out as a throaty whisper. Her own body was fighting her, giving her away.

His hands lightly caressed her. "Sure, honey, anything you say."

Well, forget it. She'd tried. "I'll just ring my service first."

The high-pitched nasal twang of the switchboard operator at Tory's answering service carried to the farthest corners of the room. That voice could wake anyone up. Maybe that was why she always worked the night shift. An emergency call from Mr. Julie Kingman in Yuma. She gave Tory the number at the motel. "Call back no matter what time you get in." Tory sighed. Couldn't she just pretend she hadn't gotten the message? "Up to you, honey," said twangy-voice and rang off.

Julie bellowed like a foghorn when she finally reached him. She'd had no doubt he'd be in his room, alone and fast asleep. Julie was a businesslike movie producer, and any starlets trying to screw their way to the top had better be in and out by 10:00 P.M. so he could be bright-eyed and ready to go in the morning. He'd come a long way in a few years, producing big money-makers out of material no one else thought would earn a dime. And when he said he wanted her to call no matter what time, he meant it.

Julie didn't waste time asking why she was out so late or wondering what he was interrupting.

"Get your ass down here right away, baby. We got problems. We got the morgue scene shot and the whole bit, and now the stupid broad who's playing the waitress breaks her arm!"

"I'm sure she didn't do it on purpose, Julie."

"Huh? Yeah, yeah. Well, we gotta come up with something else. I don't wanta reshoot. Get what I mean? So you're a smart girl. Rework that murder scene so we can use someone else." He paused, apparently waiting for her to come up with an immediate solution. Then: "Well?"

Tory had to laugh. Julie was no different from most other producers, or directors for that matter. He thought the typewriter or computer was the key to writing a script. All the writer had to do was turn it on and the magic words would pour out.

"I'll try to come up with something. I'm sure it will work out," Tory told him.

"Yeah? Well, just don't take too much time with the thinking part. I need those scenes right away. There's some little feeder plane service into here. I'll roust someone and get you on the first flight out."

"Julie! I can't! I've got a really important interview tomorrow afternoon. Can't it wait a couple of days?"

Julie struggled with what was left of his conscience. "Look, kid. I don't wanta screw up your life. We'll do some pickup shots tomorrow. But you gotta be here tomorrow night. That new stuff's gotta be shot the day after—no later, got me? Remember, kid, you're workin' for me. And I want you *here*!"

"Right, Julie. I'll leave right after my interview and dictate something on my way down. But I'm not trusting myself to some Freddie Fly-by-Night. I'll drive my own car. Then I'll be sure of getting back."

"That's a girl. Knew I could count on you. And I'll make it worth your while." He hung up, and she was sure he was instantly asleep.

Tory groaned as she cradled the phone. She'd better be able to come up with this magical solution that she'd so readily promised. It was always easy to say the job could be done, but doing it was another thing. Already she could feel the first twinges of the writer's familiar demon: Did she lack the imagination to make this work?

She turned to Michael. "Well, you got the gist of that."

"You're not really going down to Yuma?"

Tory looked at him in surprise. "Of course I'm going. It's my job." She gave him a playful grin. "And that means it's time for me to say good night."

The flash of anger in Michael's eyes was gone almost before Tory noticed it. He bent to kiss her. "Well, have fun. Let me know when you get back."

Tory locked the back door behind him. Funny, she thought. Michael likes the idea that I'm an independent woman with a career of my own, but he also likes everything to revolve around his schedule.

As she hung up her clothes and wondered what she should wear to her interview the next day, the other part of Tory's mind was still focused on Michael. His daughter Melissa's life was also controlled by Michael's schedule. The little girl spent an awful lot of time in the care of Michael's neighbor and baby-sitter, Ellen Green. Of course, it was lucky for Michael that he'd found Ellen. She was home all day with her three young children anyway, and Tory imagined that Ellen and Dan could use the extra income. And Ellen obviously loved Melissa and provided the child with a pretty good substitute family.

But when Michael worked late, Melissa either spent the whole night at Ellen's or was carried home half awake far past her bedtime. Michael insisted that his daughter was extremely mature for a five-year-old and coped beautifully with this erratic arrangement. Still, Tory couldn't help feeling that the little girl needed more consistent contact with her dad.

Yawning, she climbed into bed. Well, it wasn't up to her to tell Michael how to raise his child. But Tory was a little surprised to realize how much she cared.

The next morning as Tory made a pot of coffee, she thought wryly that whoever said people should let their minds solve their problems while they slept must have a different kind of mind from hers. She didn't have a single constructive idea about how to fix the script that was being shot in Yuma. She didn't even remember exactly which version of the script was the final one— she'd written it months before and had barely thought about it since the last rewrite.

With determination she rooted through her file drawer and pulled out the thick sheaf of papers. When she located the final shooting script and her untidy collection of notes, she set the rest of the papers on the floor and settled down at the kitchen table.

Three hours later Tory sat back with a sigh. Rewrites were the worst! She'd thought up at least five promising ways to fix this story, only to discover that some other element in the plot made them unworkable. Why had she written such a complicated story line? She'd know better the next time—keep it simple. If there was a next time.

She looked up at the clock and then leapt to her feet. She'd better get moving, or she'd be late for that interview. Zooming into the bedroom, Tory flung her robe on the bed and dashed into the bathroom to turn on the shower. As she soaped herself energetically, the script kept running through her mind. And suddenly there it was—the neat solution she'd been searching for. Hurriedly rinsing the shampoo out of her hair, Tory stepped out of the shower and wrapped herself in a towel. She knew from bitter experience that if she didn't write down at least a rough outline of her idea, it would fade away and she'd never recapture it.

In the kitchen, she dripped all over the yellow pad as she jotted down a skeleton of the new scene she planned to write. It would work—she was sure of it.

Feeling much more cheerful, she returned to the bathroom and finished drying herself. Switching on the hair dryer, Tory decided it would make a lot of sense to pack now. Then she could get right on the freeway after the interview and save some time. Let's see, she thought, I'd better take my tape recorder—I hope I have a blank tape. And I wonder what kind of clothes I'll need.

The interview took longer and the rush-hour crush was heavier than Tory had expected. The sun was setting over the ocean as she cleared the last of Los Angeles's sprawl to the south. Approaching San Juan

Capistrano, she decided to get off the highway now and grab something to eat. Then she wouldn't have to deal with the congested areas farther south. At the next exit she steered her white Miata up the exit ramp and pulled into the crowded parking lot of the nearest fast-food emporium. After a somewhat rushed meal—what did it matter, it all tasted like plastic-coated cardboard anyway—she got back in her car and headed out. Her auto club map showed that the best and fastest route was to go south to San Diego and then turn east to Yuma.

After the lights of San Diego, Interstate 8 was a dark and lonely strip of white-lined asphalt. But even if there had been more traffic, Tory would have noticed the arrogantly driven red pickup truck easing up beside her once again. Pacing her little convertible for a few moments, the grinning young man behind the wheel gave her a long, caressing look. She clutched the steering wheel and avoided his stare, her profile rigid with fear. The driver of the pickup smirked as he gunned his engine and swooped smack in front of her.

Tory exhaled slowly, still gripping the wheel with both hands. She'd written scenes like this in scripts, and she'd been pleased when people thought they were scary. But it wasn't so much fun in real life. Nervously she checked the doors, making sure they were locked. Then she glanced up at the roof of her car. That thin skin of canvas wouldn't keep anybody out if he really wanted in. Well, she just wouldn't be stopped; she wouldn't let herself get trapped.

Slowly her eyes focused on the road again. The pickup had all but disappeared, leaving two dim glowing red dots way up ahead as visual reminders of her fear. Tory sighed with relief and pushed herself back against the seat, trying to ease the tension in her shoulders. Living in L.A., she'd encountered her fair share of freeway weirdos, but incidents like this one were a lot more threatening out here by herself in the dark of night.

Then she shook her head impatiently. It's over, she told herself. Just forget it. Get your mind on something constructive, like the new scene that has to be ready in the morning. She'd better start dictating it now before she forgot the details. It had really been stupid to leave the outline at home on the kitchen table—she could see the yellow pad in her mind's eye, right there next to her coffee cup. But she'd been in such a hurry to pack and get to her interview.

Tory took a moment to gather her thoughts. Movie scripts were written in a very definite format, with the first line of each scene telling where and when the action was taking place. In addition, camera directions were often included in the script. It wasn't enough just to describe the action and make up the dialogue. Tory had had to learn a lot of new terms when she first started writing for the movies. "Cut to," "intercut," "pan," "angle on," and numerous other phrases were now part of her everyday working vocabulary. And then there were the abbreviations, like ECU for "extreme close-up" and POV for "point of view." She was still surprised at how quickly she'd learned this new language—but whatever language she used, she still had to write the new scene. With a rueful grin, she picked up the microphone of the cassette tape recorder beside her and switched it on to record.

"Interior, bar, night. Pan the audience, all male with the usual assortment of old cowboy types, young studs, couple of Indians. Close on stripper doing her act on tiny stage runway. Intercut various angles on stripper with ECUs of men's expressions as she does her finale. Cut to backstage. The stripper, as naked as we can get away with . . .''

Tory switched off the mike and stopped to think a moment. That last sentence wasn't what she wanted. Her hands mechanically guided the car as her mind focused on the method of killing off her victim. She smiled to herself as she grabbed the mike and continued.

''Forget that. Angle on stripper backing off stage with edge of backdrop in b.g. Behind the backdrop someone is holding open a gaudy dressing gown for her. Note: Camera angles for murder set up so killer remains unidentifiable. Stripper's attention still on audience as she backs toward open gown. She expects it to be there as usual. But gown is held too high. She struggles into it, then whirls around to face unseen killer. Dialogue stripper. 'Who the hell are you? Where's Jack?' End dialogue. Killer's hand slashes out with knife. Kills her. Pull back to see stripper's body on floor. Killer grabs knife and flees.''

Tory clicked off the mike and arched her back, wondering if she was halfway to Yuma yet. She stifled a yawn as an elevation sign flashed past. It seemed strange to be moving across the mountains to get back to sea level on the other side. She had left the ruler-straight freeway behind and was winding and climbing up toward the Tecate Summit.

Zooming around a curve, her white Miata pulled out to pass a dawdling pickup in the right lane. As she drew even, Tory heard the change in pitch as the pickup accelerated. She got that familiar sinking feeling—another macho creep who couldn't stand to be passed by a woman driver. Not turning her head, she glanced across—it was the same red pickup.

The driver leered at Tory, his sharp-featured face halfway out the window, waiting for her to react. Slowly the pickup drifted into her lane, crowding her little car. Her heart pounding, she eased up on the accelerator. But he dropped back with her, keeping her pinned in the left lane. She couldn't slow down any more without letting herself be trapped. She tried edging forward gently, but he stayed right with her, his front bumper even with hers. Then she heard the taunting toot-toot-ta-toot of his horn. Really frightened now, she sped up and held the Miata at a steady seventy. The pickup kept pace with her. Christ, what do I do now?

Tory checked the rearview mirror for the welcome gleam of headlights. But behind her the road was dark and deserted. She stole another look at the man beside her. The moonlight slanting across the windshield caught his mocking eyes as his mouth opened in a soundless laugh. On the flat she could have outrun him, but on the unfamiliar mountain highway, she had to brake for every curve.

They raced along side by side through the barren landscape. Tory and her opponent seemed alone on an empty planet. Rushing wind swept away all sound, and the strange rocky shadows added to her sense of unreality.

The green and white sign overhead said ''Alpine 2 miles.'' Tory shook off the frozen trance of fear. Thank God, she thought, a town, and people. She had to take that exit.

She realized she was pushing down harder on the accelerator—the road was climbing more steeply now.

Cautiously she let up on the pedal. She didn't dare risk a glance as the needle dropped to fifty-five, but she sensed the pickup slowing along with her.

"Alpine ¼ mile." Tory took a deep breath and gripped the steering wheel even tighter. It was now or never. "Okay, car," she murmured, "let's do it."

As she floored the accelerator, the Miata leapt forward, responding instantly with surprising power. The pickup's engine roared in belated reaction. Tory swung the wheel hard right, slicing across just under the pickup's nose, and careened down the exit ramp. A braking skid through the stop sign, and she was on the darkened streets of the small mountain town.

The old highway ran parallel to Interstate 8. Still shaking, Tory drove toward the lights up ahead. Nervously she watched her rearview mirror for any sign of the red pickup, though she felt certain he must have missed the exit. The street behind her was deserted.

A flashing neon light shaped like a flower welcomed her to the Edelweiss Bar and Grill. Tory pulled into the parking lot and looked around. The grocery-deli and the coffee shop across the road were both closed for the night. She was glad this place was open; she needed the sight and sound of normal people.

The twang of an old Johnny Cash tune greeted Tory as she opened the door of the restaurant. The jukebox was turned up loud, filling the place with music. Tory stopped and looked around uncertainly. After a moment she caught the eye of a lone waitress resetting the empty tables.

"Sorry, this here section's closed," she called to Tory.

"I just want a cup of coffee."

"You can get some in there." The waitress gestured with a fork toward the dimly lit bar.

Only a few of the scattered tables were occupied. At the far end of the room three young men in Levi's took turns at bumper pool; in front of the jukebox two older couples danced a neat fox-trot. The bartender was deep in conversation with the bar's sole patron, a weather-beaten balding man working on a double martini. As Tory chose a stool halfway down the bar, the bartender looked up. "What'll it be, miss?"

"Just a cup of coffee, please," she said apologetically.

He nodded. "Gimme a coffee, Doris," he yelled toward the kitchen.

Tory propped her elbows on the bar and let the welcome sounds of normalcy wash over her. Scraps of conversation carried over the noise of the jukebox: "So then I told him I wasn't putting up with any bull, and he had the nerve to say . . ."

A woman's high-pitched giggle floated across, punctuating her friend's story. "Oh, Gladys, you didn't! You're too much!"

Staring into space, Tory was startled by a voice almost in her ear. "What're you thinking about so hard?" A muscular young man in T-shirt and jeans leaned between the barstools, much too close to Tory. His forearm rested on the bar, giving her a good look at the tattoo just above his wrist: a snake, coiled and ready to strike.

She felt her skin crawl. Holding herself rigid and hoping he couldn't sense the effect he was having on her, Tory stared into her coffee cup. If she ignored him, maybe he'd go away. But he persisted. "Haven't seen you before. You new in town or just passing through?'' His insolent tone made the innocuous words sound menacing.

Tory picked up her coffee cup and sipped, scalding her tongue.

''Didn't you hear me? I asked you a question.'' He sounded hostile now.

''Just passing through,'' she said noncommittally.

''Oh, how about that? She can talk.'' He settled onto the barstool next to hers. ''Where you going, honey?''

Tory stood up. With shaking hands she pulled a dollar from her wallet and slid it under the cup. His voice followed her across the room. ''Too much of a good thing for you? How 'bout if I show you how to loosen up and have some fun?''

Forcing herself to walk at a normal pace, Tory left the bar. Surely he wasn't going to follow her outside. With a quick glance over her shoulder, she crossed the parking lot toward her car. As she fished in her purse for her keys, she looked back once more. Framed in the bar's open doorway was the man with the tattoo.

Tory felt a trickle of fear down her spine. Staring back at him under the flickering neon lights, she was immobilized by the invisible thread of tension stretched between them. If she got into her car and drove away, would he follow her? She hung suspended in indecision.

Just as Tory felt she might scream, a laughing group pushed past him and emerged from the Edelweiss. The fox-trotting couples were calling it a night. They glanced curiously toward Tory as they jingled their car keys and called loud good nights. The tattooed man stared at Tory for another long moment, then turned and vanished inside the bar.

Tory jumped into her car and roared out of the parking lot. A few moments later she was back on Interstate 8 heading east. Her hands on the steering wheel were still trembling a little, and her whole body felt stiff, unable to relax. What was going on? First the guy in the red pickup, and then the creep in the bar. She wondered if maybe she should stop writing such scary movies. Maybe all the violence and lurking terror in her scripts was setting up an aura around her that attracted menace in real life.

Don't be stupid, she told herself. Next you'll be seeing ghosts. But she had to admit that she'd been really frightened by the two incidents occurring so close together. And somehow, having things like this happen just as she'd been gleefully killing off the pathetic stripper in her script was more than a little unsettling.

A road sign proclaimed the Tecate Summit, and the wide and well-surfaced highway became a rapid series of steep switchback curves down the other side. Tory's concentration on the road seemed to push her earlier fears out of her mind for the moment. A profusion of signs warned truckers to use low gear and pointed the way to runaway vehicle ramps. How many drivers had lost control and turned desperately up those shallow slopes that ended in piles of sand and slag? Even in the Miata it was a hair-raising descent.

When she reached the desert floor, Tory felt the change in temperature. Lowering her own window, she reached over and wound down the passenger window to let the warm desert air rush through the car. Then she settled back for the long drive still ahead of her. The road unrolled straight as a die through the sand and tumbleweeds.

What would she find when she got to Yuma? Even though she'd grumbled when Julie asked her to rush down there, she was really looking forward to being on location and watching them shoot the film she'd written. Usually they kept the writers as far away from the filming as possible. Tory reran the new scene in her mind. Yes, it would work. And the film production team would like it. Especially Julie. Now he wouldn't have to reshoot anything. He wouldn't even have to cast another part; Tory was especially pleased with her ingenuity about that. The actress playing the stripper's bit part was surely good enough to carry a little more, and she would be delighted at the prospect of a larger role. Julie no doubt had the girl locked into a contract so she wouldn't get an extra cent for playing a bigger part, but maybe she'd get billing, or even a "featuring" credit. Julie was always generous about things like that—as long as they didn't cost anything.

In any event, it wouldn't hurt Tory's own career to be known as a cooperative writer. Julie might be doing B pictures now, but who knew what he'd be up to next year?

A small tumbleweed bounced across her windshield and off onto the sand. A sign announcing "El Centro 2 miles" flashed by. Turning on the car's interior light, Tory took a quick look at her map—about another hour and she'd be there.

At last the lights of Yuma, which had been just a glow on the horizon, came into focus as Tory raced toward the town. The sidewalks weren't exactly rolled up, but it was immediately apparent that exciting nightlife wasn't plentiful in Yuma—if there was any nightlife at all.

Tory laughed at herself. What had she said in her

interview today—that she felt writing was an adventure? Well, this is it, kid. Adventure City. She thought back over the meeting. She'd felt good about it, and the producer had seemed enthusiastic. But like everything else in show business, it would be "hurry up and wait." No point in wondering "what if." Her agent had her Yuma number. Agonizing wouldn't help.

Leaving the highway, Tory found the motel loop. She passed the usual collection of identical chain motels with their pretentious names. At last she reached the Wagon Wheel Inn.

Tory parked the Miata near the entrance and got out, already anticipating clean sheets and a hot shower. The clock over the reception desk said a few minutes to midnight as Tory stifled a yawn and signed in. She asked for a large envelope and a piece of paper. Standing at one end of the long desk she organized her thoughts, knowing that when she next sat down she'd be asleep.

She popped the little cassette out of her tape recorder and slid it into the envelope. Then across the paper she scrawled, "Julie, here's the new scene. Can someone type it up? It's ready to shoot." She stuffed the paper into the envelope, sealed it, and printed Julie Kingman's name on the front. "Please be sure Mr. Kingman gets this first thing in the morning." Handing the envelope to the sleepy-eyed night clerk, Tory headed for her room.

Chapter 2

Penny Seriale listened to the next section of the tape coming through the earphone, then clicked off the machine and typed on. There was no doubt she was a fast typist. The ball of the rented IBM raced across the paper: ''The stripper, as naked as we can get away with, forget that angle on stripper backing—''

It didn't look right. Penny didn't know much about movie scripts, but this just didn't make sense. Something was wrong.

She looked over at Julie Kingman. He was sitting on the edge of the motel bed with his back to her, one thick-fingered hand rumpling his thinning hair as he growled into the phone. Penny was a little afraid of him; maybe she'd just wait till he finished his call.

Turning off the typewriter, Penny looked over what she'd typed so far. Good thing she had the script to work from or she'd never know what to put where. This whole movie business was a lot more confusing than she'd expected, and it certainly wasn't very glamorous. She'd been really excited when the office temp agency

told her she'd be working for a film company on location. But she'd been stuck in this office by herself the
whole time and had never seen any filming. And when
she did see movie people, all they did was yell at her.
Penny sighed and gazed out the window at the motel's
swimming pool. At least she could take a quick dip at
lunchtime.

Julie slammed down the phone. "That jerk—does he
think I woulda hired him if I wanted to do his job
myself?" He turned and looked expectantly at Penny's
silent typewriter. "All done? Good, let's take a look at
it." He held out his hand for the pages.

"Well, um, no, Mr. Kingman, I have a little more
to do—"

"What is this, your coffee break? You in a union,
too?"

Penny stumbled a little over her words. "No, Mr.
Kingman, I—well, I didn't want to interrupt you, but
this part doesn't make sense. There's something
wrong."

"That's not your problem!" Penny flinched as his
voice rose. "Just type what's on the goddamn tape!"

The door opened. "Morning, Julie. How does it
look?"

Tory stood in the open doorway and surveyed the
production office. It was the corner guest room of the
motel's first floor. One bed had been taken out, and
the space was filled up with a desk for the typist and
various tables heaped with papers. A desktop copier
had supplanted the TV, and the mirror was covered
with taped-up schedules, lists of phone numbers, and
important reminders. On the inside of the plate-glass
window was a map of the area; that day's production
schedule was taped to the glass facing outward.

"Aw, Christ, she's not done typing it yet. See if you can straighten out her problem."

Tory smiled sympathetically at Penny as she moved to look over her shoulder. "Oh, I see." She laughed. "When I said 'forget that,' I meant get rid of the whole first part of the sentence. Just cross out everything up to 'angle on stripper' and start a new line with those words in caps."

Penny nodded and switched on the typewriter. Over the clatter, Julie said to Tory, "Come on, we'll grab a cup of coffee. My treat."

"Good, I haven't had breakfast yet."

Going out the door, Julie turned back to Penny. "When you're done, make ten copies and bring them to us in the coffee shop."

Just the short walk to the other building was enough to make Tory appreciate the air-conditioned cool of the coffee shop. Sipping her orange juice, she settled back and listened to Julie's troubles.

"Honest to God, kid, you wouldn't believe this broad, Debra. Thinks she's a combo of Marilyn Monroe and Katharine Hepburn."

"Difficult, huh?"

"You ain't kiddin'. And that's not even the word for it. She'd got that dumb little Artie pantin' after her like she's a bitch in heat—I guess you never met my sister's kid. Why I have to teach him this business I don't know. Anyway, she's driving everyone crazy and fucking up— pardon my French—fucking up the production schedule like you wouldn't believe." He took an enormous slurp of coffee. "Now of course Kevin says he can't work with her. And John just pussyfoots around. He's got the idea she needs something better than a good slap on her cute little butt. Meanwhile I'm watching money go down the drain. If I bring this turkey in on budget it'll be a minor miracle.''

''Poor Julie.'' Tory was careful to keep her amusement from showing. Julie always had something to moan about. Now he sighed heavily.

''Shoulda had my head examined when I hired her as the lead.''

He looked up as Penny approached their booth. ''Here they are, Mr. Kingman, all ten copies.''

''Okay, kid. I'm going out to the location now. I'll be back at lunchtime. If Ed Prince calls from L.A., be sure to get a number where he'll be.''

Tory took the sheaf of pages. ''Julie, maybe I'd better look through these quickly.''

Maneuvering his heavy, compact frame out of the booth, Julie signaled for the check. ''Yeah. You can ride out there with me, read them to me in the car.''

Slouched in the comfortable front seat of the big rental car, Tory put on her sunglasses and began reading aloud.

    60 INT. BAR—NIGHT
      PAN the audience, all male with the usual
      assortment of old cowboy types, young
      studs, a couple of Indians.
    61 CLOTHES ON STRIPPER

Tory broke off and laughed as she scrabbled for a pencil in her bag.

''What's so funny?''

''Oh, she typed 'clothes on' instead of 'close on,' and it's about the stripper,'' Tory explained. ''It just looks funny on the page.''

She felt a quick pang of sympathy for Penny. It must

be hard for an inexperienced girl to translate the odd
movie lingo, especially from a tape. She realized that
her own mind had automatically interpreted "INT." as
"interior" as her eyes scanned the page.

As soon as she'd made the correction on all ten copies, she continued reading the new scene aloud to Julie.

61 CLOSE ON STRIPPER
    doing her act on tiny stage runway.
62 INTERCUT
    various angles on stripper with ECUs of
    men's expressions as she does her finale.

                    CUT TO:

63 BACKSTAGE
    ANGLE ON STRIPPER
    backing off stage with edge of backdrop in
    b.g. Behind the backdrop someone is hold-
    ing open a gaudy dressing gown for her.
    Note: Camera angles for murder set up so
    killer remains unidentifiable.
    Stripper's attention still on audience as she
    backs toward open gown. She expects it to
    be there as usual. But gown is held too high.
    She struggles into it, then whirls around to
    face unseen killer.

                   STRIPPER
    Who the hell are you? Where's Jack?

    Killer's hand slashes out with knife. Kills
    her.

PULL BACK
to see stripper's body on floor. Killer grabs
knife and flees.

Tory finished reading and looked across at Julie expectantly. "That's it, Julie. What do you think?"

"Sounds good. It'll work great." Julie's voice boomed enthusiastically. "I knew I could count on you, kid." He flashed Tory a smile. "Of course we're gonna need a new location. The one we've got lined up won't work for that backstage stuff. Good thing we haven't shot the stripper yet."

Julie turned left off what seemed to be the main drag and tooled along Sixteenth Street, past small houses interspersed with new-looking apartment complexes. Tory gazed around with interest.

"I always wonder how you guys find locations to fit the stuff I write. It'll really be a treat to see some actual shooting. What are they doing today?"

"They should be winding up that street scene in front of Jean Anne's apartment. Then they'll do some pickup shots—the local market, some street stuff—before they break for lunch. Nothing this afternoon; we'll do this new scene of yours late tonight."

"You're going to try to shoot it tonight? Things are moving right along."

Julie looked surprised. "Sure, why not? We were gonna do the original stripper scene tonight anyway. All she has to do different is die on camera."

Tory laughed. "Aren't you lucky I didn't write in more than one line of dialogue?"

He laughed, too, as he waved at the uniformed cop and pulled up behind the equipment truck parked at the curb. "Yeah. With any luck at all, we'll be out of this hotbox this time next week."

Tory got out of the car and narrowly avoided tripping over the tangle of cables strewn across the sidewalk. Just up the block was a nondescript white stucco apartment building; its row of green doors would look fine on film. Knots of people stood around looking sweaty and irritable. If this was late spring in Yuma, what could the summer be like, Tory wondered. A group of spectators clustered across the street, among them two little boys struggling to control a small but eager terrier.

The camera crew was just finishing another runthrough. Tory heard some incomprehensible muttering about problems with the focus change as they trundled the camera dolly along the planks laid in the street.

Taking the copies of the new scene from Tory, Julie tucked them under his arm and bellowed, "Artie!"

His curly-headed, bespectacled nephew trotted up. "Yes?"

"We need a new location for tonight." He thrust some pages at Artie. "As soon as you've got it set, tell Penny to fix the production schedule."

"Tonight? You want to shoot it tonight?"

"Yeah, so get moving." Julie turned to Tory. "Why don't you run this copy over to the script girl and make sure she plugs it in the right place?"

He moved off toward a tall man who was watching the camera crew as they got into position. Tory recognized John Hartnell's spare figure and his longish graying hair; as director of the film, he'd attended a couple of the story conferences in Julie's office back in L.A. As John turned to greet Julie, one of the cameramen called, "Okay, Mr. Hartnell, we're ready."

A short, intense-looking young man immediately sprang into action. He strode purposefully along the sidewalk, calling, "Places, everybody. This is going to be a take. Quiet on the set!"

John turned toward the equipment truck. "Debra? We're ready for you, sweetheart. Let's try for a real winner this time."

A sulky-looking blonde glared at John from her chair in the shade cast by the truck. With an exaggerated sigh, she put on her high-heeled backless sandals, then stood and walked slowly into the sun.

Tory walked over to the script girl's umbrella-shaded chair. "Girl" was sort of a misnomer. The fair-skinned redhead was a well-preserved fifty, dressed in a no-nonsense outfit of walking shorts, tank top, and flip-flops. She was recapping the bottle of sunscreen she'd been slathering on her legs.

"Hi, I'm Tory Ryan."

"Oh, you're the writer—how nice. I'm Sally Manganaro."

Tory held out the pages. "I've got a new scene to slot into the script—"

"Okay, this is it," a voice shouted. "Quiet, everybody!"

Sally turned to the fat script that lay open across her lap. "Hang on a minute. They may actually shoot something now."

"Camera rolling," the cameraman said over his shoulder to John.

"Sound rolling," called the sound man from his small stand of sound equipment situated well behind John but with a clear view of the action.

One of the crew members held the clapboard in front of the camera—scene 21, take 8—and dropped the clapper with a loud click. He ducked out of the way as John called, "Ready, Debra? Okay—action!"

Debra sauntered along the sidewalk toward the apartment building, the camera tracking soundlessly behind her. Her high-heeled sandals accentuated the suggestive sway of her hips, and she tossed her blond mane with every other step. She was about halfway to the other tape mark when the little terrier broke loose and charged in front of the camera. The camera dolly jerked to a stop as John said resignedly, "And that's a cut. Dennis?"

As the short young man went into action again, Tory thought that an assistant director's job wasn't much fun. All he ever got to do was tell people to be quiet. She watched him corral the dog, carry it back to the boys, and give them a stern warning about interrupting the shooting again.

Standing a little apart from the knot of spectators was a man of about thirty. Tall and thin, he wore chino pants and a pressed short-sleeved shirt, rubber-soled moccasins and white socks. In spite of the sun, his skin was peculiarly white, and his eyes were pale. With his dishwater-blond crewcut, he looked like a holdover from the fifties who had just emerged from a cave. He stared disapprovingly at the little boys, twisting what looked like a narrow strip of braided leather around his hands. Then he walked silently toward the equipment truck. Stopping close to Tory, he stared hard at her. "Mixed blood, those children. Mixed blood, bad blood." Before Tory could react, he had padded silently away.

Sally made a face. "That guy gives me the creeps."

Tory said nothing, but she shivered with distaste. Thank goodness he'd left.

John's patient voice floated through the heat. "Debra, we're going to try it once more. You're doing fine, but this time I want you to be more subtle. Don't forget, Jean Anne is pretending she doesn't know there's anyone watching her.''

Julie said in a hearty tone, ''Yeah, kid, let's get it right this time and we can wrap this up and move on.''

''Well, no, Julie.'' John sounded apologetic. ''We still have the dialogue to do.''

''What?'' Julie's scream expressed outraged disbelief. ''What the hell have you been doing all morning? Where's that script?'' He stomped over to Sally, trailed by John and Debra.

Sally pointed wordlessly to the open script in her lap. Julie read down the page.

19 EXT. STREET—DAY
   Jean Anne walks along the sidewalk, sunglasses in place and hips swaying, dressed in tight shorts, halter top, and high-heeled sandals, and carrying a small sack of groceries. Behind her a four-wheel-drive Jeep with shiny paint creeps along the curb lane following her.

20 CU JEAN ANNE
   as she senses someone watching her. A smile flits across her face. She hitches her purse strap higher on her shoulder and then fluffs out her hair with spread fingers, shaking the tawny mane in the sun.

21 POV FROM JEEP—DOLLY SHOT
   From behind the wheel Alan watches her sashay toward the faceless apartment building. He guns the Jeep enough to catch up with her.

22 FULL SHOT
   as Alan pulls up beside Jean Anne. She

continues to look straight ahead as if she doesn't know anyone's there. Alan leans across the seat and opens the passenger door.

ALAN
It's a hot day. Why don't you let me buy you a drink before you go to work?

Jean Anne turns with a little smile, but when she sees who it is her mouth curls into a sneer.

JEAN ANNE
Oh, it's you.

ALAN
Come on, Jean Anne.

JEAN ANNE
Once was enough. Buzz off.

She tosses her head haughtily and steps quickly into the entrance of the apartment building. Alan watches her go, then roars off, leaving a streak of rubber on the road.

Julie looked up from the script. "What dialogue? You got four lousy lines here. Jesus H. Christ, this ain't supposed to be *Gone with the Wind*. What's the holdup?"

"Well, we had a few equipment problems, and then

Debra's been having difficulty . . ." John let his words trail off.

Julie rounded on Debra. "Listen, doll, this is just a dumb little scene. Get off your high horse and do like the man tells you. All you got to do is walk!"

Not wanting to hear anymore, Tory moved quietly around the front of the truck. On the other side a tanned, good-looking guy in his late thirties was entertaining some of the crew members. Tory caught the end of his comment: "So if she can't walk, what do you think will happen when she talks?"

As the others snickered, his gaze rested on Tory. The sun glinted on her shiny cap of dark curls and gave her tanned skin a rosy glow. "What have we here? A fresh young face come to brighten our day. Welcome to the funny farm. I'm Richard, the mad makeup artist." He stepped back and squinted at Tory through the frame of his hands. "Oh, yes, perfect! Don't tell me—let me guess. You've come to replace darling Debra, queen of the multiple takes."

Tory's big brown eyes crinkled with laughter. "No, sorry. I'm Tory Ryan, the equally mad scriptwriter."

"Oh, well, you can brighten our day anyway." He called to an older woman talking to a dark, attractive man. "Rose! Kevin! Come right over here. I've got a treat for you." As they approached, he said grandly to Tory, "Here's Rose Murphy, our fabulous wardrobe mistress—without her we'd all be running around in rags. And of course you'll recognize the gorgeous Kevin Dean, our leading man. Kevin has the dubious pleasure of working with our own Miss Debra."

"Now, Richard," Rose admonished. Then she smiled kindly at Tory. "Hello there."

"Hi, I'm Tory Ryan."

"Oh, how nice to meet you. Did you just get here?"

"Yes, late last night."

Kevin shook his head in mock dismay. "A script-writer on the set can only mean one thing—revisions. Really, I liked it the way it was."

"Don't worry, Kevin, I'm sure Tory wouldn't deprive you of a single torrid scene with Debra—" Richard broke off. "Uh-oh."

On the opposite sidewalk the pale crew-cut figure paced along toward the spectators who still goggled at the movie-making.

"It's Straight Arrow, our ever-present minder of morals."

"Oh, Richard." Rose's voice was calm. "He's not bothering you."

"He'd better not." Richard wasn't bantering anymore.

Dennis's urgent voice cut across the awkward moment. "Places, everyone! This will be a take! Makeup! Wardrobe!"

Recovering his light tone, Richard said, "Come, Rose. Duty calls!"

The group dispersed and Tory followed them around the truck. While Richard dabbed the shine of perspiration from Debra's forehead and nose, Rose carefully readjusted the angle of the bow at the back of Debra's halter. Tory couldn't see that it looked much different when Rose had finished, but she knew that the big screen would magnify every minor detail.

At last the cameraman said, "Camera rolling," the sound man started his tape, the clapboard clicked, and John said, "Ready, Debra? Action."

This time Debra managed to walk to her finish tape without mishap. John smiled his relief. "Cut, and that's a print. Let's get ready for the next setup."

Tory looked on in amazement as everyone began bustling around. It looked like total confusion, but she knew everyone's actions had been skillfully choreographed. She was watching the boom man position the microphone over Debra's head when a man's voice spoke almost in her ear.

"They dwell in the tents of wickedness."

His tone was one of tightly controlled fury, and Tory spun around. Not ten inches away were the pale eyes of the man Richard had called Straight Arrow; he was staring over her shoulder at the activity beyond. The strip of braided leather was wrapped around one of his hands, while with the other he fingered the free end. Shaken, she quickly walked away.

Luckily the rest of the morning's shooting moved right along. Julie's highly vocal presence seemed to have pushed Debra out of her sullen mood, and the dialogue went without a hitch.

"It's a wrap!" Dennis, like any assistant director, loved making this announcement. Everyone greeted the end of the workday with enthusiasm. He moved self-importantly across the set. "Don't forget—ten o'clock call tonight. Check the production office for the new location. Ten o'clock call tonight!"

Rapidly and efficiently the crew members began stowing their gear in the equipment trucks. Tory looked around for Julie—he and John, deep in conversation, were walking toward Julie's car. He obviously expected her to find her own way back to the motel.

Rose emerged from the wardrobe and makeup trailer, car keys in hand. She stopped to extract a pair of clip-on sunglasses from her purse.

"Are you driving back to the motel?"

Rose looked up at Tory, adjusting the glasses. "Sure. Do you need a ride?"

"Yes." Tory smiled wryly. "I rode out with Julie, but he seems pretty busy."

"Oh, yes, he's always busy. I don't know where he gets his energy."

They reached Rose's rented Escort and got in. "Oh, dear, it's awfully hot in here, isn't it? Why don't you roll down your window until the air conditioning gets going?" Rose started the engine, then fastened her seat belt and carefully adjusted the rearview mirror. She arranged her purse beside her, released the hand brake, and pulled cautiously away from the curb.

Driving along the city streets, Rose kept up a stream of conversation. "My, it's nice to have the afternoon off. I'll have time for a swim and a nap before dinner. I must say I find this desert heat a little debilitating. Guess I'm getting old!" Her pleasant laugh endeared her to Tory.

"I wasn't prepared for this myself. Has it been this hot the whole time?"

"Oh, we've had a few cooler days, but mostly it's been broiling, just like today. By afternoon people's tempers seem to get a bit frayed. But it's a real nice, friendly crew, and on the whole everyone gets along fine. Did you get a chance to meet everybody?"

"Well, I met quite a few people, but I'm still not too sure who's who. I'm not used to being on the set."

"Oh, you'll get to know your way around in no time."

"I hope so. I just got a little confused. For a while I thought that guy Richard calls Straight Arrow was part of the crew."

"Oh, no, he just hangs around and watches. I think he must be lonely. You can't help feeling a little sorry for him."

"Yes," Tory said dubiously, "but he's kind of scary. He crept up behind me and said something about the tents of wickedness, and he sounded really spooky."

"Oh, dear." Rose's concern was genuine. "He's said some things that upset Richard, too. But I'm sure he's harmless."

Tory was quick to agree. "I'm sure he is. It's just that driving down here I had a couple of encounters with obnoxious guys. I know it's stupid, but they really frightened me, and I guess I'm still nervous. It makes me wonder if I'm doing something to attract weirdos. Do you think it could be my perfume?" Her attempt at lightness didn't quite come off. As Rose pulled into the parking lot of the Wagon Wheel Inn, Tory added, "Your plan for the afternoon sounds pretty good. A swim and a nap will make me feel much better."

Waking up later in the cool, dim motel room, Tory was momentarily disoriented. Then she saw the luminous dial of her travel alarm clock. Almost six o'clock—she'd slept for quite a while. She must have been really tired.

She wondered how Michael was doing. He'd seemed a little annoyed night before last and had left in such a rush he'd forgotten his briefcase. She stretched and yawned. Oh, well, he had a key. Tory hoped he'd picked up his stuff yesterday and found the note she'd left for him. There was no reason for him still to be upset, but he sometimes got things all out of proportion. He could be mad at her for days, and she'd hardly know what it was all about. But of course he was worried about his experiments. Besides, he was intelligent, sexy, and good-looking. She felt lucky to have found him.

Slipping on her robe, she padded to the window and opened the heavy drapes. The afternoon sun was still bright, and the pool was full of splashing bodies. She smiled at the sight of an older couple sitting side by side. The man had rolled up his pant legs, and they were dangling their feet in the water. Tory knew her mom and dad would love this place—oh, my God, she thought, today's Dad's birthday. I'd better call them. Good thing I sent that tape measure gadget off to him last week. And this is a good time to call. It's eight o'clock there, and they'll be finished with dinner. Quickly she dialed her parents' number.

"Hi, Dad, it's Tory. Happy birthday!"

"Hi, honey, what a nice surprise!" She heard him call to her mother, "Margaret! It's Tory." Into the receiver he went on, "She's getting on the other phone. Thanks a lot for the rolling tape measure, honey. It's going to be a big help. I've already tried it out and it works just fine."

"Oh, good, I'm glad. I was hoping you didn't already have one. Did you have a nice birthday?"

"Yes." His voice was a bit strained.

"Do you have company or something, Dad? You sound kind of funny."

"No—Margaret, are you on? Well, Tory, it was real nice of you to call and wish your old dad a happy birthday, and thanks again. I'll just let you talk to your mom."

She heard the click as he hung up. "Mom?"

"Hi, Tory. Gosh, Daddy really loves that thing you sent him. He's measured everything but the kitchen sink. And how are you, dear?"

"I'm fine, Mom. But is everything okay there? You and Dad both sound a little odd."

After a short pause her mother said, "Well, I was hoping it would all blow over before we talked to you, but it looks like it won't. Carrie's here with the two kids. She says she's left Doug for good.''

"Oh, Mom. You mean she's living with you, with Kim and Ricky?"

"Well, it's just for a while, until . . . Oh, Tory, it's just awful!''

Tory heard the catch in her mother's voice. "My God, Mom, what happened?''

"Well, I'm not sure I understand it all, but you know Carrie was involved in that hospital benefit, and they just loved what she did and they asked her to be on the board. Well, of course she was thrilled, but Doug didn't want her to do it because the board meets on weeknights and he wants her home with him and the kids.''

"She left him because he didn't want her to go to these meetings?''

"That's what it sounds like. I guess she was real disappointed, but Doug works such long hours, and of course he feels—''

"But, Mom, what's she going to do?''

"I don't know. Carrie gets so emotional about things. I'm sure they can work it out. I just hope she doesn't do something foolish.''

"Oh, Mom, how awful. How's Dad taking it?''

"Well, it hasn't been easy for any of us. You know how outspoken your father can be. And Carrie's in floods of tears and on the phone with Doug for hours at a time. Of course the kids are upset, and who can blame them? Your Dad gets pretty impatient with them, though. We're all on edge.''

"Wow. I'm really sorry to hear about it. I sure hope they can work things out. Can I talk to Carrie for a minute?''

"She took the kids over to see Aunt Alice, but I'll be sure to tell her you called."

"Okay, but I'm not at home—I'm in Yuma, Arizona. They're shooting one of my scripts here."

"In Yuma—goodness, that's exciting. Is there a number where we can reach you?"

Tory gave her mom the number and said good-bye, then hung up with a sigh. What a mess! She could imagine what things were like at her parents' small house with her older sister and the two kids there. What she couldn't grasp was what in the world Carrie thought she was doing. To walk out on her marriage of nine years over a hospital benefit—it didn't make sense. There had to be something more going on.

Carrie's life was so different from Tory's that it was hard to know what she was going through. Pretty and popular, Carrie had made it through one year of college before dropping out at age nineteen to marry Doug. Tory had always found him a bit on the boring side. Was it possible he'd stepped out of character and was carrying on an affair or something? No, she didn't believe it. A hard worker, he was obviously crazy about Carrie and the children, a real family man.

Well, she'd just have to wait and talk to Carrie. It all sounded pretty serious, but her mom was right: Carrie did tend to get hysterical over trifles. Maybe it would blow over. She hoped so—what would Carrie do on her own with two young children?

Moving away from the phone, Tory dressed quickly and went down to find something to eat. At the dining room entrance she paused. Julie and John were sitting together at a table for four, but Julie had a stormy look. She certainly didn't want to get caught in the middle of their argument.

As the hostess approached, menus under her arm, Kevin Dean came up behind Tory.

"Table for two?"

Kevin and Tory exchanged a glance. "Why not?" the actor said.

The hostess smiled brilliantly and led them to a table overlooking the pool. "Here you are, Mr. Dean. Your waitress will be right with you."

Sitting down, Tory looked around in mock awe. "I think I'll eat with you every night. They really give you the royal treatment!"

He returned her smile. "Yes, the best table at the Wagon Wheel Inn in Yuma makes it all worthwhile."

The waitress appeared and they ordered, but when she left the conversation lapsed. Kevin looked preoccupied and worried, so Tory amused herself by making up life stories for the other diners. In the back of her mind she mulled over the distressing news from her family.

When their food arrived, Kevin shook off his distant air. "I'm sorry—I'm not being very good company. I had a very upsetting phone call right before I came down."

"That makes two of us." Tory smiled briefly.

"Well, what do you say we declare a moratorium on problems for this evening? After all, someone worked hard to make this a memorable setting for fine dining." He gestured around the room.

Tory took in the wagon wheel chandeliers, the horseshoe brands on the vinyl-covered banquettes that were echoed in the design of the plates and napkins. On the far wall a life-size mural depicted cowboys squatting around a campfire under a stormy sky. Sets of longhorns were strategically arranged on the other walls.

Tory's full, sensuous mouth curved in a smile, and Kevin watched her appreciatively. She had more than healthy good looks, he thought. There was an aura of vitality about her that he'd bet would come across superbly on camera. He wondered if she'd ever done any acting. Probably not—she didn't have that veneer of pretension most aspiring actresses had.

Tory laughed and looked at Kevin. "You're right—the decor definitely is memorable."

"Yes, I'm just sorry I left my tooled leather boots and my Stetson at home." He signaled for another beer. "But enough of that—tell me about you. Did you leave a husband at home, wishing he were here in this glamorous location?"

"No, I'm not married. What about you?"

"I'm not either, at least not anymore."

"Oh," Tory said feebly. She could never come up with an appropriate response to a statement like that.

He shrugged. "Well, it was probably all for the best. The only sad part is that I don't see enough of my daughter."

"How old is she?"

"She's just turned three—my little fairy princess." He pulled out his wallet. "Here she is. I know it sounds corny, but she's the joy of my life."

A dark-eyed laughing tot dimpled at Tory from the photo. "She's darling. Just wait till she gets older—she's going to be a knockout."

Parental pride softened his features, and Tory thought with a pang of Carrie and her kids. No matter how hard it was for Carrie and Doug to deal with their marital problems, at least they were both adults. It must be even worse for the children.

Chapter 3

By 11:00 P.M. the Rumpus Room had undergone a transformation. Cables snaked across the floor, the tables had been clustered near the small stage in one corner, and floodlights flashed brightly through the normally dim room as the crew moved them here and there.

Tory thought Artie had done pretty well to find this place on short notice. The bar was about what she'd had in mind. The stage would work fine as soon as the crew got the curtain hung to make a backstage area, and the crowd of extras was just what she'd envisioned—a little seedy-looking but not derelict.

As John Hartnell stepped up on the stage, Dennis's voice cut through the babble. "Attention, please, everybody!"

The men at the tables looked up at John expectantly.

"Hi, I'm John Hartnell, the director of the film. I want to thank you all for being here. We won't be ready to start shooting for a little while, so I'll fill you in on what's going to happen. Some of you may have already guessed that this lovely young lady is going to provide you with a little entertainment." As he gestured toward the actress playing the stripper, appreciative hoots and whistles rose from the crowd. John smiled. "That's just what we want. You're here to enjoy yourselves and have a good time and just act natural. But"—he held up a hand—"there are a couple of important things to keep in mind. Keep your language clean. We'll be recording sound as we're shooting and we don't want to get an X rating." They all got the in joke and laughed. "For the same reason, no obscene gestures, please. And—this is very important—you must stay in the seats you're in right now. Of course, since the beer is free, you'll all probably need to make a quick trip at some point." They chuckled again. "But be sure to return to the same seat afterward." He looked at his watch. "I think that covers it. You should all have signed a release by now. If anyone hasn't, please hold up your hand and someone will bring one over. This is just a formality that says you know we're shooting a movie here and you give us permission to use footage of you if we decide to. Okay, the beer and popcorn are on us, so sit back and have a good time." He jumped down to a scattering of applause.

While John spoke, the camera, lighting, and sound crews had been setting up to shoot part of the stage scene. The actress, dressed and made up, now stood at stage center while the crew fiddled with adjustments. Richard added a touch of purple lip liner and moved back from the girl to see the effect. "Perfect! You're all ready for your debut, love," he called to her with a grin. Then he saw Tory standing alone at the edge of the stage and ambled over to her. "If it isn't our writer in residence! And how do you find the real-life version of your vision?''

"Well, this place is perfect." Both of them gazed around the room. The extras looked suddenly stage-struck. As the moment approached, they seemed afraid even to lift their beer mugs lest their movement spoil the picture. ''But these fellows look awfully subdued. I hope they'll liven up a little.''

Richard snickered. ''Oh, I wouldn't worry about that. A few more free beers and they'll be as lively as we can stand.'' He stiffened and the smile left his face. ''There's one, though, who won't be.''

Tory followed his glance. The man he'd nicknamed Straight Arrow was sitting at a rear table, hunched over a Coke. Though he was with a bunch of other men, he had an air of being totally alone, almost as if he were encased in glass. Tory realized that the braided leather strip dangling from his left hand was in fact a bolo tie. She'd seen some like it in the motel gift shop, complete with hammered silver sliders. It was obviously a popular tourist item down here. But in Straight Arrow's hands it took on a sinister appearance. ''What's he doing here?'' Tory breathed.

''Who knows? He'd just better stay in his seat.'' Richard's voice had a distinctly threatening tone. Then he took Tory by the elbow and positioned her behind the camera's line of sight. ''Fun and games are about to begin,'' he whispered with a laugh.

At long last everything was ready. The stripper's music started, and as the camera rolled, the actress began to dance. Unconsciously Tory tapped her foot to the insistent rhythm while the girl bumped and swayed in her scant costume.

* * *

"Come on, baby, light my fire!" Down the street from the Rumpus Room, the familiar whine of the Doors' old hit tune shook the flimsy walls of Hank's Hangout. On a runway that was little more than a couple of planks three feet above the barroom floor, a bored-looking young woman shuffled her feet and swung her hips more or less in time with the music.

A young marine took another swig of beer and thumped his mug down on the bar. "Do it, Dorothy Jean!" he called out. But the girl's blank expression didn't change, and she continued to chew mechanically on a wad of pink bubble gum.

Dorothy Jean could have passed for pretty if she'd been about fifteen pounds lighter. But as it was, her costume didn't do much for her chunky figure. It looked suspiciously like the top to a pair of baby doll pajamas. Red with a black ruffled border and spaghetti straps, it hung open from the elasticized bustline, exposing her naked belly. The sheer nylon fabric swung back and forth over a pair of black bikini panties. To complete the outfit, she wore shiny red vinyl backless sandals—the style unkindly known as hooker shoes—on her dirty bare feet. Her silver toenail polish was chipped and uneven.

The crowd at Hank's Hangout was an odd mixture of clean-cut fellows on a night out from the nearby marine base and seedy locals who knew where to find the cheapest drinks in Yuma. A few women of indeterminate age were deep in conversation with their escorts. Only some of the younger marines paid any attention to Dorothy Jean's inexpert performance.

The pounding music wound down at last, and Dorothy Jean moved wearily to the end of the runway. Cautious in her stiletto heels, she put one hand against the wall to steady herself as she stepped down. Her finger-nails, bitten to the quick, were poignant evidence that she lacked the hard veneer of a professional.

The blond bartender gave her a grin as she passed. "Another day, another dollar, right, kid?"

Dorothy Jean smiled in return. "You got it, Eddie." She continued toward the back of the bar. A middle-aged man, his blue work shirt strained over his paunch, lurched off his stool into her path. "Hey, doll, wanna come home with me?"

Dorothy Jean shook his damp hand off. "Get lost," she muttered nervously. Moving quickly away, she reached up to push her curls off her neck. She thought again that it was about time to touch up her hair color. Maybe she'd try a different brand this time. The last time it had turned out a little more carroty than the package promised. Still, she thought, it looked a lot more exciting than her own mousy brown.

A short corridor led to the ladies' room and, next to it, Dorothy Jean's "dressing room." This was in reality a broom closet—the door had been removed and a curtain strung across the opening. She pushed it aside and switched on the light.

Dorothy Jean sighed with relief as she stepped out of the ridiculous shoes. Peering into the small mirror on the wall, she saw the brown roots at her hairline—definitely time for a touch-up; she'd do it tomorrow morning.

She sighed again and took off the red costume, then reached for her T-shirt, which hung on a nail in the wall, and started to pull it on. As her arms groped for the sleeves, a gloved hand twitched the curtain aside. Dorothy Jean's face was still covered by the T-shirt when the long-bladed knife plunged into her back.

The gurgling cry that escaped her was drowned out by the jukebox's wail. She fell forward against the wall. The knife was withdrawn quickly. It slashed again, this time into the soft skin of her neck. Then it clattered to the floor as Dorothy Jean's body crumpled slowly, her head still grotesquely shrouded in the gaudy T-shirt. The curtain dropped back in place over the doorway.

Washing glasses behind the bar, Eddie glanced again toward the hallway. It had been almost twenty minutes—what was taking Dorothy Jean so long? He dumped out the beer he'd drawn for her; it was warm and flat by this time. He knew she couldn't have left without his noticing—her purse was still tucked under the bar where she always left it for safekeeping. Christ, what was keeping her?

Eddie dried his hands and walked over to Bert, the other bartender. "Take over for a minute, will ya? I'm just gonna see if Dorothy Jean's okay. She's been in there long enough to change three times."

Bert nodded and Eddie ducked under the flap of the bar. In the corridor he knocked on the ladies' room door. Hearing no response, he tried the doorknob. It was unlocked. He opened the door and found the small room in darkness. "Dorothy Jean?" he called uncertainly. He pushed the door wide so that the light from the hallway revealed the empty interior.

Eddie turned away with a puzzled frown. Then something caught his eye. Beneath the lower edge of the dressing room curtain he glimpsed a row of silver-painted toenails. Two quick strides and he flung the curtain aside. "Dorothy Jean, are you—" The words died in his throat as he took in the ugly scene. "Holy Christ!" he whispered.

The body lay wedged awkwardly against the wall,

and the floor was covered with blood. For a wild moment he thought she'd been beheaded. Then reason reasserted itself, and he bent quickly and pulled up the sodden T-shirt. Dorothy Jean's eyes stared sightlessly past him.

Eddie stepped back, shaking violently, and sagged against the corridor wall. "The cops," he said aloud. "I've gotta call the cops." He walked unsteadily toward the pay phone at the end of the hall. After fumbling awkwardly for change, he dropped a coin in the slot and dialed the well-known number.

"This is Eddie at Hank's Hangout—" He broke off to swallow convulsively, and the voice on the other end spoke resignedly.

"Yeah, okay, we'll send a cop. Is he still swinging or did he pass out already?"

Eddie's sweaty hand clutched the phone. "No, no, you don't understand. Somebody killed Dorothy Jean." He glanced apprehensively toward the curtained alcove and saw with horror a line of his own bloody footprints leading to where he stood. "Oh, Jesus!" With a sob Eddie dropped the phone.

Two o'clock in the morning. Tory rubbed her eyes and yawned. She'd always thought writing scripts was slow; now she could see that hers was probably the speediest part of the whole business. And at least if she didn't like what she'd written, she had only herself to blame. It must be very frustrating for the director to shoot a scene over and over just because a light was in the wrong place or the microphone boom was in the shot or a truck rumbled past. John was awfully patient. Tory didn't see how he could remain so calm.

But at least the crowd shots were finally finished. The only things left to do were the close-ups of the stripper and the killer. The crew was busy shifting lights and cables and mysterious pieces of equipment toward the backstage curtain.

"Okay, folks, thanks a lot." Dennis's voice made it clear that the "audience" was dismissed. Several of the men drifted toward the door, but others hung around, unwilling to let go of the limelight. "You've been a great audience, but I'm sure you're all tired by now. So, thank you and good night."

Tory watched with amusement as Dennis, looking like a harried sheepdog, tried to herd them all toward the door. Some of the men sat on at their tables and others edged forward, mesmerized by the glimpse of Hollywood's inner workings.

At that moment two uniformed sheriff's deputies strode into the Rumpus Room. As they stood surveying the scene, Dennis hurried over to them. "What can I do for you, officers?"

The heavyset deputy turned to look at him. "Sheriff's Department, Deputy Hurd. Who's in charge here?"

"We're shooting a motion picture, and I'm the assistant director. How can I help you?"

"I think we'd better talk to whoever is running the show."

"That's Mr. Kingman. He's standing right over there on the stage, but he's awfully busy right now. Maybe you can tell me what it's about?"

"Thanks." The deputies turned away and walked purposefully in Julie's direction. "Mr. Kingman?"

"Yeah?" Julie glanced down from the edge of the stage. "If it's about the permits, talk to Artie. He's got all that stuff somewhere. Hang on, I'll find him." He looked around for Artie's curly head.

Deputy Hurd held up a hand. "No, sir, it's not the permits. There's been some trouble near here, and we need some information. I understand you're in charge."

Julie nodded vigorously. "Yeah, sure, anything I can do." His restless glance fell on John Hartnell, who was deep in discussion with the actress who played the stripper. What could they have to discuss at this point? He'd better see what it was all about. His gaze rested on Tory; then he turned back to the deputy. "I've just gotta check on something, but I'll be back in a minute. Meanwhile you can talk to my scriptwriter. She knows everything." He raised his voice. "Tory! C'mere for a minute, kiddo."

Julie introduced her to the deputies and hurried off to the back of the stage where John still stood talking.

"We're checking on various people's whereabouts this evening, ma'am, and we want to know who's been here tonight and what time they arrived and left."

"Oh." Tory sounded a little overwhelmed. "Well, we've been shooting here since about ten o'clock, but— Do you mean just the cast and crew, or all the extras who were here in the bar? I'm not sure what this is all about."

The deputies exchanged a glance. Then Hurd said, "I guess there's no reason not to tell you. There's been a murder in another bar in town, and we're trying to pin down anyone who might have arrived here late or left early."

"Oh, how awful," Tory said. "Well, the cast and crew have all been here since ten o'clock and we're all still here working. Now, let's see—I'm sure the local people we used as extras had all arrived by eleven o'clock, because that's when we started shooting. A lot of them left about half an hour ago when we finished those shots, and the rest of them are still here, kind of hanging around.'' She gestured vaguely toward the men near the stage. ''Does that help?''

The big man nodded. ''So you're saying that no one arrived or left between eleven and about one-thirty, right?''

''As far as I know. But of course the doors weren't locked, and these people weren't glued to their chairs. They got up and went to the bar or the bathroom or whatever. They weren't supposed to leave, but I couldn't swear they didn't.''

Hurd closed his notebook and said resignedly, ''I see. Well, thanks. I suppose there's a list of all these people's names somewhere.''

''Oh, sure, they all signed releases before we started. I'll just find Artie and he can—''

She stopped in mid-sentence. A tall dark man in uniform had appeared at her side, and both deputies turned their attention to him. ''Captain Fleming,'' Hurd said.

''How's it going?'' He looked about thirty, but his air of easy assurance gave him an undisputed authority. As he stood listening to what the deputies had learned, Tory felt invisible. He'd hardly acknowledged her presence.

At last he turned cool gray eyes on her. ''What kind of scene are you shooting here?''

''It's a murder scene. In the script, a striptease dancer is stabbed backstage by a psychopathic killer.''

All three men stared at her without speaking. As the silence lengthened, Tory felt the hot flush of embarrassment rise up her neck to her cheeks. Maybe it did sound a little heartless when she said it like that, but they didn't have to look at her as if she were the psychopath.

Finally Captain Fleming said dismissively, "All right. Thanks." He turned to his deputies. "We'll pick up that list of names and get moving."

Tory gazed after them as they strode off. Even in a small town like Yuma, it seemed, murder really did happen. Then she thought, Damn! I really hate it when I blush like a silly teenager. You'd think I'd have grown out of it. Her annoyance shifted to the source of her discomfort. Cops! They were all alike. Give them a uniform and they couldn't resist showing off their power. Sometimes she really understood why Michael hated anything to do with the police.

But as she watched them talking to Artie, Tory admitted to herself that the three policemen hadn't done anything to complain about. It was just that awkward moment when they'd stared at her without speaking that had made her feel uncomfortable. And after all, it wasn't their job to put her at ease—they were investigating a murder. But the memory of Captain Fleming's unreadable gray eyes lingered in her mind.

Chapter 4

The next morning Tory checked to make sure she had her key and then stepped out of her room into a blaze of sunshine. She quickly pulled out her sunglasses. She wasn't ready for so much brilliance before she'd even had her coffee. She went down the steps and skirted the pool.

"Morning, Tory!" Rose's cheerful voice carried over the laughing shouts of the swimmers. She sat at a shaded table on the patio with Kevin and Richard. Tory made her way over to them.

Kevin smiled up at her. "You're looking bright-eyed and bushy-tailed this morning."

Tory laughed. "More than I was at three A.M., anyway."

Rose patted the empty chair next to her. "Join us, why don't you? We've just ordered."

"Thanks." As Tory slid into the seat, Richard gave her a speculative look.

"Seen the paper yet, Tory?"

"No, I just woke up." Tory smiled at the waitress

who was filling the coffee mugs. "That smells great. And I'd like a large orange juice and a toasted English muffin."

As the waitress moved away, Richard folded his newspaper carefully and passed it to Tory. "Do read the lead article. I'm sure you'll find it fascinating."

Tory stared at the heavy black type of the headline: "Dancer Slain in Dressing Room; Local Girl Planned Career in Nursing; Police Search for Assailant."

The accompanying photo showed a high school graduate with a sweet smile. Tory read on, horrified at the details of the murder at Hank's Hangout. She looked up, but before she could speak, Richard said, "Sounds familiar, doesn't it? Did you arrange it yourself as promotion for the film, or do you have second sight?"

Tory shuddered, and Rose said reprovingly, "Now, Richard, it's nothing to joke about. That poor girl."

"It's horrible." Tory put the paper down beside her chair, her eyes wide behind her sunglasses. "It really gives me the creeps. I can't believe it."

Rose patted Tory's arm consolingly. "I know, dear. It's a strange coincidence. But do try not to let it upset you."

Including both Kevin and Rose in his innocent look, Richard said, "Well, they always say life imitates art. I guess death does, too." He put a hand on Tory's arm. "Do let us know who's next, won't you, Tory? It would be such a pity to go without having one's affairs in order and all."

Tory's face went pale beneath her tan, and Kevin jumped in. "Don't worry, Richard. Only girls get killed in this script, remember?" It wasn't the most tactful remark in the circumstances, but it served its purpose. Richard fell silent, and Rose turned the conversation into safer channels. But Tory found it difficult to shake off a feeling of dread.

Of course, it was a coincidence. What else could it be? How macabre that the details in the news story were so similar to her script for a dumb B movie. The scene she'd made up wasn't even supposed to sound like real life. It was the movie equivalent of escape fiction—total fantasy. But here it was, happening to an ordinary young woman who had her whole life ahead of her. That girl had been a living person not long ago, and she'd been killed virtually at the same moment they'd been shooting the murder scene Tory had written, almost as if her words had leapt off the page and become reality.

Don't be stupid, Tory told herself angrily. It *is* just a coincidence. If I knew all the details, it probably wouldn't sound similar at all. But as the toasted muffin sat cooling in front of her, Tory knew she couldn't eat a single bite.

The location for the afternoon's shooting was north of town along the Colorado River. They'd found a place where a bend in the river formed a sheltered cove: a short stretch of sandy beach led up to a grassy glade surrounded by overgrown bushes and a few scattered trees. A path to the left of the clearing led to a campground crowded with trailers and tents. It wasn't exactly the remote, secluded spot Tory had envisioned, but it would work fine. She reminded herself that the camera's selective eye could produce a look quite different from the real setting.

Tory remembered writing this scene. She'd wanted to give Alan, the killer, a reason—however crazy—to go off the deep end. But Jean Anne, the heroine, couldn't do anything deliberately to set him off, or the audience wouldn't identify with her. She'd worked it out pretty well, she thought, by having Jean Anne go on a picnic with a nice young man and having Alan follow them and skulk in the bushes to spy on their lovemaking.

A crowd of curious onlookers had wandered over from the campground, eager to watch a film being shot. Debra and Paul Wilder, the young actor who played her boyfriend, were settled on a blanket with picnic things strewn around them. Tory watched as Dennis hurried importantly around, organizing the spectators.

"You'll have to keep that radio turned off, madam, or I'm afraid we'll have to ask you to leave."

Tory smiled at the confrontation between short, intense Dennis and a large lady in curlers and sunsuit. But as the woman turned away in a huff, Tory stiffened. Straight Arrow—what was he doing here? He must have followed them from Yuma. She realized that he'd been hanging around every time she'd been on the set. He'd even been at the Rumpus Room last night. But wait a minute—she was sure he'd been there when they started shooting, but she hadn't seen him at all after the first few takes. He must have left early; Tory felt certain she'd have noticed him later on.

She'd better tell the cops about him. This was just what they were asking about, anyone who left before the shooting was finished. And he was weird enough— Tory shivered at the turn her thoughts were taking.

"Cheer up. Things can't be as terrible as that." It was Artie, grinning his perpetual grin. Just then Dennis's familiar command rang out.

"Quiet on the set! This is a take!"

Artie and Tory watched as Debra and Paul ate fried chicken with every appearance of enjoyment. Artie gave

Tory a smirk. "If I was on a picnic with her, I wouldn't waste any time eating chicken!"

Tory smiled unwillingly—Artie was so much in character. When the take was over, she grasped his arm. "Artie, I want you to do something for me. You know that guy who hangs around all the time—over there by the tree? Find out his name, will you?"

"Sure, Tory—got the hots for him?"

This time Tory wasn't amused. "I want to give his name to the cops, do you mind?"

The set was suddenly a beehive of activity again as the crew set up for the next shot. Giant silvery reflectors were moved here and there, and shouts filled the air—"A little to the left, Joe," "Check that angle—okay?" "Hold it, lemme take a look." It was amazing how much time it took to get ready for a scene that would only last about a minute on the screen.

Dennis sprang into action once more. "I'm sorry. You'll have to leave," he told the group of onlookers. "This will be a closed set from now on. Yes, that's right, no spectators. Sorry." Tory realized that they were about to shoot Debra's nude scene. Of course it was really only topless, but it was smart to get the onlookers out of the way. An ill-timed catcall or whistle could spoil the whole shot.

God, it was hot here. Debra and Paul were probably looking forward to their dip in the river. Tory headed over to the ice chest in search of a cool drink. As she straightened up, a can of Dr Pepper dripping in her hand, a toneless voice spoke in her ear. "Evil woman . . ."

Tory whirled around. Standing so close he was almost touching her was Straight Arrow! He snapped his leather thong between his hands as his pale eyes stared into hers.

With a strangled gasp Tory slid past him. She walked quickly away and with relief spotted Sally Manganaro sitting in her chair, the inevitable bottle of sunscreen by her side. Julie and John stood in front of Sally.

As Tory approached, her heart still pounding, she heard Julie say to John, "Don't make me sorry I gave ya a break, ya hear?" Then he stomped off.

John looked after him for a moment and then turned to Sally. "You've got that now?"

"Oh, sure." Sally was imperturbable.

John hurried off to find Lars Swenson, the director of photography. Sally glanced at Tory. "Hey, what's up?"

"Oh, nothing." Tory finally managed to open her Dr Pepper with still shaking hands. "It's just that weirdo—you know, the one Richard calls Straight Arrow—he came up behind me and scared the hell out of me. Called me an evil woman—at least I thought he did. Now I realize he must have been talking about Debra. He probably doesn't approve of picnics on the grass," she wound up with an attempt at humor.

Sally shook her head in disgust. "Oh, him. I don't know why he bothers to come and watch if he doesn't approve."

"I like your attitude." Tory laughed. "Well, what's happening now?"

"Oh, the obligatory sex scene. Surely you remember that? The little confrontation you just missed was John being director and full of it and Julie being producer with his eye on the schedule."

Tory looked over Sally's shoulder at the open script.

29 EXT. PARK—DAY
It is the same clearing where Jean Anne

and Peter had their picnic. The lake shimmers in the background.
ZOOM ONTO LAKE
where the two of them, in swimsuits, frolic in the water. Laughter and splashing turn into heavy kissing. Then Jean Anne pulls away and splashes Peter again.

                    JEAN ANNE
          Come on! I'll race you!

STAY WITH THEM
as they splash toward shore and run across the small sandy beach.
30 CU BLANKET
on the grass where Jean Anne flops down, panting. Peter drops down beside her.

                    JEAN ANNE
          I won!

Peter leans down and fastens his mouth on hers for a long kiss.

                    PETER
              (smiling down at her)
          No, I won.

She is lying on her stomach, he on his side next to her. He unties the top of her bikini and runs his hand down her bare back.

                    PETER
          God, you're beautiful.

She rolls up on one elbow, facing him. Her
bikini top lies on the blanket and her breasts
glisten with water.

JEAN ANNE
Do you really think so?

PETER
You know I do.

He pulls her to him in a long embrace.
31 CLOSE ON
Alan, hiding in the bushes watching them.
His face reflects his agony and his mouth
twists into a grimace.

As Tory finished reading the scene, she looked quizzically at Sally. "What's the problem?" she asked.

"There's no problem with the script," Sally assured
her. "The point is that John wants to change your camera directions and do this whole scene in one shot."

"One shot?"

"One complicated shot," replied Sally with mean-
ing. "His idea is to set up the camera there." She
pointed to where John and Lars were conferring. "He
plans to zoom out to the water, pull back as they come
up to the blanket, and tilt down on their scene together.
Then, instead of cutting to another shot of Kevin in the
bushes, he's going to slowly move the camera down to
level with Debra's head and tilt up and have Kevin in
the bushes behind her. He'll slip focus to pick up Kevin's expression over the soft focus of Debra and Paul
kissing."

"Wow."

"Of course, it'll be terrific if it works, but Julie's afraid they'll waste so much time getting it right that we'll lose our light and we won't get it at all today. He wants John to play it safe and do it in three separate shots."

Tory shrugged. "Well, let's hope it works, then. I'd hate to have to come out here in this heat another day."

"You and me both," said Sally with a grin.

From the picnic blanket John called out, "We're just about ready. Kevin?"

Kevin and John trudged up into the bushes while Lars put his eye to the camera. "A little to the left and down more," Lars yelled. Obediently Kevin scrunched into an uncomfortable position behind a thicket. "Perfect!" the cameraman called. "Hold it right there, Kevin."

John leaned over and patted Kevin on the shoulder. "Just keep your eyes on Debra and stay in character. I know it's not very comfortable, but it's going to look great."

John climbed down from the tangled underbrush and walked over to where Debra and Paul waited at the water's edge. "Okay, kids, ready for your dip?"

Debra dipped an experimental toe into the river and quickly drew it back. "This water's freezing! I can't go in there!"

Stifling a sigh, John said patiently, "Now, Debra, I'm sure you can manage. This is going to be a great scene for you."

Debra frowned prettily. "But—"

"And the sooner you get in," John went on, "the sooner you can get out again. So let's get moving, okay?"

Paul grabbed Debra's hand. "Come on, Debra, it'll feel great once you're in!"

The two of them waded out into the water, Debra emitting little shrieks. "This is crazy! It's much too cold! I'll be absolutely blue when I get out!"

Lars readied the camera while Dennis reminded the crew that this would be a take. Tory crossed her fingers for John as the camera started to roll.

John picked up the megaphone and called out over the water, "Okay, Debra, Paul, let's start splashing!"

The scene progressed beautifully. They did their frolicking and kissing. Debra pulled away, splashed Paul again, said her line, and the two of them waded toward shore and ran across the beach.

"Cut!"

John walked down to the water's edge. "Debra, I know you're not an Olympic athlete, but you can't just prance across the sand. Run, girl! Really run. You did it just fine when we rehearsed it, so I know you can."

Debra gave him what she considered an engaging pout.

"I'll tell you what." John reached in his back pocket and pulled out his wallet. "I'll give you five dollars if you can beat Paul to the blanket."

"For real?" Debra was amazed.

He nodded solemnly. Sometimes the Method really worked.

They started again, and this time Debra ran like a champ. Reaching the blanket, she flung herself down and immediately rolled over with a howl of pain. "Shit!"

"Cut!" John yelled again. He walked over to the blanket. "What happened?" he asked her.

"I landed on a goddamn rock! I'm probably gonna have a huge black-and-blue mark on my hip!"

Debra's voice carried through the whole clearing.

Richard turned to Tory. "In that case, it's lucky she's only going to take off her top."

Tory laughed. Then she saw Kevin straighten up from behind the thicket and stretch. Poor guy, his knees must be killing him, she thought. She was glad to hear Dennis call out, "Okay, folks, we'll take five. But keep it down."

Paul had leapt to his feet. "Oh, poor you," he exclaimed to Debra. "I'll get you an ice pack!"

As he ran off, John helped Debra up. "Dennis!" he shouted crossly. "Get someone down here to smooth out the ground under this blanket!" He turned back to Debra. "What a thing to happen! And it was going to be a perfect take—you looked absolutely terrific. Really radiant and glowing—sensational."

Debra put a hand up to her hair. "Did you really think so?"

"Absolutely."

Paul ran up, clutching a sodden paper napkin filled with ice. "Now show me just where it hurts, Debra." He knelt beside her and applied the ice pack gently to the spot she pointed to.

A pleased smile struggled with the pout on Debra's lips.

"A little lower down, Paul—oh, that feels good."

A few feet behind Tory, Artie watched Debra with greedy longing. "Debra, baby, *I'd* like to make you feel good," he said almost inaudibly. Then he pushed his glasses back up on his nose and turned away abruptly.

"That's fine, Debra," John said. "Just keep that ice on it for a few minutes while Richard fixes your makeup again. You're being very brave." He patted her shoulder and then, motioning to Richard, climbed up to where Kevin was doing deep knee bends.

"I know this isn't easy, Kevin, but I really think this next take will do it. So, if you'll just get down again in position, I'll have Lars line things up. Remember, your face will completely fill the screen at the end of the shot, so keep that wonderful agonized expression."

"That's no problem, believe me," Kevin muttered as he hunkered down again in the bushes.

"There, that should do it," Richard told Debra with a final flick of the makeup brush. "You're quite the queen bee, aren't you? Paul here is even down on his very knees!"

Debra's reply was cut short by John, who hurried up to say, "Okay, are we all set now? Good. I just know this next take will do it." He smiled encouragingly as she walked back down to the water with Paul.

"Action!"

The scene was going perfectly. Paul untied the strap of Debra's bikini top and ran his hand lovingly down her back. Then Debra gave a shriek of laughter and wriggled away. "Paul, stop! You're tickling me!"

Disgustedly, John called, "Cut!"

Debra folded her arms coyly over her bare breasts. "Oh, I'm *so* sorry, John. I just couldn't help myself." She directed her big blue eyes at Paul. "Your hands just drive me wild," she told him in a carrying voice.

Then from up on the hill, a shout of rage silenced them all. "You little bitch! I'll drive you somewhere!" Everyone looked up to see Kevin thundering down the hill. "Don't you ever think at all? I'm squashed up here with the goddamn mosquitoes, and you're fucking up this scene six ways from Sunday just so you can keep everyone's eyes glued on your bare titties as long as possible. You cheap piece of ass, wait till I get my hands on you."

Debra shrieked and cowered behind Paul as Kevin advanced on her. He looked truly enraged. Even Tory felt a trickle of alarm. How far would he really go?

Then Rose was at Kevin's side. "Oh, Kevin, it's really been a difficult afternoon, hasn't it? You must be exhausted, waiting up there so patiently. And it's so hot. Let's go find something cool to drink. I think I saw some iced tea."

Kevin allowed himself to be led away, still muttering angrily. "What's she trying to do, ruin my whole career? She really is a first-class bitch."

Rose handed him a can of iced tea. "Now, Kevin, you know Debra isn't worth getting so hot and bothered about."

He turned on her. "She's not worth shit!"

Rose gazed at him shrewdly. "There's something else on your mind, isn't there?"

Kevin looked startled. "What do you mean?"

"You've seemed so edgy and unlike yourself recently. I'm sure there's something bothering you. Now, I certainly don't want to pry, but if you need someone to talk to, you know I'd be only too happy to help."

Kevin stared at her for a moment, then bent to kiss her cheek. "Rose, you're the only sane person around here. What would we do without you?"

Everyone pretended that nothing out of the ordinary had happened, and miraculously the next take of the scene went without a hitch. John called, "Cut and print!"

Dennis, for the first time showing some normal human emotion, made his announcements with relief. "That's a wrap, folks! Go on back and have a nice evening. See you tomorrow."

Tory made her way toward the parking lot and ran

into Julie. He had just driven back to the location from the production office in Yuma. "How's it going, kiddo?" he asked. "You leaving the sinking ship?"

"No, Julie, everyone's finished for today."

"John pulled off that shot?" He sounded disbelieving.

"Yes," Tory assured him, "and it's going to look terrific. I wouldn't say it was easy, but he did it."

"Great!" Julie smiled broadly. "I always figured he was a dynamite director. Who cares about his problems?"

He bounded off and Tory watched him go. She wondered what he had meant about John's problems, but she didn't have time to think about it. A petulant voice spoke up behind her. "Don't ask me to run any more of your errands." It was Artie, his damp hair plastered to his forehead. "I thought that guy was gonna hit me when I told him you wanted to know his name!"

Tory looked at Artie, her expression a combination of concern and disbelief. "You told him I wanted his name!"

"Yeah, sure. When I asked him what his name was, he said, 'Who wants to know?' So I told him. Boy, he's really a creep!"

"Well, what's his name?"

"I dunno. He wouldn't tell me."

"Terrific. Nice job, Artie, thanks a lot." Tory didn't want to hear Artie's reply to her sarcasm. She stalked off toward her car, but underneath her seething she felt a little frightened. Maybe Straight Arrow had been referring to her after all when he'd said "Evil woman." What was the matter with Artie, Tory wondered angrily. Didn't he have the brains he was born with? Why had he told that creep that it was Tory who wanted to know his name? It was too late now, but Tory wished she hadn't given Straight Arrow any reason to single her out as a target for his hostility.

When she arrived back at the motel, she stopped at the production office to take a look at the schedule. Penny Seriale stopped filing her nails and smiled up at her. It occurred to Tory that Penny's job must be pretty dull.

"Hi, Tory. How did it go today?"

"Long and hot, but we're still on schedule. You're lucky you weren't out there in that sun."

"Yeah, I guess so," Penny said doubtfully. "Oh, a guy was in here looking for you just a little while ago."

"Oh? Who was it?"

"I don't know. I never saw him before. He was, you know, sort of blond."

Tory's heart sank. Could it have been Straight Arrow? Was he so bent out of shape he'd actually come here looking for her?

"I didn't know if you were back yet or not," Penny continued, "so I told him where your room was and said he should go knock on the door. But I guess you weren't there. Anyway, he sounded like he was going to hang around and wait for you."

Belatedly Penny noticed Tory's look of concern. "Did I do the wrong thing?"

"No," Tory said thoughtfully. In the long run it didn't make any difference. He could have found out her room number anyway. Well, it was still bright outside even though it was seven o'clock at night, and there were plenty of people around. No point letting her imagination run away with her. What she needed was a long, cool shower. But as she climbed the steps to her room, she carefully scanned the motel walkways. There was no sign of Straight Arrow.

Inside her room Tory pulled off her sundress and stepped out of her sandals. She walked through the dressing room area and into the bathroom. Shedding the rest of her clothes, she reached in and turned on the shower. Just as she was putting one foot in the tub she saw there was no soap. At least she'd noticed before she was dripping wet.

Stepping back out into the dressing area, Tory reached for a bar of soap sitting beside the sink. At that moment she heard a loud series of knocks. Tory froze. From where she stood, she could see the door to her room shuddering under the blows of a heavy fist. Even with the drapes closed she felt totally exposed. And of course she hadn't bothered to put on the chain lock. Then over the roar of the shower she heard a man's voice calling, "I know you're in there." He pounded again on the door and rattled the doorknob trying to get in.

Oh, my God, she thought, what do I do now? Instinctively Tory grabbed the skimpy hand towel and clutched it to her. Should she call the switchboard? But she couldn't make herself step out farther into the room to reach the phone.

He wasn't going to stop knocking and go away. Finally Tory called out, her voice shrill, "What do you want?"

"Come on, Tory, open up. It's me, Michael."

"Michael!" She flew across the room and yanked open the door. As he stepped into the room, Tory flung her arms around his neck. "Wow! What a welcome," he said with a little laugh.

"Oh, Michael, I'm so glad you're here!"

Michael held her close. "If I'd had any idea I'd be greeted like this, I'd have been here sooner."

Suddenly Tory looked over Michael's shoulder and pulled away abruptly. Standing close behind him was his daughter, Melissa, her blue eyes round with astonishment. "Oh, my gosh! Hi, Missy. Look, the shower's still running. I'd better go shut it off." Aware she'd been babbling, Tory ran back into the bathroom and slammed the door.

Leaning against it, she thought, Slow down, Tory, take it easy. As her breathing settled to a more normal rate, she reached in and turned off the water. Thank goodness she'd brought her robe into the bathroom with her. She slipped it on and belted it tightly around her. Then she opened the door and walked into the room.

"What a surprise!" She smiled at Melissa, then turned to Michael. "What are you two doing here?"

"My rats all got sick and died," he told her flippantly. "The experiments had to be suspended. So I decided to come down here and sweep you off your feet." He saw her look of puzzled disbelief. "Actually, I missed you."

"Oh, Michael," Tory said softly.

He pulled her to him and kissed her. "Where's the best place to eat around here? Missy and I want to buy you the biggest steak in town."

While Tory quickly showered and dressed, Michael and his daughter had a lengthy conversation with the desk clerk about Yuma restaurants. Soon Tory joined them in the lobby and Melissa announced, "Guess what? We're going to the D-Bar-Q! Doesn't that sound neat?"

Tory knelt down in front of the little girl. "It sure does,

Missy. But you know what? I was so surprised to see you that I didn't get to say hello properly. Got a hug?''

She held out her arms and the child ran into them, throwing her own small arms around Tory's neck. Touched by the girl's eager embrace, Tory swung Melissa off the floor and held her tight. ''Now, that's what I call a hug,'' Tory said. Then she smiled across at Michael. ''I think we're all ready to eat.''

Once the three of them were settled in a big booth at the D-Bar-Q steak house, Melissa had lots of questions about the movie. Tory told her about the little terrier that had interrupted the shot the day before. ''Maybe he wanted to be in the movie,'' she told the little girl, and was rewarded with a delighted laugh. ''Then today,'' she went on seriously, ''the star of the movie had to go swimming in the river, and she said the water was so cold it would make her skin turn blue. She was afraid she'd look blue on the film.''

''Did she get blue goose bumps?'' Melissa tried to look serious as she asked this question, but she dissolved in helpless giggles as soon as the words were out of her mouth.

''I bet she did.'' Tory laughed along with the child. ''Must have looked pretty funny, huh?''

Between bites of steak she recounted a few of the other amusing things that had happened on the set in the short time she'd been in Yuma. For once Michael seemed really interested in her impressions, and Melissa hung on her every word. When they were all full to bursting and Michael was calculating the tip, the little girl said shyly, ''Tory? Do you think I could come and watch them make the movie?''

Tory reached over and pushed a wayward strand of blond hair off the child's face. ''I don't see why not,

Missy. I'll ask to make sure it's okay. But tomorrow everybody has a day off, so we'll have to wait till the next day.'' She looked quizzically at Michael. ''How long are you going to be here?''

''Oh, a couple of days at least.'' He stood up and looked at his watch. ''But now I think it's bedtime for little girls.''

No sooner had Michael started his car than Missy's eyelids began to droop, and in a moment she was sound asleep in the backseat. Michael glanced over his shoulder, then said to Tory, ''Well, it sounds like you've been having a great time down here. You movie people sure have all the fun, don't you?''

''Well, it hasn't all been fun,'' Tory said slowly.

He looked at her expectantly. ''What do you mean?''

''Oh, I don't know,'' Tory said with a nervous laugh. After a pause, she went on, ''This weird guy has been hanging around the set all the time, and I think he's kind of scary.''

Michael's glance was unreadable. ''What are you talking about? Did something happen?''

''No, not really. I'm sure I'm overreacting.'' Tory was already sorry she'd brought it up.

''But who is he?'' Michael's tone was insistent.

Reluctantly Tory told him about Straight Arrow and his strange mutterings and ominous presence. ''And now, thanks to stupid Artie, he knows who I am and that I was going to report him to the cops,'' she wound up. ''I just hope he doesn't turn up again. He gives me the creeps.''

Michael turned and smiled at her. ''Don't worry, sweetheart, I'm here to protect you now.''

At the motel, Michael carried his half-awake daughter to their room. Alone in her own room, Tory hung up her clothes and began getting ready for bed. Staring into the mirror as she brushed her teeth, she suddenly realized how strange it was that she hadn't mentioned last night's murder to Michael. She hadn't even told him how it replicated her script in such an uncanny way.

She turned out the bathroom light and walked toward the bed. I guess I don't want to think about it, she acknowledged to herself. It's too scary. But it *was* just a coincidence, she told herself firmly. She climbed into bed and picked up her book.

Half an hour later Tory heard a quiet knock at her door. As she let him in, Michael told her, "Well, the cat's asleep, so now the mice can play." Pulling her roughly into his arms, he bent to kiss her. "God, I missed you."

Tory was caught off-balance. For a moment she saw the two of them as a furtive couple sneaking into a sleazy motel room in search of a one-night stand. She felt an unaccustomed shyness and stood awkwardly as Michael turned to lock the door. "What about Melissa?" she whispered.

"Don't worry—it would take an earthquake to wake her, he whispered back. "And I'll go back before morning."

Then he took her in his arms again, and her absurd embarrassment vanished. His cool skin burned against hers, and her whole body seemed to come alive under his touch.

Chapter 5

Richard stood at the pay phone near the motel pool, listening to the ringing at the other end of the line. Eight o'clock in the morning and it was already blistering. How nice that they all had the day off. He would rest up in an air-conditioned bar all day and—

"Hello?"

"This is Richard."

"Yeah?"

"Well, you told me to call at eight."

"Oh. Yeah. Hang on."

Richard heard unintelligible murmurings and then another voice came on.

"Richard."

"Yes."

"Okay. Here's the deal. There's a souvenir shop on Avenida Juarez in San Luis, about six blocks on the left after you cross over into Mexico. There's no number, but it's next door to a record shop called Discoteca. Be there at five-thirty this afternoon. Ask for Sam. Tell him you're a friend of Ricardo's." There was a pause. "You got that?"

"Yes. But . . . what is it? I mean—"

"I don't know. You'll find out when you get there. But don't worry—Sam has never let us down."

"All right. I'll be there at five-thirty."

"Right. And we'll be hearing from you." It wasn't a question.

"Yes, of course. Well, good-bye, then."

There was a definite click at the other end of the line. Richard hung up thoughtfully. He went back to his air-conditioned room and flopped down on the bed.

In the coffee shop of the Wagon Wheel Inn Tory smiled across the table at Michael and Melissa. "It's so nice to have you here."

Michael gave her a grin. "Well, it's nine-thirty and we're ready to go. Aren't we, Missy? What's on the program for today?"

Tory looked startled. "Did I forget to tell you? Since this is our day off and there's no shooting, a bunch of us were planning to go down to a Mexican beach area called El Golfo. I'd better talk to John, I was going to drive down with him."

"Who's John?"

"He's the director, a real nice guy," Tory said absently. Then she caught his frown. "Oh, for heaven's sake, John's over fifty, Michael." She reached over and patted his hand. "He's not my type."

His face cleared. "Well, that sounds like fun."

"Oh, great," Missy piped up. "Can I bring my swimsuit?"

"You'd better," Tory told her with a laugh. "Otherwise, how can you go in the water?" Then she turned to Michael. "Can we take your car?" He nodded and she went on. "I'll just let John know. I'm sure the guy at the front desk can tell us how to get there."

The desk clerk knew all about El Golfo. "Oh, yeah," he told them. "Just go along toward the Ramada Inn and take a left. The road curves around, and when you come to a light, take another left and you're on the highway. You can't miss it."

Settling into the passenger seat of Michael's black Mustang, Tory smiled wryly at him. "I guess they don't believe in maps around here. Hope that guy was right. 'You can't miss it' always makes me nervous."

Michael grinned and pulled out onto the road. "You've lost your faith in human nature." He turned and looked over his shoulder at his daughter in the backseat. "Buckle up, honey. We're on our way."

He followed the desk clerk's directions, turning left and curving around a golf course. He pulled up at the stoplight and pointed to a prominent sign—"To San Luis"—and the arrow pointing left.

Almost immediately they left Yuma behind. Miles of cultivated fields stretched out on both sides of the highway. Small houses stood surrounded by dusty yards, their fences keeping in an occasional bony horse, its head drooping in the heat. In less than half an hour they reached the border.

No other cars waited at the two-lane crossing point, but a steady stream of pedestrians flowed in both directions. "Where are they going?" Tory wondered aloud as she looked around at the short string of shops—dime store, supermarket, coin laundry, drugstore. That seemed to be all there was of San Luis on the Arizona side.

"Got me. Maybe the grass is just greener on the

other side.'' Michael nodded to the border guard waving him through. ''On to El Golfo!''

When they got there, the beach was as lovely as the Yuma tourist brochure had promised. The smooth white sand and sparkling clear water made the hot dusty drive seem worthwhile. But it certainly was primitive. Tory was glad John had warned them to bring bottled water and food.

Several of the cast and crew were already there as were a number of Mexican families and groups of young people. Tory spotted Sally Manganaro ensconced against a folding back rest under an umbrella and headed toward her. But Missy, squealing with delight, kicked off her sandals and raced down to the water's edge. Tory took the beach bag and picnic sack out of Michael's hands as she smiled fondly at the small figure already ankle-deep in the gentle wavelets that washed the shore. ''Looks like you're on lifeguard duty. I'll drop this stuff and be down in a second.''

Sally looked up and gave Tory a friendly wave. ''Glad you made it. Isn't this heavenly?''

''It's certainly a nice change of scene,'' Tory said with a laugh.

Gesturing toward Michael and Melissa paddling in the water, Sally said, ''That must be your boyfriend. And his little girl?''

''Yes,'' Tory said. ''Isn't she cute? And she's such a nice kid. I'll do all the introductions when I can persuade them to get out of the water.'' Pulling off the sundress she'd worn over her bathing suit, she rolled it up and stuffed it into the beach bag. Then she strolled across the wide beach to join Melissa and Michael.

Missy was standing at the edge of the water, her face puckered as if ready to burst into tears. Instinctively

Tory took the child's hand and then looked out into the surf where Michael stood waist-deep. "What's wrong?" she called.

"Nothing," he called back, his voice irritated. "She got knocked down by a wave and now she won't try again." He paused as a breaker engulfed him, then bobbed up as it passed. Then he shouted to Missy, "Come on, Missy, you know how to swim. Be a brave girl—it's only water!"

But the little girl still hesitated as the waves lapped at her feet. Tory looked at her and said encouragingly, "Want me to swim out to your dad with you, Missy? Would that help?"

Missy planted her feet more firmly in the sand. "No," she said. "I don't want to. It's too scary."

"Okay," Tory told her understandingly. After all, she thought, these waves are a lot bigger when you're only three feet tall. She looked out at Michael standing in the water. "It's a little too rough for her right now, Michael." She had to raise her voice over the sound of the surf. "Maybe she'll try it later."

He stared at the two of them for a moment. Then without a word he strode toward the shore. When he reached them, he spoke to Tory, ignoring his daughter completely. "If you hadn't interfered, she would have done it."

Tory looked at him in exasperation. "You told me yourself that she tried, but the waves knocked her down. She's only five, Michael. She got scared."

"She's got to learn." His mouth set in a stubborn line.

"Oh, for heaven's sake." Now Tory was angry, too. "Not everyone's perfect like you. Give her a break."

His face grim, Michael looked coldly at Tory. Then

without a word, he turned and walked up the beach toward Sally's umbrella.

Wow, I guess I really put my foot in it, Tory thought as she watched Michael march through the sand. Maybe I shouldn't have butted in. After all, I don't have a child myself. . . . Then she looked down at the tense little face beside her. No, she realized, a child shouldn't be forced to do something that frightened her so much.

But now what? she wondered. Michael was pretty angry. Perhaps it would be best to ignore the whole episode. She reached down and took Missy's hand. "Come on, honey," Tory said, her voice artificially bright. "I'm hungry, aren't you? Let's go get some lunch."

The movie group was collapsed on the sand, slurping cold drinks and munching on slices of watermelon. Michael stood next to Kevin, a cold beer in his hand. He smiled at the two of them as they approached, and Tory realized with relief that, as far as he was concerned, the incident was over.

"Help yourself," said Kevin indistinctly. He spat out a few seeds and gestured toward the enormous melon.

"Did you all meet?" Tory asked. Without waiting for an answer, she went on, "This is Michael Canfield, and this is his daughter Melissa." Tory waved a hand at the recumbent bodies. "Michael, Missy, these people are part of our terrific cast and crew." She bit into a slice of melon. "Mmm, who's responsible for this treat?"

Lars Swenson laughed. "We passed a stall beside the road, and I could not resist."

Sally spoke from under her umbrella. She looked a little like a Martian with sun hat, sunglasses, and zinc oxide ointment masking her nose. "Tory, there's lots of potato salad and stuff in the ice chest, and I'm sure we didn't eat all the sandwiches. Help yourselves. I don't want to lug that stuff back to Yuma.'' She included Michael and Melissa in her friendly smile and said to the little girl, ''What do you feel like eating, honey?''

''Well, we brought some fruit and stuff,'' Tory began.

''Oh, don't worry about depriving us,'' John Hartnell said. ''You know Sally; she brought enough for an army.'' He peered into the ice chest. ''Let's see— coleslaw, potato salad, roast beef sandwiches, with or without mayonnaise. What can I give you?''

Tory and Michael heaped food on the paper plates Sally had of course provided. Melissa carefully picked out a sandwich and some melon and folded herself cross-legged on a towel to eat. ''Hey, thanks,'' Tory said. ''I didn't realize how hungry I was—all this fresh air and exercise.''

As they sat down in the sand, Debra edged over and leaned her forearm on Michael's shoulder. ''Oh, my, that potato salad looks so delicious. Could I just have one teeny tiny bite of it?'' Her kittenish voice made the request sound both helpless and suggestive.

''Yeah, sure.'' Michael sounded surprised.

Tory concentrated on her own plate as Debra leaned even closer, one scantily covered breast casually brushing against Michael's arm. ''I really shouldn't. I've got to be so careful of my figure.'' Playfully she added, ''Just make sure John isn't looking. You don't mind if I use your spoon?'' She reached down into his lap.

''Debra, for goodness' sake!'' Sally spoke sharply. ''Cover yourself up. You're starting to get burned.''

''Oh, dear, am I?'' Debra peeled down the edge of

her bikini top. "I guess I am. But it's too hot to wear my beach robe." She looked at Sally's umbrella-shaded chair. "Maybe I'd better—"

"If you won't wear your robe, you can use some of my sunscreen." Sally's voice was brisk. "Make sure you put it all over yourself, especially your face and chest."

Debra grimaced. "But that stuff is so yucky. I can't—"

"Oh, for God's sake," John broke in. "Sally's right."

Debra looked at him defiantly. "I don't see why I have to do what she says."

Into the awkward silence Lars said soothingly, "But, Debra, I do not wish to see your beautiful face all peeling and red when I look through the camera."

Debra stared at him. Then she snatched up the sunscreen and said sulkily, "Oh, all right, if you're all going to make such a fuss."

The four members of the crew, who had watched this exchange with detached boredom, now made signs of preparing to depart. Harry, the small, wiry sound man, stood up and stretched. "Guess we'll see you all back in Yuma."

"Where are you off to?" Kevin asked.

"The track in Mexicali," Harry replied.

Jimbo heaved himself to his feet. A huge bear of a man, he was ideally suited to his job as key grip, shifting all the heavy equipment from place to place with seemingly effortless ease. The navy anchor tattooed on his upper arm was dwarfed by his enormous biceps. He grinned at the group lounging on the sand. "Got any pesos you want me to lose for you?" He chuckled at his own wit and gulped down the remains of his Coors. "Want me to take the ice chest back, Sally?"

"No, thanks, Jimbo. I think we'll be able to manage if we all lift it together."

"Okay." He turned to Stu, the young cameraman, and Bill, the electrician, who never seemed to utter a word. "Ready when you are, guys."

Stu brushed the sand from his legs. "Bye, Lars. Bye, everyone."

Harry picked up his towel. "So long, everybody."

Jimbo grinned. "Yeah, *hasta la vista*."

Bill gave them a silent wave as they turned toward the road.

The remaining group sprawled like slugs on the sand. The combination of hot sun, food, and beer seemed to have immobilized them. Only Melissa had any energy at all. She moved off the towel and began covering her legs with the fine white sand. When they were completely buried, she moved them gently and watched the silvery streams cascade off her thighs.

Tory looked at Michael. He was lying on his back with one arm flung across his eyes, and he seemed to be dead to the world. She wondered what was going on. She just didn't get it. One minute he was in a cold fury with her and Melissa and the next he was his usual charming self. It was as if that whole business down by the water never happened. Puzzled, she gazed at his face, half hidden by his arm. Michael was a complicated person; she wished she understood him better.

After a while Melissa got bored with burying her own legs. She moved over to where her father lay and picked up a handful of sand. Letting it trickle slowly onto his chest, she watched it mound up and slither off.

"Dad, want to make a sand castle with me?" she asked when he sat up.

"In a minute, honey," he told her absently as he gazed longingly out toward the deeper water.

Kevin followed his look. "I bet you'd like to get in a real swim," he said to Michael in instant understanding. "Tell you what. I'll keep an eye on Melissa while you and Tory go get wet. Take your time. I'm an expert sand-castle builder."

"Hey, thanks." Michael flashed Kevin a grateful glance. "Come on, Tory, let's go."

They ran down to the water and plunged into the cool surf. The salty waves were buoyant and friendly, nothing like the rough whitecaps of the Pacific coast. Swimming out, Tory kicked lazily and looked back at the beach. Kevin's dark head was bent close to Melissa's blond one as they piled up a large heap of wet sand.

"Tory, let's swim out to that sailboat," Michael called out. "Look at that guy!"

"What's he doing?"

Tory watched in amazement as a brown young man swung high up over the water in a rope swing. The spinnaker of the sailing yacht had been loosened at the bottom, and as the wind caught it, the rope swing swooped up and then swiftly down again.

They reached the boat and were laughingly pulled up over the side by a group of young people. They were from Santa Barbara, the boat's owner explained, and had decided to explore up the Gulf of California from their mooring at Cabo San Lucas. When Michael said he was fascinated with the sling swing, they insisted he try it.

Tory sat on the luxurious deck, sipping a tall glass of iced tea and watching Michael stand poised and ready as he gripped the sides of the swing. His tall, rangy body was surprisingly agile and muscular. Tory caught her breath as she watched the wind carry him up and away. How could anyone think that was fun? she wondered. She shuddered. The whole idea was terrifying.

"Tory, that was absolutely incredible!" Michael said as he got out of the swing. "You must try it."

She laughed. "You can take my turn for me."

"But it's great! Come on!" He reached for her hand to pull her to her feet.

"No, really, Michael—"

"Try it just one time. I know you'll love it."

Annoyed at his insistence, Tory said, "You know anything like that gives me the shakes. Please don't push me. You go ahead and enjoy it."

"For God's sake, Tory." He stared down at her, his eyes unreadable. "You're too smart to let a silly fear like that govern your life. You could get over it if you'd just try!"

His voice was raised, and the boat's owner intervened. "Maybe she'd better not, if she—"

Michael turned away and, embarrassed, Tory tried to smooth things over. "He can't stand it that I'm not perfect," she said with a deprecating laugh.

As she watched Michael soar through the air again, she found herself wishing he'd stop trying to "improve" her character.

But when Michael was finally ready to leave, with profuse thanks to the yacht party, his annoyance seemed forgotten. They dived overboard and with long, easy strokes headed back to the beach.

By four o'clock they had all had about as much sun as they could take. Kevin and Michael carried the ice chest to John's car while Tory helped Sally gather up all the gear. Melissa folded up their towels and tried to brush the sand off her legs.

As John, Lars, and Debra drove off in John's car, Kevin turned to Michael. "Sally tells me she knows a great place to eat in San Luis. Why don't the three of you meet us there for dinner?"

Michael and Tory exchanged a glance. "Sure. Sounds good."

Sally gave Michael directions and said, "We'll meet you there at six."

Michael pulled his Mustang out onto the paved road. "Nice people. Kind of an unlikely-looking couple, though," he commented.

"Kevin and Sally? Oh, they're not a couple. Kevin is our leading man. You saw him in that film *Don't Walk Home Alone*. He's Kevin Dean. And Sally is our script girl. Her job is to keep track of all the shots that are taken and make sure the props are all the same, and like that. She's really well organized. Without her the whole thing would be in a total mess. I'm sure Kevin came down with her because he couldn't stand being stuck in a car with Debra. It's just as well that there isn't much more to shoot," she added. "Tempers seem to be a little ragged on the set."

When they reached the small border town of San Luis at about five-thirty, the streets were full of local shoppers. Shoe stores, dime stores, drugstores, and markets seemed to predominate along the main street. In the late afternoon heat, street vendors were doing a brisk business with their hand carts of various colored liquids to pour over crushed ice.

"Wow. This sure isn't like Tijuana," Tory remarked. "There are hardly any tourist shops."

"Well, this is all farmland around here. I suppose

this must be the big city where they come to do their marketing.''

Tory was looking out the window. ''I guess you're right.'' Then she said, ''There's one place for tourists, though. Look at all those sombreros and big pots.'' She stared at the little souvenir shop. ''That's Richard!'' Craning her neck as they cruised by, she exclaimed, ''What in the world is he doing with all those piñatas? He must have at least a dozen of them.'' She settled back in her seat. ''That's very peculiar.''

The green neon sign of the Casa Verde restaurant was straight ahead. ''Hope this place is air conditioned,'' Michael commented as he pulled into the parking lot. ''We're a little early, but I could use a cold beer.''

A solemn-looking young man ushered them to a table and snapped his fingers for a waiter. ''*Dos cervezas, por favor*,'' Michael said with a smile. Glancing at Melissa, he added, ''*Y una* Coca-Cola.''

The spotless white walls were festooned with a collection of old musical instruments and painted trays. On the tables, brilliantly striped serapes were crisscrossed to serve as tablecloths. Colorful pottery held tortilla chips and fiery hot sauce. Fingering the edge of a serape, Melissa said, ''This is neat.''

Tory smiled in agreement and then said, ''Let's go find the ladies' room before our drinks arrive, Missy.'' Slinging the beach bag over her shoulder, she took the child's hand and walked toward the back of the restaurant.

Luckily the ladies' room was clean and spacious. Tory helped the little girl out of her sandy bathing suit and fished out clean clothes from the beach bag. When they'd finished washing, Tory asked, ''Missy, do you want me to fix your ponytail? That wind on the beach made it kind of tangled.''

"Well . . ." Melissa looked at Tory shyly. "Do you know how to make braids?''

"Sure. Let's find the other elastic band you put in the bag.''

As she brushed out the fine golden hair and divided it evenly for braids, Tory realized how easy it would be to get really attached to Melissa.

When they returned to the table, the drinks were there. Michael leaned back in the woven palm and leather chair and took a large swallow of beer. "Just what I needed.''

He had just ordered some guacamole when Sally and Kevin appeared. "You're not drinking beer!" Sally exclaimed. "This place has the best margaritas in the world!''

"Well, then, by all means let's have some!" Tory's festive mood bubbled over in laughter. Sally grinned back, and then turned to Kevin.

"How are you feeling now?''

He smiled wanly, and Tory asked quickly, "What's the matter?''

Even in the soft glow of candlelight, he looked pale under his tan. "I've got a terrible headache,'' he said apologetically. "And I didn't bring my pills. Sally offered me some aspirin, but I can't take that.''

"Did you get too much sun?'' Tory asked in concern.

"No, I don't think so,'' he replied slowly. "I'm afraid it's mostly tension. Spending the day with Debra probably wasn't a good idea. She really gets on my nerves.''

"I've got some pills that might be just what you

need," Michael said helpfully. "They don't have any aspirin in them. They're prescription tranquilizers. I get them from a guy at the lab who's using them in a series of experiments."

"Well . . ." Kevin said uncertainly.

"I've used them. They're perfectly safe," Michael went on. "But they're fairly strong. Half of one would be plenty. And you probably shouldn't drive for several hours afterward." He looked questioningly at Kevin and Sally.

"That's okay," she said quickly. "I'm driving tonight."

"Well, I'd certainly appreciate it," Kevin said gratefully.

Michael opened a small metal box and took out a white tablet. He split it with a knife, and Kevin quickly swallowed it. Then they turned to the serious business of choosing from the menu.

At about the same time Richard Reed joined the short line of cars waiting to go through the border crossing back to the United States. When his turn came, the U.S. customs official leaned down to his open window. With a glance into the back seat, which was filled with brightly colored piñatas, he asked straight-faced, "Did you buy anything in Mexico, sir?"

"Fifteen piñatas, officer!" Richard's voice held a manic gaiety. "My sister sent me down here especially to buy them—all different," he rattled on.

"Would you open the trunk, please?"

Richard hopped out of the car and quickly opened the trunk. It was also filled with piñatas. "See what I mean? Don't you think they're just the thing for a fifteen-year-old's birthday party? It's *so* original."

The customs man looked at him steadily. "You didn't buy any liquor? Or anything else?"

"Oh, no," said Richard in his almost falsetto voice. "Just the piñatas."

"Okay. Move along, please. And drive safely."

Richard drove across the border and headed north toward Yuma. Once he was well past the guards he began muttering under his breath. "Goddamn idiots. They could have at least warned me it was piñatas."

Chapter 6

Filled to the brim with tostadas and shrimp Casa Verde, Tory and Michael gratefully saw the lights of Yuma spread in front of them. Melissa, of course, had fallen asleep as soon as they got into the car, and Tory thought how fortunate it was that backseats of cars were so well adapted to be travel beds for children. As they drove into the parking lot of the Wagon Wheel Inn, she said to Michael, "Our home away from home. Luckily we can leave tomorrow."

"Tomorrow?" Michael said in surprise. "But I thought you'd have to stay on longer."

"Oh, no. There's no reason for me to stay on. I was planning to drive back to L.A. in the morning."

He parked the car in a slot near the steps to her room. "What's the rush? We'll never come back to this area again, and I was sort of looking forward to spending some time with you. You know, kind of a holiday."

"That sounds nice." Inside she was glowing; Michael seldom spent time away from his lab. She wasn't going to turn down this chance. "Let me think . . . I guess I don't have anything planned that I need to get back for right away. And I'd love a little vacation. Sounds great!''

"Good." Michael got out of the car and leaned in to lift his sleeping daughter from the backseat. "I'll take her in and get her settled, but it's still early. How about if we meet in the bar in half an hour or so?"

"Will Missy be okay all alone?"

Guiltily Tory realized that she hadn't been worried about Melissa the night before, and she was glad when Michael answered, "Oh, sure. She hardly ever wakes up, and she's five, after all. She knows how to call the desk, and I'll tell them where I'll be."

Later, as they sat in a booth in the dark motel bar, Michael told Tory, "You know, I don't have any idea what this film is all about."

"Oh, Michael, you won't approve. You'd really rather not know."

"Don't be silly. I want to understand what you're doing. Tell me about it."

"Okay," Tory said dubiously. "Just tell me when I reach your saturation point." She launched into her story. "It's about this guy who's madly in love with a gorgeous blonde. She goes out with him once and decides she's not interested in him, so she dumps him. But he's a little bit crazy."

Uh-oh, Tory thought, that was a mistake. Michael hated to hear people use the word "crazy," or misuse it, as he always reminded her. She looked at him nervously and hurried on. "Anyway, he starts following her around, and he sees her making love to another guy. So he flips out. First he slashes her tires, then he breaks into her apartment and kills her dog. He kills a strip-tease dancer who's also a blonde. Then he moves on to kill her neighbor and then a girl she works with. Finally he tries to kill her, but of course she's saved in the end by the cops.'' Tory watched Michael's stony expression as he took a swallow of Mexican brandy. ''I knew you wouldn't like it. But that's what they wanted.''

''I understand that that's what the public wants, Tory. But sometimes you disappoint me. I'm sure you could be a really fine writer. It offends me to see you cheapening yourself by pandering to the public taste for trash.''

''Michael, I don't think that's fair—''

''And besides,'' he broke in, ''don't you think you have an obligation to give your audience some real insight into why people behave in an antisocial manner?''

''I knew you'd disapprove of the whole idea.''

''That's not the point. Even though it's just a potboiler, don't you feel it's important to explain how these things happen? You know that so-called crazy behavior is the product of the unbearable stresses in our society.'' He saw Tory's defeated expression. ''Now, Tory, you know I have the greatest belief in your intellectual powers. That's the whole point. You *know* that there is no such thing as 'crazy.' There are only normal responses of different individuals to known or unknown environmental pressures. We can't always know what stresses a particular person is responding to. Even in the kind of commercial stuff you're writing, there's no reason you can't provide a more truthful view of life and human emotion.''

''Well,'' Tory said uncertainly, ''it's not easy to make all that into an exciting story line.''

Michael smiled. ''Come on, now, honey, you don't have a contract that says you have to tell out-of-date lies. Give them the real truth.''

Looking away from his intense expression, Tory saw Lars Swenson standing alone at the bar with a drink in his hand. "Oh, there's Lars!" she exclaimed, a note of relief in her voice. She waved to attract his attention and called, "Hi! Come on and join us."

As Lars slid into the booth, Michael said to him, "I saw you out there in the water today. You looked like quite a serious swimmer."

Lars smiled modestly. "Oh, not really. I just try to keep in shape. But the water is not really my first love. I am from Sweden, you know, and there everyone is a skier."

"Oh?" Michael was clearly interested. "Where do you ski?"

"Here in this country I have a share in a place at Mammoth, and I go to Sun Valley a few times. But each year I go home to ski in Sweden, too."

Michael was an avid skier, and Tory could see that they were warming up for an extended session of comparing slopes and trails and probably brands of ski equipment as well. She glanced at her watch and then said, "Listen, I'm going to go up and try calling my sister. I'll be back."

As the door to the bar closed behind her, Tory drew a deep breath. It was unfortunate that this movie script centered on a crazy, obsessed man; a different kind of story wouldn't have bothered Michael so much. He might still have considered it a potboiler, but it wouldn't have pushed his buttons the way this one did.

He really was insistent about not labeling people "crazy," and Tory could understand why he felt that way. She often tried to imagine what it had been like for Michael, living in foster homes for much of his childhood. She could almost hear the other kids teasing him because his mother was "crazy" and in the "loony bin." No wonder he didn't like anyone to use those words. Perhaps that was what had led Michael into psychology—the need to understand what had happened to his mother.

In her room, Tory put through her call. When her sister answered, she said, "Hi, Carrie. How are things going?"

"Oh, Tory," her sister said breathlessly. "I'm so glad you called. I know Mom and Dad told you what's been happening, and it's so hard for me to know what to do. Doug does love the children, and I believe he loves me, too, and the kids need him. But *I* need me, if you know what I mean. Sometimes recently I've felt positively suffocated with pressures and responsibilities and duty and all. Well, anyway, it's real difficult and I'm not at all sure I'm handling it right. But I've got to watch out for myself after all, not only for me but to make sure the kids have a mom who's not totally nuts when all's said and done . . ."

Tory listened patiently, trying to make sense of her sister's rush of words. She wished she had a better grasp of what had actually happened. But it was hard to really feel someone else's troubles, no matter how much one cared.

"Tory, do you think I'm wrong to want to be me for myself?" Carrie went on. "I mean, of course I love the kids, and Doug, too, and I want to do things for them and make them happy, but why can't they let me do things for myself and make me happy, too?"

Tory took a moment to collect her thoughts. "If you're asking if I think you should have a life and interests of your own, of course I do."

"You don't think I'm being totally selfish, then?"

"No," Tory said sadly, "I just wish you and Doug could find some less drastic way to solve your problems. But, Carrie," she said strongly, "I really do feel you will be able to work things out. Have you thought about some kind of counseling? I think it might . . ."

A few minutes later Tory hung up the phone, not sure that she had been much help. Then she glanced out the window and saw Richard walking quietly along the balcony toward the stairs. As she went to the window to close the drapes, she reflected on how different her own life had been from Carrie's.

Who would have ever thought a girl from the small town of Geneva, Ohio, would end up in Los Angeles as a scriptwriter? That hadn't been her plan when she went off to the University of Chicago on a scholarship. Her parents had been a little worried about their baby girl living and going to school on the south side of Chicago. The area's rough reputation had definitely reached Geneva. But Tory was intent on becoming a historian, and the school's reputation in the humanities, as well as its offer of financial assistance, had finally convinced Mom and Dad.

She'd loved living in the big city. And to her surprise she'd found lots of boys eager to take her out. Amazingly, her lean tomboy figure had blossomed, and she enjoyed the new feeling of desirability. She had studied hard, but somehow she'd managed to have a lot of fun, too. She'd spent a good deal of time in the cheap bar on Fifty-fifth Street, just off the campus, that was a hangout for some of the most interesting students and professors. Some of her best college memories were of being there with a glass of beer, alternately arguing about Toynbee and cheering for the Blackhawks playing on the big color TV over the bar.

Tory had taken a movie production course in her senior year as a lark. The visiting professor was a handsome young director with a lot of Hollywood charm, and there had been an instant attraction between them. Tory had found the class fascinating, and she had been thrilled when the professor said her writing was first rate. But she'd felt guilty about the affair they'd become caught up in. And when Justin left at the end of the quarter to return to his wife and family, Tory had said good-bye with both relief and regret.

After graduation, Tory hadn't been sure what she wanted to do. Working for a Ph.D. in history somehow didn't have much appeal anymore. And she couldn't see herself teaching history in high school. So when her roommate broke up with her boyfriend and decided to go to Los Angeles for the summer, Tory jumped at the chance to go along.

Kathy said that her cousins would be happy to put them up, but Tory knew when she saw it that the house was too small for long-term guests. When after a long-distance call, Kathy announced, with stars in her eyes, that she and Bob were getting married after all, Tory realized she had to make a decision. She didn't want to go back to Chicago, and she certainly couldn't continue to stay with Kathy's cousins. Then she remembered Justin's parting words: "If you're ever in L.A., look me up. I really do think you have what it takes to write for the movies."

He was the only person she knew in Los Angeles, and after a moment's deliberation, she picked up the phone.

"Hello, Justin. This is Tory Ryan." Into the silence that followed, she added, "From Chicago."

"Oh, yeah, hi, Tory. Gee, how are you?"

Plunging right in, she told him her predicament and wound up with "So I thought I'd take you up on your offer to help me find some sort of job. I need to make a little money so I can rent an apartment."

Once he realized that she wasn't interested in rekindling the romance, Justin couldn't have been more helpful. He arranged for her to house-sit for a friend of his who was going to Europe, and several phone calls later, he'd gotten her a chance to try rescuing a script in trouble. By the end of the summer, she was ensconced in her beach house in Venice and was working on her first project with Julie Kingman.

Tory's thoughts returned to Carrie. She was glad she hadn't tied herself down at nineteen, as her sister had done. But at age twenty-six she was beginning to wonder if she'd ever find a man with whom she would want to share the rest of her life. Although Michael was being very attentive here in Yuma, Tory suspected that once they were back in L.A. his work would again come first in his life. Was she asking for the impossible, or did she just somehow get involved with guys whose goals didn't mesh with her own?

Tory picked up her purse and started out of her room. Maybe she was misjudging Michael. After all, he had come all the way down here to see her. Maybe things would all work out when they got back to L.A. She supposed she would just have to wait and see. She pulled the door closed behind her and started toward the steps, then lifted a hand to greet the man coming up the stairs.

"Hi, Richard."

He looked at her blankly for a moment. Then Tory could almost see his habitual charm sliding into place. "Hi, gorgeous," he replied with a quick smile.

Remembering her quick glimpse of him in San Luis, Tory asked, "What in the world are you going to do with a bunch of piñatas, Richard? I've been dying of curiosity ever since I saw you in that shop in Mexico."

Disconcerted, Richard stared at her. "Oh," he said. "Well, I promised a friend I'd get some for him."

There was an awkward pause. Then Tory said, "That was nice of you."

"Yeah, I'm a nice guy," he told her in an approximation of his usual teasing tone. He added quickly, "I've got to run—people to see, places to go." With a quick grin, he moved past her, clutching something to his chest under his windbreaker.

That was a little weird. But then, Richard was often a little weird. Tory shrugged. She didn't want to know what he was up to, she thought as she headed back toward the bar and Michael.

In his room, the door carefully chained and bolted, Richard took the two large film cans from under his windbreaker and dumped them onto the bed. Then he went to work on the piñatas. He found the opening in the first one and gently pulled out a sealed plastic bag of white powder. Now that he knew how to do it, the rest came fairly quickly.

Once he had the fifteen plastic bags on the bed, he opened up the empty film cans. He started to pack the cocaine into the cans and then stopped. A little smile flashed across his face.

From his big makeup box, he took out a razor blade and one of the small plastic bags he kept to put wet sponges in. Then, after carefully slitting open one of the bags of cocaine, Richard poured about a third of the powder into the other little plastic bag. This he sealed neatly with tape and placed in the film can. The original packet, now two-thirds full, he sealed and buried at the bottom of his makeup box. He never allowed anyone to use his makeup kit, but anyone who did see it would think it was some sort of face powder.

Richard efficiently packed all the rest of the packets into the two film cans and sealed them with wide white tape. With a large felt-tip pen he wrote a title, *Cry for Help*, on each tape, and added a small x. Now the cans looked like all the others that would be sent to the film lab in L.A. Only the guy in the lab would notice the small x and take care of that "film" personally.

Chapter 7

The next morning Tory was lounging in bed, taking advantage of the unaccustomed opportunity to be lazy. Her phone rang, and when she picked it up, Michael said, "Hi, sweetheart. How about some breakfast? Let's go sit by the pool and decide what we want to do today. It's the first day of your vacation, after all."

Tory laughed. "Sounds okay to me."

She found Michael and Melissa at a table by the pool, and while Michael caught the waitress's eye and ordered an enormous breakfast, Tory ducked inside to the front desk. She collected an assortment of maps and fliers describing the local tourist spots and places of historical interest. When she got back outside, Penny from the production office was standing beside the table.

"Oh, Tory, I've been looking for you. Mr. Kingman called. He wants you to go out to the location right away."

"What for?" Tory asked in dismay.

"I don't know, but he said it was real important."

"Oh, dear. Couldn't you just say you couldn't find me?" Tory looked at Penny's expression. "No, I guess you couldn't. Oh, damn. Where are they shooting?"

"They're at the apartment today. You know, Jean Anne's apartment?"

"Oh. Well, okay, Penny, I know you didn't mean to ruin my morning."

Tory took a sip of coffee and set down the cup. "Michael, I'm really sorry about this. But it's probably nothing at all—just some line they want changed and as long as I'm still around, Julie wants me to do it. I'm sure it won't take more than an hour at the most. Why don't you and Missy stay and have a swim here? I'll zip out there and get back as soon as I can."

Michael gave her a look of cool displeasure. "This was supposed to be our vacation."

Surprised, Tory replied, "It is. I'm sure this won't take long."

"Sometimes I don't know where your priorities are." His whole body expressed disapproval and annoyance.

Now annoyed herself, Tory said quickly, "But, Michael, this is my job. I came here to work, after all. When it's your work that interferes—" She broke off. Missy's eyes were wide and her face looked pinched, almost fearful. "This isn't the time to discuss it," Tory told Michael firmly. "The sooner I get out there, the sooner I'll be finished. You two can decide what you want to explore so we can leave as soon as I get back." She dropped the handful of brochures beside his plate and hurried toward her car.

The streets of Yuma shimmered in the hot sun, and Tory flipped down the sun visor to shield her eyes. All that talk last night about what a great writer she could be sure didn't mean much when her work interfered with his plans. She didn't like his attitude one bit—and this wasn't the first time, either. It was something they were going to have to work out at some point.

She signaled for a left turn and realized that there was another aspect of Michael's reaction this morning that bothered her. This was not something to quarrel about in front of his daughter. Missy had looked really worried. Tory thought it must be hard for the child to cope with her father's hostility, especially when it often seemed to come out of left field. It was hard enough for Tory herself to deal with it, and she was a lot older than Missy.

After parking behind the equipment van, Tory got out and surveyed the location. Julie of course was embroiled in an argument with John and Lars. Tory walked over to Sally. "What are they shooting today?" Maybe she could fix the problem right now and leave as soon as Julie had okayed it.

Sally answered laconically, "The dead dog—starts at scene thirty-nine." She handed the script book to Tory, who started reading.

39 EXT. JEAN ANNE'S APT. BUILDING—DAY
    FULL SHOT
    of Jean Anne's front door as she opens it
    from inside, comes out, and pulls it shut be-
    hind her, giving it a good yank to make sure
    the lock clicks. She's wearing a skimpy
    sundress and high-heeled sandals and is on
    her way to work.
    PULL BACK
    as her heels CLICK along the pavement.
    From the side of the building, Alan peers

around the corner. He moves out into view
and watches her walk away.

40 FULL SHOT

of Alan as he pries open a side window of
Jean Anne's apartment. Dog YAPPING
from inside.

41 INT. JEAN ANNE'S APT.—DAY

Alan is just climbing into Jean Anne's bedroom through the window. Her dog, a tiny
Yorkshire terrier, stands in the middle of the
room, BARKING furiously. Ignoring the dog
for the moment, Alan looks around the
room, then picks up her nightgown from the
floor and strokes it longingly. Then he
places it carefully on the bed and crosses
to pick up the dog.

42 INT. JEAN ANNE'S LIVING ROOM—DAY

Alan enters from bedroom carrying dog. He
freezes as he hears Jean Anne's clicking
heels outside and a key turned in the lock.
Alan drops the dog and slips into the coat
closet near the front door.

Jean Anne enters the apartment as Alan
pulls the closet door closed. The dog
BARKS furiously and dances between the
front door and the closet door.

JEAN ANNE
Now, now, Jojo. I know you're happy
to see Mama, but I just came back to
get this letter I forgot to mail.

She stoops and picks up the dog and kisses
it. Carrying the dog, she crosses to the cof-

fee table, picks up an envelope. She kisses
the dog again and puts it on the floor. Then
she shoves the envelope into her purse.
She heads toward the front door.

JEAN ANNE
Bye, bye, Jojo. Mama has to go to
work. Be a good boy and I'll see you
when I get home.

Jean Anne goes out the front door and
closes it behind her while the dog BARKS.
Alan comes out of the closet and picks the
dog up again. Grabbing its head in one
hand and its little body in the other, he
quickly snaps its neck.
He lays the dog's body on the floor just inside the front door.

ALAN
(softly)
Bye, bye, Jojo.

He turns and heads into the bedroom.
43 EXT. JEAN ANNE'S APT. BUILDING—
DAY
Alan climbs back out her bedroom window,
looks around, and runs toward the back of
the building.

Tory riffled through a few pages till she came to the
scene in which Jean Anne returned from work.

51 EXT. JEAN ANNE'S APT. BUILDING—
   NIGHT
   Jean Anne, in the same skimpy sundress,
   walks quickly to her front door, fishes the
   key out of her bag, and pushes open the
   door.
52 INT./EXT. JEAN ANNE'S DOORWAY—
   NIGHT
   She takes one step inside and switches on
   the living room light. As the room lights up,
   Jean Anne sees her dead dog at her feet.
   She SCREAMS.

JEAN ANNE
Oh, my God! Jojo!

She drops to her knees beside the dog's
body, tears streaming down her cheeks.
She picks up the tiny body.

JEAN ANNE
(brokenly)

Jojo. Jojo.

Julie walked over just as Tory finished reading. She
looked at him with a puzzled expression. "It looks okay
to me."

"You wouldn't say that if you'd been here long,"
Julie said aggressively. "How I ever let you write a dog
into this turkey, I'll never know!"

"Has the dog been giving you problems?"

"Not the dog! The dog is okay as long as you don't
mind the handler who's worried the goddamn lights are
too hot for its delicate coat or the breaks every time

we're ready to start shooting so that the little darling can have a drink of water 'cause it's not used to this dry desert climate, and then, of course, it's got to have its little mouth wiped and its coat brushed. Oh, and yeah, then it's got to go out and pee 'cause it's drunk all that water. No, the dog isn't any problem.''

"So what's wrong?" She wasn't in the mood to listen to his tirade.

"What's wrong! I'll tell you what's wrong. Debra can't stand the beast. She practically throws up when it gets near her. And the shit really hit the fan when she had to pick up that goddamn corpse." Julie paused to take a breath.

"What did you do about that anyway?" Tory asked curiously. "Did you have to drug the dog, or what?"

"Naw. Artie went down to the pound and got a body."

Tory blanched, but her curiosity overcame her squeamishness. "But what if they didn't have a Yorkie?"

"Sweetheart, you wouldn't believe it, but whatever you're looking for, they can come up with it a day later." He sighed heavily. "But that's not what I got you down here for. I want you to write a new ending."

Tory stared at him. "What?"

"Yeah. This ending stinks. Yesterday, while you guys were all down to the beach, I was lookin' over this script again. The ending's all wrong—too corny, too sentimental, you know what I mean, kiddo? This is supposed to be a scary picture. The girl can't get rescued at the last minute like in some old western. We gotta send 'em out of there with a chill down their spines. So I want ya to come up with something that will really weird them out."

Tory tried to collect her thoughts. "But, Julie—"

He patted her shoulder. "Stick around the set. I wanta hear what you come up with before you start writing."

She opened her mouth to protest, but Julie was already yelling, "What's the holdup over there? We're on a budget, you guys, so let's get things moving." He stomped over to the group huddled around the camera.

Damn, Tory thought. This was ridiculous. And what was she going to do about Michael and Melissa? Then, unwillingly, she considered what Julie had said. Maybe he was right—she had always been a sucker for a happy ending, the knight in shining armor on the white charger. This movie probably did need something a little more macabre. But how could she do it so they wouldn't have to reshoot anything? Julie would have a fit if it needed more time or money. Let's see, she thought. How about if . . .

She walked over to the trailer to find a copy of the script. "Hi, Kevin," she said in a preoccupied way.

He was standing face to face with a tall, dark-haired teenager. The boy was saying, "I don't want to cause you any problems, Dad, but I just can't live with her. I mean, she's driving me crazy. I can't take it anymore."

Kevin had a hunted look. "But, Greg, I told you, it's just not possible. I'm away so much on location, and there'd be no one home to take care of you. You're just a kid; you've got to be in school. I just don't see how it could work." Christ, he thought, what a time for this to happen. Why can't the kid stick it out for another year and a half, till he's eighteen? I know it's rough; I lived with that bitch for ten long years, but after all, he's in school, he's got things to do. All he has to do is come home to sleep. I can't deal with having a teenage kid around; it's hard enough getting parts without that.

Greg was still staring at him with pain in his eyes. "Dad, really, I won't get in your way. I promise."

John's voice floated across. "Cut, and that's a print. Good girl, Debra, I knew you could do it. Let's take five, everybody. Debra dear, go and relax, and we'll get Richard to make you all gorgeous again."

Before Kevin could escape, there she was, looking prettily wilted. She sank into a chair. "That was the worst experience of my whole life. Wasn't that just awful, Kevin, that poor little dead thing?" Debra glanced over at Tory, a little distance away, and raised her voice. "How could you ever have written that scene, Tory, so gruesome and pathetic? I've learned my lesson. My agent's just going to have to tell people that I can't do these scenes. It drains all my emotional energy."

Tory didn't respond, and Debra turned her attention back to Kevin. "But who is this handsome young man? I haven't seen you before—I'd remember."

Unwillingly Kevin said, "This is my son Greg, Debra."

"Your son? Kevin! You've been keeping him a deep dark secret. I didn't know you were old enough to have such a big beautiful grown-up son. How old are you, Greg?"

"Sixteen." Greg stood awkwardly, glancing from her to his father.

"I think you'd better go on back to the motel, Greg," Kevin said. "I'll talk to you when I get back."

"Oh, Kevin, you're such an old fuddy-duddy. I bet Greg would love to stay and watch his ol' daddy do his stuff. And I'd love to have someone new to talk to for a change." She looked innocently from Kevin to his son. "You don't want to go back to that boring motel, do you, Greg?"

"Well . . ."

"Of course you don't, and I don't blame you a bit. Your dad's forgotten what it's like to be young and eager." She looked over his shoulder. "Oh, Richard, guess what? This gorgeous thing here is Kevin's son! Isn't he naughty for never telling us he had a son who's all grown up?"

Richard stepped toward Debra with his makeup sponge in his hand. "Stop drooling, darling," he said cattily. "I have enough repair work to do already." He glanced at Greg. "Out here for long?"

"I don't know," Greg replied uncertainly.

Kevin cut in. "As long as you're here, Greg, let me show you around the set."

"But I don't want to hold you up, Dad."

Kevin laughed shortly. "Don't worry about that. I have to hang around until Debra gets through this next scene. We have plenty of time."

Debra shot Kevin a venomous glance, and Richard cackled with glee. "Guess you're not top of the pops, sweetie pie." He chortled at his own wit.

Soon they were ready to resume shooting, and Tory could see why Julie was all worked up. Debra seemed incapable of relating to the dog at all. And the dog's handler hovering about just made things worse. The retakes continued, with everyone wilting under the hot lights. Tension on the set became almost unbearable. Tory realized she couldn't think at all in this pressure cooker. She had to get out of there. But she certainly wasn't going to tell Julie that now. He looked as though one more word would set off an explosion. If only they'd get this damn scene right, she could talk to him and then leave.

Guiltily she decided she'd better call Michael and let him know what was happening. Even if she left right now, she couldn't go off and explore with him and Missy. She had to come up with an idea and then write it. Oh, dear, she thought, Michael was not going to be pleased.

Tory headed for the temporary phone that had been installed at the location. As she picked it up, her glance rested on the little collection of spectators who always seemed to gather wherever a film was being shot. And of course, there he was—the pale, intense man they all now referred to as Straight Arrow. Grimly she hoped he'd stay out of her way. Today was not the day for one of his sinister pronouncements.

Someone finally answered the phone at the Wagon Wheel, but the switchboard girl couldn't find Michael. "Please leave a message that I called," Tory said. "Tell him to go ahead and do whatever he's got planned without me. I'm going to be tied up for most of the day."

After hanging up, Tory looked around once more for Julie. There was that cop, Captain Fleming, standing near the equipment truck. Too bad such an attractive guy had to be so arrogant, she thought. She wondered if he was married—she suspected he was horrible to live with.

She glanced at him again, and he looked up and motioned her over. With a martyred sigh, Tory joined him.

"Hello, Ms. Ryan. I'm Captain Fleming; we met the other night."

"Yes, I remember." Tory's tone was neutral.

"I'm glad I caught you here. I have a few questions I'd like to ask you."

"What about?"

"Ms. Ryan, I can't say that Yuma is a crime-free area, but we don't have many murders here. And I couldn't help being struck by the similarities between the murder of that dancer the other night and the scene you told me you were shooting."

Tory stared at him. "What are you saying?"

"I'm not saying anything. But I don't know much about the movie business and I thought you could help me out." He smiled at Tory, but she didn't smile back. "Who had access to the script?"

"Everybody. It's what we're working on after all."

"All these people have copies?" His gesture took in the whole location.

"Sure—" Tory stopped abruptly. Then she said slowly, "Well, that particular scene wasn't in the original script. The original murder scene couldn't be shot because the actress in it broke her arm."

When she didn't go on, Captain Fleming prodded, "And then?"

Unwillingly Tory continued. "I had to write in the stripper's murder instead. I wrote a rough outline in Los Angeles and then dictated the script pages on my way here. It was typed up in the morning and we shot it that night. I'm not sure who got copies of it."

"So nobody knew who was to get murdered until you got here?"

"It sounds as if you think it's my fault that girl got killed." Angry spots of color appeared on Tory's cheeks.

"Not at all." Captain Fleming flipped through his notebook. "Let's move on to something else. Arthur Silverstein said that you wanted to report someone to the police. Is that true?"

"Arthur Silverstein?" Tory repeated blankly. "Oh, you mean Artie!"

Captain Fleming waited a moment. Then he said, "The man you wanted to report—I understand you've seen him several times on the set. Is he here now?"

Tory looked across the street. "Yes—the guy with the crew cut."

The captain followed Tory's glance, then turned back to her. "That man frightened you?"

"Yes," Tory said warily.

"What did he do?"

She began to blush. This was going to sound so stupid, she thought angrily. Taking a deep breath, she launched into an account of Straight Arrow's disconcerting habit of playing with that leather thong and the way he kept creeping up behind her and muttering bizarre comments. "I know it doesn't sound like much," she wound up defensively, "but it was really scary at the time."

"I see. And that's what you wanted to report?"

"No! What I had planned to tell you, and the reason I tried to find out his name, was that he left during the shooting on the night of the murder—or at least I think he did. Maybe now you could ask him a few questions and stop bothering me!" Help! she thought. Now it sounded as if she had made that up to justify her hysterical female fears. She glared at the cop in frustration. Why had she let him maneuver her into looking like such a fool? She wished she could match his cool imperturbability.

"What's the matter?" a male voice said behind her.

Tory had been so caught up that she hadn't even seen Michael approach. She turned to him, relieved. "Oh, it's nothing. Captain Fleming just likes to play tough cop.''

She regretted the comment as soon as she'd made it. What a stupid thing to say. Michael tensed, his face a stony mask. Tory knew he had a thing about cops; he had nearly come to blows with a policeman who stopped him for speeding one evening. She felt flustered and out of control. What was the matter with her anyway? Why get Michael embroiled in this interview? It would only make things worse.

Captain Fleming closed his notebook and nodded to Tory. ''Thanks, Ms. Ryan,'' he said matter-of-factly.

She took Michael's arm, and with a thunderous look at the captain he turned away. Tory glanced back and saw the policeman looking after them thoughtfully.

''What's going on?'' Michael still sounded upset. ''I thought you were coming right back to the motel.''

''Oh, Michael, Julie wants me to rewrite the ending now! The thing is, I guess he's right; the ending is kind of feeble the way I wrote it. But I can't think here with everything going on. I'm going to tell Julie I'm leaving, and I'll try to come up with something back at the motel where it's quiet.''

''For God's sake, Tory!'' Michael's green eyes glittered with anger. ''I come all the way down here to see you and you barely spend ten minutes of your precious time with me. First you go off, quote, for an hour, unquote, and now it's going to be the whole damn day!''

Luckily Missy was still sitting in Michael's car, and Tory let her annoyance boil over. ''Look who's talking! I didn't ask you to come to Yuma.'' She saw his scowl deepen. ''Michael, it's not that I don't want you here— I'm thrilled that you drove down. But I came here to work, and that's my first obligation. Surely you can understand that.''

After a long pause, Michael said quietly, "Right. I'll leave you alone. Maybe late this afternoon you could take a few minutes off. Missy wants to show you how much her backstroke has improved.'' Without waiting for a reply, he turned away.

Tory watched him stride toward his car. So far this had not been a great day. And now she had to come up with a fabulous and entirely new ending for a film she thought she'd finished with months ago.

Late that afternoon as the film crew straggled in, Tory, Michael, and Melissa were sitting by the pool, dripping wet and with their legs dangling in the water. Tory had tried to work for most of the day, frantically coming up with and then discarding new ideas for the film's ending. Finally she'd given up, hoping that the distraction of a swim would generate new creativity. On the way to the pool, she had met Michael and Missy, who were just returning from a visit to the old Territorial Prison, one of Yuma's few tourist attractions. Michael greeted Tory as if their quarrel earlier in the day had never happened, and Tory was happy to leave things that way. Soon all three of them were relaxing beside the pool.

"You guys certainly have the right idea, escaping from the heat," Sally said as she flopped into a chaise.

"I think the heat has fried my brain," Tory said. "I've been groping for ideas for this new ending all afternoon, but all I came up with is a blank. So I gave up. I needed a break.''

"Yes, it has been a long day for me, too,'' Lars agreed.

John emerged onto the patio. "Well, everyone." He

included them all in his look. "The man at the desk tells me there's a fabulous Mexican restaurant nearby called the Latin Quarter. It's where all the locals go. I suggest that we all meet there for dinner. I, for one, am starving!"

"Sounds like a good idea," Jimbo said. There was a general nodding of heads.

"We all deserve a treat," Debra chimed in.

"Count me out, my dears." Richard pressed a melodramatic hand to his brow. "I don't think my delicate tummy could take Mexican food after the day we've had." He blew them a kiss and went off toward his room.

Lars checked his wallet. "Julie only pays for meals in this motel. Perhaps I can cash one of my checks—"

John interrupted him. "I'll loan you some money, Lars. It can't be that expensive. How 'bout you, Rose? You coming along?"

"I don't think so." She smiled sweetly at them all. "I'm on a bit of a budget. A swim and a sandwich at the coffee shop will suit me fine." She said to John, "Thank you anyway. I'll see you tomorrow." With a wave she was gone.

"That's Rose for you," said Dennis. "I've worked with her on three films, and she's never spent a dime. Don't know what she's saving it for. She certainly earns enough."

"Perhaps she's a secret bettor." Harry laughed. "See her often at the track, Jimbo?"

Jimbo looked at Harry in confusion. He wasn't sure if his leg was being pulled. "Rose?"

Sally frowned in puzzlement. "It is strange, now that you mention it. I know she lives alone. Maybe she banks it all for her old age." She shrugged. "Well, that's her own business.'' She looked at John. ''How dressy is this place?''

''Sally.'' John laid a hand on her shoulder. ''Tonight it's come as you are.''

Sally laughed cheerfully. ''Good, because I'm too tired to change.''

''Well, I'm not!'' Debra exclaimed. ''If I don't have a quick shower, I'll just melt into a little puddle right here and now.'' She stood up. ''I'll only be a minute. Don't go without me!''

Lars looked after her retreating figure and then dropped down into the chaise next to Sally's. ''I think I will drink a beer. For Debra, a minute could become one hour.''

''If she's not down here by six-thirty, we'll leave her a note and go,'' John said with a smile.

Tory stood up. ''Well, I certainly can't go anywhere in this wet bathing suit.''

''Right.'' Michael stood up, too. ''Come on, Missy, let's go get ourselves ready for a night on the town.''

As he and the little girl left, John chuckled. ''There's no rush, Tory. Knowing Debra, I think you've got time to have a beer. Besides, I'm dying to know what dramatic new ending you've dreamed up for us.''

Tory sighed. ''Everything I think of seems so corny. Have you got any thoughts?''

Before he could reply, they heard Debra's scream.

Chapter 8

"Oh, my God! The movie's coming true again!"

The group at poolside looked up to see Debra, her face white with shock, running out of her room. Lars was out of his chair in a flash and bounding up the stairs to the balcony. "Debra! What is wrong?"

She pointed wordlessly toward the open door of her room. Lars entered cautiously. The closet door stood ajar. As he approached, he saw it—the limp body of a small brown dog hung by its neck from the closet pole.

Lars shook his head in disgust. Pulling out his pocketknife, he cut the cord and lowered the body to the floor. He wrapped it in one of the clean towels stacked by the sink. Then he went outside to where Debra stood trembling and pale. Putting his arm around her shoulders, he called down to John. "I think you had better fetch the manager."

When the manager heard what had happened, he expressed profound dismay and went off to call the police. Lars coaxed Debra downstairs.

"Oh, Debra, what a dreadful thing to happen," Tory

said with sympathy. "You must have been scared out of your wits."

"I was," Debra answered shakily.

Sally shook her head. "Whoever did that has a pretty perverted sense of humor."

" 'Sick' is what I'd call it," Tory replied soberly.

Artie had joined them by this time. "Debra, this is really terrible. Can I get you something to drink, or maybe some tea?" Debra seemed grateful for his attention, and Artie bustled around ordering a pot of tea and some honey for her.

Feeling as if she'd been kicked in the stomach, Tory sat down and rested her head in her hands. What did this mean? Why did it seem that someone was taking scenes from her script and turning them into real life? It couldn't be happening—but apparently it was. She felt sick and irrationally guilty.

Suddenly Michael was sitting in the chair next to hers. "Well, Missy's thrilled. I let her watch TV as a special treat, and she's glued to some game show in the room." He gestured toward the group of people who still stood talking in low voices. "What's going on?"

Shakily Tory told him what had happened. "Can you imagine?" she wound up. "It's so horrible, and it makes me feel responsible. I know I'm not, really, but somebody is making my script scenes come true." She shuddered convulsively and hugged herself.

"Mmm." Michael might have said something more, but Tory swept on. Now that she'd started talking, she couldn't seem to stop.

"Who could possibly have done something like that? It must have been someone like that weird guy we call Straight Arrow. I mean, it had to be someone so repressed and fanatical and so afraid of human contact that he can't express himself except in these really sick ways. I wonder if he could possibly have sneaked into her room—''

Michael looked at her coldly. ''You sound as if you know all about it. You should charge for these psychiatric diagnoses.''

''For God's sake, Michael, it doesn't take much insight to see that whoever did this needs help.''

Before Michael could reply, the police arrived and were told what had happened. One of the deputies settled down at a poolside table to gather what information he could from the group on the patio. Meanwhile Deputy Hurd started the seemingly futile task of knocking on doors to find out whether anyone had observed anything.

Deputy Hurd pounded on the door of Richard's room. He wasn't sure anyone could hear him over the noise of the television inside, but after a few moments Richard's face appeared in the narrow opening behind the chain lock. ''My goodness! Don't tell me someone called out the militia just to get me to turn the volume down.'' He giggled engagingly.

''Would you mind opening the door, sir? I have a few questions to ask you.''

''Questions?''

''Routine, sir, we've had a disturbance in the motel.''

The door closed and after a few seconds opened all the way to admit the deputy. He glanced curiously at the room's other two occupants. The young men were dressed almost identically in cowboy boots, Levi's, and skintight T-shirts. Their narrow hips were encircled by wide leather belts with intricate turquoise and silver buckles. One wore a single earring while the other had a slender chain around his neck. They stared at him, one sprawled on the bed farthest from the door, the other curled up on the floor between the beds.

Stepping inside, Deputy Hurd took a long, slow look around the room, his speculative gaze finally resting on Richard's face.

Richard jumped in quickly. "What can I do for you, Officer? Anything to aid the forces of law and order."

Hurd just stared at him. Then he stepped back and closed the door firmly. He was looking at an upside-down ashtray on the little counter between the beds. "Coke?" he said to Richard.

Really flustered now, Richard replied archly, "I beg your pardon?"

Moving surprisingly quickly for an older man running to fat, Hurd strode to the bedside table and lifted the ashtray. Underneath it was a piece of motel stationery with a small mound of white powder on it.

The boy on the floor gave a sudden high-pitched laugh and then quickly clapped a hand over his mouth.

Hurd turned to Richard. "Easy enough to get this analyzed," he said in a conversational tone. "And I think we all know what the lab will find."

Richard said nothing. His eyes were held unwillingly by the deputy's steady stare.

After a moment Hurd went on. "If I turned this in, I bet my boss would be real happy—might even give me a bonus."

Still staring at the deputy, Richard drawled slowly, "He might. But if you didn't . . ."

The silence lengthened between them as the television blared in the little room. Finally Hurd nodded as if satisfied. He said briskly, "Let's take care of these questions." He asked how long they had been in the room and whether they had noticed any unusual activity outside.

"Why, no," Richard answered. "What's this all about?"

Hurd told them about the grotesque discovery Debra had made. Richard laughed nastily. "It couldn't be more appropriate, could it, for a dog like her?" Hurd didn't say anything and Richard went on, "Oops! I shouldn't have said that, should I? But seriously, we didn't see a thing."

"Can you think of anyone who dislikes her enough to do something like that?"

"Oh, everyone dislikes her—she's such a bitch. But if you're asking who dislikes her the most, well, let's see. I imagine our boy Kevin wouldn't mind seeing Debra upset. And of course the great director doesn't care for her much. You might ask him about it, although I really think his problems are with young girls. Debra's too old for him, I expect. Anyway, there's just a wealth of possibilities."

"How about you? Do you dislike her, too?"

"Oh, of course I do. But you can't think for a moment that I'd do something as sordid as playing about with dead animals. Not my style at all, I assure you."

"Well." Deputy Hurd closed his notebook. "I guess that's about it." He stood unmoving in front of the television screen.

"Thanks so much, Deputy—do I call you Deputy? It sounds so quaint somehow—anyway, you've been terribly kind and considerate and we certainly do appreciate it." As Richard kept up his stream of chatter, he turned his back and took out a well-filled money clip. Pulling out several bills, he stuffed them into one of the hotel envelopes and dropped it carelessly on the table near the door.

Hurd moved toward Richard. Without seeming to look at it, he scooped up the envelope and slid it into his pocket. "If I have any more questions, I'll let you know." His bland words echoed in the room as he let himself out.

The other deputy had finished talking with the people near the pool, none of whom had anything useful to tell him.

John said tentatively, "Well, I guess we can go and have some dinner now."

Sally nodded. "We do have to eat something, after all." She turned to Debra. "Come on. I'll go up to your room with you and wait while you get ready. I think you'll feel much better if you come with us. A change of scene is a good idea."

Debra said shakily, "Thanks, Sally," and the two of them moved toward the staircase.

Tory shivered under the towel she'd wrapped around her shoulders. She simply couldn't keep up cheerful chatter with all these people. "I'm sorry, John," she began apologetically, "but I'm just not in the mood for dinner on the town. I think I'll stay here and have a sandwich."

"Okay, Tory," John said sympathetically. With a pat on her shoulder, he went on, "Get a good night's rest. You'll feel better in the morning, I'm sure."

"I hope so." Turning to Michael, she said, "But you and Missy need to eat something. Why don't you go ahead—"

"No," Michael cut in, "Missy's tired. She needs a quiet evening for a change. But I can't face eating in the coffee shop here. Tell you what—I'll run out and pick up some pizza and we'll have a picnic in the room.''

Tory looked at him gratefully. "I'll go and change, then. See you in a bit.''

Stepping out of her wet bathing suit in her room, Tory felt chilled. Thinking that maybe a shower would help, she stood for several minutes under the stream of warm water. Her thoughts kept returning to the pathetic little creature someone had killed. When she'd written the scene in which Alan killed Jean Anne's dog, she hadn't really been able to imagine how Jean Anne would feel. Now she knew. But Debra's real-life experience had been even more macabre than Tory's script. It was so meaningless; it wasn't even Debra's dog. Tory shivered in the steamy little bathroom and tried to push the whole thing out of her mind.

By nine o'clock that evening she was back in her own room getting ready for bed. Missy's eyelids had begun to droop before she'd even finished her pizza, and she'd been asleep minutes afterward. Tory was glad that the little girl hadn't been at the pool to hear about the gruesome incident in Debra's room. She hoped no one would talk about it in front of Missy tomorrow. She herself hadn't felt like talking, even to Michael. Wasn't it lucky that he'd suggested eating in the room? They'd watched an old Jacques Cousteau program about porpoises that had kept all three of them interested and almost eliminated the need for conversation.

Michael hadn't seemed pleased when she said she was going to sleep early and made it clear that she didn't want him to join her later. But she felt strongly that she needed to be by herself tonight—surely he should be able to understand that.

The next morning Tory awoke full of energy. John

had been right; a good night's sleep had let her put yesterday's events into perspective. A fresh breeze had sprung up overnight, cooling the air to a delightful eighty-two degrees. She met Michael and Missy for breakfast, and when she put down her coffee cup Tory said, "Okay, today's the day. I'm going to get the new ending figured out and typed up in record time."

Michael smiled at her. "Right. We'll stay out of your way. I thought we might go have a look at these old gold mines"—he pointed at the fanciful tourist map printed on the place mats—"and I think the desk clerk has some detailed maps. Do you want us back for dinner?"

Tory laughed. "Michael, you know that when I say record time I mean in the foreseeable future. Once I get the idea worked out, I'll have to catch up with Julie and talk it over with him before I can start writing. I just plan to have this thing finished before I go to bed tonight."

"Okay. We'll drop by later today for a progress report." He stood up and then bent to kiss Tory's hair. "Work hard, honey. Come on, Missy, let's get into our exploring clothes."

Within minutes after they left, Tory was settled in a shaded corner of the patio with a copy of the script, a thermos pitcher of coffee, and a legal pad. By noon she had the whole new ending for the story blocked out in her mind. Luckily she found Julie in the production office, talking on the phone. As soon as he hung up, she said, "Okay, Julie, I've got the problem solved." She told him the idea she had come up with.

Julie's heavy features creased into a smile. "I love it. Just what the doctor ordered. You're something else, kiddo. How do you come up with these things?"

"Well, you won't believe this, but I got the idea from the place mats in the coffee shop. There's a tourist map printed on them—you know, gold mines and ghost towns—and I was reading it this morning—"

"Great." Julie stood up. "Get it written up as soon as you can. Got a typewriter?" When she shook her head, he rushed on. "No problem, you can use Penny's. She doesn't have anything to type right now, so she can sit here on the bed and answer the phone and do her nails. I'll grab Artie when I get to the set and he can go check out this ghost town. You got the map?"

"Sure." Tory laughed. "We can get plenty of them from the coffee shop."

"Yeah, right." Julie grinned at her. "Talk to you later, sweetheart."

A few hours later Tory had roughed out the scenes she'd talked over with Julie. She stood up and stretched to get the kinks out of her shoulders. It was time for a break. She poured herself a cup of coffee—how many cups did that make today? Far too many, she thought, but never mind. She'd be out of this pressure-cooker situation shortly.

She wondered how Carrie was doing and hoped the fact that she hadn't heard from her or her parents was good news. Carrie might have gone to Toledo to try to work things out with Doug. Tory decided to call home and see how things were going.

"Hi, Carrie."

"Oh, hi, Tory." Carrie sounded more cheerful than she had the other night. "I was going to call you."

"Well, what's happening?"

"Everything's going really well. I mean, I think things are going fine. I hope you think so, but I know

Mom doesn't.'' Carrie paused for breath and went on. ''Anyway, I'm not going back.''

''Oh, Carrie.''

''No, Tory, I've made up my mind. This is the best thing for me right now, and I think it's best for all of us. I'm not going to be any good to anyone until I find out who I really am. It's time I got myself together and worked all that out,'' she told Tory. ''You know Doug and I were so young when we got married. We've both grown, but it seems we've grown in different directions. Do you know what I mean?''

''But, Carrie, you and Doug always seemed so happy.''

''I guess it did look that way to everyone else—at least I hope it did. But you know, we haven't really been happy for a long time, or anyway I haven't.'' Carrie stopped, as if trying to gather her thoughts and find some way to make Tory understand. ''Doug has this ideal of a home-loving wife and mother who's content to keep the cookie jar full and entertain when necessary and make sure the house is spic and span. I didn't mind doing all that; actually I liked it. But even though Doug talked about my doing other things—going back to school, getting involved in politics, taking some art classes and finally getting serious about my painting— he never really expected or wanted me to do any of those things. He just liked talking about it. But when this benefit thing came up and everyone thought I did a fabulous job and asked me to be on the board, he just said no, it would take up too much of my time.''

''Carrie, you don't mean you're leaving your husband because of a committee meeting for some stupid benefit?''

''No, Tory, that was only the symbol of everything

else that was going on," she replied, and Tory was surprised at the intensity in her sister's normally serene voice. "Honestly, he and I have gone around and around on this stuff for years. Only I was so sure that I had to have this secure home life and this great big wonderful husband who came home to me every night. Everyone always said I was so lucky, and I was ashamed to admit I didn't think so, too. And actually it is plenty hard to think of giving all that up."

"But what are you going to do?"

"I really don't know. Find myself, I hope." Carrie sounded both embarrassed and determined. "Tory, really, it's not as half-baked as it sounds. Aunt Alice is dying for me to move in with her. She'd love to take care of the kids after school—of course, I'd pay her to do that—and she's got that huge old house. So that would get us out of Mom and Dad's hair and give us a rent-free place to live for a while. And George Clinton—you remember him, he married Sue Esterbrook—has this software development company here in town, and his office manager just quit. He said I could give the job a try and see how I do. It isn't a guarantee or anything, but it seems as if I'm pretty good at organizing things, so I think it might work out."

Carrie paused, as if waiting for Tory to comment. But Tory didn't know what to say. Finally Carrie said earnestly, "I guess you must think I'm throwing my life away and ruining everybody else's happiness into the bargain. Tory, please understand. As unhappy as I've been in the last few days, this is the first time I've felt alive in years. I've got to do it. And it's now or never. Another five years of being unhappy won't make breaking away any easier."

All kinds of questions were racing through Tory's

mind: How did Doug feel about the separation? How were the children taking it? Wouldn't Carrie find it hard to exist without the luxuries that Doug's salary bought? Carrie didn't know anything about business. Would she be able to make a living for herself and the kids? Wouldn't she be lonely without Doug? But Tory sensed that this was not the time to ask questions. Finally she said, "You sound very sure."

"I am," Carrie said strongly. "I know this isn't going to be easy, and I know there'll be times I'll regret giving up that security. But, Tory, I was suffocating. I was turning into a plastic doll that Doug had created. I need to be on my own so I can be who I am, and I need to meet people who will deal with me as the real person I am, with faults and good points and all that, instead of the imaginary person Doug thought I was."

Tory nodded slowly. "I think I do understand, sort of. But this is really a surprise to me."

"It's a surprise to everyone." There was a bitter edge to Carrie's voice. "Little homemaker Carrie really does have a brain. She's a real person after all."

"Oh, Carrie, I didn't mean that. It's just that I have to get used to thinking of you in a new situation."

"I know." Carrie's voice softened. "It's good to talk to you, Tory, and it's good to have a chance to spill all this out. I'll let you go now—the kids are about ready for supper."

"Carrie." Tory hesitated. "I love you."

"I love you, too, Tory. Bye."

Chapter 9

Music thumped steadily from the little house on the eastern edge of Yuma. Its insistent refrain poured exaggerated promises into the hot night air of the desert. Out here where the streets disappeared into sand, the peeling wooden shanties looked insubstantial, ready to collapse at the first hard gust of dry wind. On the other side of the John Deere sales lot were open fields, their green rows fed by the still water in the irrigation ditches. A row of old railroad cars, their slats as weather-worn as the shanties, stood huddled beside a water tank, put out to pasture like ancient horses.

Dennis, the movie's assistant director, looked doubtfully at the house and peered at the numbers beside the door. This was the right place—he glanced at the slip of paper in his hand, but he knew before he looked that the address was the one written in Richard's elegant script. And besides, all the other houses were dark except for the ghostly glow of a television set here and there.

Squaring his shoulders, Dennis walked up onto the

porch and knocked firmly. A young blond man opened the door. High-heeled cowboy boots and tight leather pants were surmounted by a short leather vest worn over his bare chest. A leather headband studded with turquoise medallions held his fine straight hair in place, and a silver star glittered in one earlobe.

"Hi," he said sweetly. "I'm Bob. Who are you?"

Dennis swallowed nervously. "I'm, uh, Dennis Sullivan."

"Oh, Richard's friend! Come in, come in. But no last names, dear—we're all on a first-name basis here." He laughed and pulled Dennis through the tiny entryway into the living room.

The air was blue with smoke and the sweet cloying smell of hash. Dim red light bulbs revealed a roomful of couples swaying and clinging on the hardwood floor. As Dennis stood blinking, a tall dark woman materialized beside him. "I'm Georgette. Dance with me, you gorgeous creature!"

Her voice was surprisingly husky. As she laid her cheek against his, Dennis felt the unmistakable rasp of stubble. A shiver of excitement ran through him.

"Your first time, sweetie?" Georgette's voice was gently mocking. "Oh, I'll have to introduce you around."

When the music trailed off into sullen drumbeats, Georgette raised knowing eyes to his. "Come on, love, let me help you get started."

Placing a hand-rolled cigarette between Dennis's lips, Georgette lit it for him with a silver lighter. As always, the first deep drag made Dennis a little dizzy. His tensions seemed to melt away in the circle of warm friendliness. Placing his hand trustingly in

Georgette's, he allowed himself to be led through a doorway.

In the next room Richard was carefully applying false eyelashes over the doe-eyes of a young Mexican boy. He stepped back to admire his handiwork, and Dennis despairingly wished he had Richard's style. Of course he could never afford it—Richard's Gucci loafers and belt gleamed expensively, and the Italian silk shirt and well-cut black trousers fit him like a second skin. Dennis's own lavender shirt and white pants suddenly seemed tacky, even gaudy, though he'd chosen them with care and saved them for a really special evening. He looked at the floor as Georgette cried, "Richard! You've got to do Dennis next! And I know exactly the right outfit for him, the blue with the sequins, if someone hasn't taken it already."

As if in a dream, Dennis sat down in Richard's makeup chair, while Georgette pawed through a trunkful of shimmering clothes. "Here it is!"

Twenty minutes later Dennis stared awestruck into the mirror. He almost couldn't believe it, and yet anything seemed possible tonight. A beautiful face stared solemnly back at him—huge dark eyes rimmed with black, a plum-colored Cupid's bow mouth, and on his cheek a glittering blue star that matched the dress. And the dress! Low-cut, with a narrow slit skirt, and sequined straps over his pale shoulders. Georgette's dark face appeared in the mirror. "Blond, I think, for tonight." The wig's tousled curls completed the transformation.

He sat down, and Georgette knelt to strap on delicate sandals with stiletto heels and tiny golden buckles. Standing, he hardly felt the narrow straps biting into his ankles.

"Darling, I'm jealous!" Georgette cried. "You're an absolute vision of loveliness!"

Dennis stepped away from the chair and tottered on the insubstantial shoes. He wanted to float.

A hard brown hand grasped his elbow. Dennis looked up into an unsmiling face. He'd seen this tall man, bulging with muscles and maleness, watching silently as Richard performed his magic. Dennis smiled demurely, or perhaps deliriously, as they merged into the primitive music, the dance.

Richard stood apart, music pulsating all around him, couples swirling and glittering, sighing and embracing. He loved feeling that he'd created, orchestrated, this heady mixture. Smiling, his brush poised for another awakening, he turned to see who was awaiting his ministrations.

Watching Richard smooth a film of gold glitter shadow on a young man's eyelids, Bob felt a pair of arms snake around his waist from behind. A chin rested on his shoulder, and Georgette's voice whispered in his ear, "Isn't Richard just fabulous? What he does with that box of makeup is just obscenely exciting! Bobby, I don't know how you find people like that, and here in Yuma! You're a fucking marvel, you know?"

Bob couldn't hold in his smirk of pleasure. "He's just someone I met the other day at the Golden Dragon. He is good, isn't he?"

"Good?" Georgette shrieked. "Sweetie, this is only the most fantastic party of the century. It's historic!" A knock sounded at the door of the little house. "Now, who can this be? You stay right here, Bobby. Let me play hostess!"

Georgette slithered through the haze of dancing bodies toward the dim entryway. Outside on the porch stood a tall, slender man dressed entirely in black. On his head he wore a dark, close-fitting cap.

"Hello, handsome. I'm Georgette. Oh, I'm glad I saw you first!"

The stranger's knife slashed out like a snake through the open doorway, and with a strangled gasp Georgette doubled over, then slumped to the floor. The tall man stooped to slash twice more. Then he turned and walked swiftly off into the darkness.

"Georgette? Who is it? Who's there?" Bob wove his way through the crowd. Coming into the hall, he froze as he took in the lifeless body sprawled awkwardly across the doorstep. The door stood open. A light breeze ruffled Georgette's dark wig, which now lay askew, revealing the short-cropped hair beneath.

"Georgette!" he screamed. He dropped down beside the pathetic figure and raised one of its hands to his lips.

Instantly there was bedlam, high-pitched shrieks and sobs of fear mingled with confused hysterical questions.

"Oh, no! Not Georgette!"

"There's so much blood!"

"Oh, I can't look!"

"Did you say 'killed'?"

And from the back of the room: "What happened?"

Bob, sobbing beside Georgette and refusing to let anyone else touch the body, looked up at the sound of heavy footsteps on the porch.

"*Qué pasa?* What the fuck's going on?" A burly Mexican from the house next door stood hands on hips, flanked by his two hefty teenage sons. "This time I call the cops. You're screaming to wake the whole neighborhood this time of night." He glanced down at Georgette. "What's the matter, she sick?"

Bob's cheeks were wet with tears. "She's dead," he sobbed.

The Mexican crossed himself quickly. *"Madre mía."*

His son was staring at the body in fascinated horror. He tugged at his father's arm and whispered, "Dad, that's a guy!"

A spasm of disgust crossed the man's face. Then, putting an arm around his son's shoulders, he said quietly, "Pray for a lost soul." He looked at Bob. "I will call the police now."

By this time someone had turned off the music. The partygoers stood huddled in little groups, sobbing and consoling one another. They talked feverishly among themselves, desperately trying to absorb what had happened. Only Richard seemed to have some grasp of the situation. Rapidly and efficiently, he packed up his equipment and closed the lid of the box. Then he seized a wastebasket and moved through the two rooms, emptying ashtrays into the basket and opening windows. He hurried into the bathroom and dumped the partly smoked joints into the toilet. After flushing them down, he opened the medicine cabinet in search of a room deodorizer. Ah, a can of floral scent! He shook it briskly. Then he put his finger on the nozzle and walked through the house. When the can was empty, he dropped it behind the couch.

Dennis stood immobilized in shock. Tears of grief and self-pity rolled down his cheeks. He heard the sirens start up in the distance.

"Dennis, I think you'd better change." Richard's voice was urgent in his ear. "I'm getting out of here."

Richard gave him a little shove, and Dennis stumbled forward, but his left ankle twisted under him and he fell heavily. Moaning, he tore the blond wig from his head and threw it under a chair. Why did this have to happen to him? It wasn't fair!

Dennis fumbled frantically with the straps of his sandals, but his fingers couldn't get a grip on the tiny buckles. Swearing, he tried to yank the damn shoes off his feet, but the flimsy-looking straps were made to stay on. He screamed with frustration. Sodden and disheveled, Dennis sat weeping on the floor as the squad cars drew up in front of the house.

Chapter 10

Tory quickly grabbed the ringing phone and glanced at her little travel alarm. It was only eight o'clock—hadn't she told everyone she wanted to sleep in this morning? Who in the world could be calling at this hour?

"Hello?"

"Ms. Ryan? This is Captain Fleming of the Sheriff's Department. I'm sorry to trouble you, but I need some information. I'm down in the motel coffee shop now. Could you join me here?"

Startled, Tory replied, "Okay. I'll be down in a few minutes."

Did she have time for a shower? Well, he could wait a little longer—at least until she was awake and presentable. She'd been up late the night before, but the long hours of work had been worth the effort. The new ending was finished and sitting on Julie's desk in the production office. In fact, Julie had probably already read it through, marked any minor changes, and had Penny make enough copies so that the scene could be shot today.

As she showered and slipped into a sundress and sandals, Tory felt pleased with herself. The new scene really worked well—just what the script doctor had ordered. But it had been a marathon session of writing. Michael and Missy had dropped into the production office late in the afternoon to find her with pages scattered everywhere and what must have been her four hundredth cup of coffee cooling beside the typewriter. She'd greeted them in a preoccupied manner, thankful that Michael seemed to have gotten over his annoyance about the time she was spending on rewrites. She supposed he and Missy had gone out with Lars and John for an early dinner. She hadn't seen them again before finally turning out the lights and staggering up to bed.

Tory paused in the doorway of the coffee shop and looked around. Captain Fleming stood up and signaled to her. As she started toward his booth in the far corner, she couldn't help responding to the smile that warmed his intelligent face. He remained standing until she got there and then shook her hand before gesturing for her to sit down.

"Thank you for coming down, Ms. Ryan. Can I offer you some breakfast?"

Suddenly she realized she was starving. That club sandwich she'd eaten at her typewriter last night was all she'd had for dinner, and so much focused thinking must have burned a lot of calories. "Sure!" she said with a grin.

He followed her glance to his own assortment of empty plates, evidence of his recent enormous breakfast. "I recommend the Number Eight," he told her with mock seriousness. To her questioning look, he rattled off, "Choice of juice, eggs and sausage, home-made biscuits with or without gravy, and a short stack of hotcakes on the side.''

The waitress arrived with a steaming pot of coffee, and Tory told her, "I'll have the Number Eight—no gravy."

She thought Captain Fleming looked a little surprised. "I didn't have much dinner last night," she told him, "and you made it sound so tasty!"

He laughed and then said quietly, "I'm sorry if I woke you up, but we've got another murder case." He paused as the waitress brought Tory's juice and cleared away his dishes. When she had left, he went on. "I gather I offended you in some way the last time we spoke, but I really need your help."

Tory's eyes remained on her coffee cup as she said, "I'll be happy to help you in any way I can, but I don't understand—"

"It appears that the murder last night also bears a marked resemblance to one of the killings in your script."

She looked at him wide-eyed. "What do you mean?"

"A young man attending a party went to answer the door and was stabbed to death in the doorway."

"But—"

"Yes, I know. However, the killer may not have known it was a man. The victim was in drag."

"Oh." After a moment she said, "I can see that there is a similarity. How in the world did you find out about it?"

"Two members of the movie company were also at the party," he said. He didn't volunteer their names, and Tory realized she'd just as soon not know. "I have a copy of your script, but I don't know when I'll have a chance to read it. I thought you could tell me the story. After all, you're the person most likely to re-member the details," he said earnestly. "You see, Ms. Ryan—"

"I can't stand this 'Ms. Ryan' business. Please call me Tory," she broke in.

Captain Fleming raised a quizzical eyebrow. "Short for Victoria?"

Tory made a face. "Yes. A little old-fashioned, isn't it?"

A sympathetic grin lightened his somewhat austere features. "Believe me, I understand. How would you like to go through life as Zacharias?"

"I wondered what the Z on your nametag stood for," Tory laughed. "It's about as bad as Victoria."

"Well, my friends are nice enough to call me Zack." He grew serious again. "Anyway, Tory, you do see that it just can't be coincidence. First the dancer's death, then the dog in Ms. Scott's room, and now this. Some-one seems to be trying to re-create in life what you've already created on paper. If I know the whole story, maybe it will give me an idea about how to approach this, or at least help me figure out if anyone else is in danger."

His gray eyes watched her gravely as she gathered her thoughts. "Okay. Well, here goes. A guy falls for a gorgeous girl. She goes out with him once, then de-cides he's a drip and refuses to go out with him again. He has all these fantasies about the two of them falling in love and having a whirlwind romance. He starts fol-lowing her around, and then he spies on her out in the woods making love to another guy. At that point he kind of goes off the deep end. He slashes her tires, kills her dog, kills a stripper who looks sort of like her. Then he kills her best friend and another girl who works with her. Finally he grabs her to take her away with him. He drugs her and drives off, but she comes to when they're out in the desert. She fights for control of the Jeep; it crashes, and she's killed. Now he completely flips out. He picks up her body and starts talking to her as if she's alive—a bunch of stuff about how happy they're going to be together—and then he carries her across the sand toward a ghost town where they'll live happily ever after.''

His eyes crinkled with amusement as she paused for breath. ''People really pay you to write this?''

''Oh, yes,'' Tory said flippantly, ''murder's really in this year.'' She stopped abruptly, realizing what she'd just said, and stared at him, her dark eyes horrified. ''Oh, God, I got so carried away, I forgot what—''

He interrupted her gently, laying a hand briefly on her arm. ''It's okay. I know you're used to thinking of murder as make-believe.''

''Yes,'' Tory said, grateful for his understanding. ''It's different when it happens in real life.''

Zack nodded. Tory couldn't think of him as Captain Fleming anymore—he could be awfully nice when he tried.

''Okay,'' he said, ''let's get back to the movie. How much of it has already been filmed?''

''Well, the fantasy scenes were shot in a studio in Los Angeles.'' Tory thought for a moment. ''I guess what's left to film are the killings of the friend and the co-worker and the death of the heroine. She was originally going to get rescued by the police.'' She grinned at him and went on. ''But Julie decided that wasn't scary enough, so I wrote her death scene yesterday.''

''Which one of your characters gets killed at a party, like this person last night?''

''That's the heroine's friend,'' Tory replied.

''So,'' he said, ''if the killer is really following the script, the people who might be in danger are the heroine and the girl she works with. What does your heroine do for a living?''

''She's a cocktail waitress.''

''Oh, Lord.'' He rubbed his eyes wearily. ''Who knows how many waitresses there are in Yuma? But of course,'' he went on, ''we can't be sure this guy plans to kill a cocktail waitress. He may be leading up to someone else entirely. This guy who got killed last night was a clerk in a shoe store. Maybe we should check on his friends or something. I just don't know—it's complicated.''

Tory nodded thoughtfully. ''Yes, it's hard to know what kind of similarities this guy is looking for.''

''You know,'' Zack said slowly, ''it's possible that someone wants to kill Ms. Scott.''

''Debra?'' Tory sounded surprised. ''Why do you say that?''

''Well, the dog was found in her room, and after all, she's the heroine of the film. I don't want to scare you, but it's possible that you're in danger, too. You're one of Ms. Scott's female co-workers.''

Tory shivered. She said quickly, ''But that's ridiculous! The two people who have been killed had no connection with us. None of us even knew them! It's only the method that has anything to do with the film.''

''That's not quite true. Two crew members were at that party last night. I don't suspect them, but I'm certain there's a link to you people that I haven't yet figured out. Nothing happened until you arrived in town.''

Fear she wasn't willing to recognize made Tory quick to anger. A flush prickled her skin. ''Sounds as if you've made up your mind that one of us did it! It would be a lot easier for you, wouldn't it, if a stranger to Yuma was causing all your problems. Of course nothing happened until we got here—nobody could have seen the script until then. But you don't want to admit that one of Yuma's fine upstanding citizens could be a serial killer! I bet you never even checked on that guy I pointed out to you!'' She stared at him defiantly.

Zack sighed. "His name is Gary Barton," he said quietly. "He lives with his mother here in town, and he operates a small gun repair business out of his garage. He has an alibi for last night and for the afternoon and evening that Ms. Scott found the dog. We're still checking him out, but it seems pretty unlikely that he killed anyone, unless there's more than one murderer.''

He gazed at Tory steadily, but her expression didn't change. He sighed again and opened his notebook. "I'd like to ask you a few more questions. How well do you know the other people working on the movie?''

Tory put down her fork in exasperation. "Hardly at all. I mean I've worked for Julie before, but writers don't usually go on location. I'm here only because this stuff needed to be rewritten.''

"When did you arrive?''

Prodded by his questions, Tory soon felt she had accounted for every waking minute since she'd come to Yuma. "Fine," he said. "And now I need to know a little background. Are you married?''

"No." This was such an invasion of her private self!

"So that tall blond fellow is a boyfriend?''

"Yes. And before you even ask, his name is Michael Canfield, he's a research psychologist at UCLA, and he has nothing whatsoever to do with movies or scriptwriting. He came down here to see me because I thought

I'd be finished working and he wanted us to have a vacation.''

"I see." He sat there for a moment longer, as if he intended to say more. Then he shook his head and stood up. "Thank you for your patience. I appreciate your help." He picked up the check and walked toward the door. Tory stared after him, her face reflecting her conflicting emotions.

Getting into his car, Zack thought about Tory. It wasn't surprising that she had a boyfriend—she was good-looking and intelligent. He smiled briefly. She probably didn't know how attractive she looked when her cheeks flushed and her eyes sparked with anger. As he turned the key in the ignition, he reflected that the surprising part was that she wasn't already married.

Inside the coffee shop, her cup refilled and the table cleared, Tory sat on, gazing out the window at the big semis rolling along the highway. She wondered if she'd overreacted to some of Zack's questions. It must be frustrating to have two unsolved murders and no idea where to start looking for the killer. But she didn't see why Zack needed so much personal information. She hoped he wouldn't interview Michael, too.

She stared blankly through the big window. If the police started asking Michael a lot of personal questions, he was going to hate it. He was such a private person. Tory thought he was sorry he'd ever told her anything about his life.

He had opened up only one time, when he told Tory about his mother. Did he blame his father, killed so uselessly in a boating accident before Michael was old enough to know him? she wondered. No. Michael never blamed anyone. But maybe his mother's problems explained why he sometimes seemed so controlled, so remote and unwilling to become involved.

That wasn't entirely true, Tory reminded herself. He loved Missy, and she adored him. And he was affectionate and attentive to Tory when he was with her. But sometimes, she admitted unwillingly, it seemed as though their relationship was all on the surface—as if she couldn't get close to what was inside him.

Tory sighed. He had such a clear idea of where he wanted to go. He wanted to discover why people behaved in certain ways under unbearable stress and to share that knowledge with the rest of the world. Tory admired his sense of purpose. But why did she feel that he didn't want what she had to give him?

Startled, Tory looked up as Artie slid into the booth across from her and announced, "There ain't no such thing."

"What?" She couldn't imagine what he was talking about.

"I went out there, just like that map said, twenty-five miles, but there's nothing there."

"You mean there's no ghost town?" Tory was finally catching on.

"That's right. Just a couple of piles of stones and four million miles of sand. I asked at that ranch, just like they said to, and the lady there told me to take the track on the other side of the highway. She said there wasn't anything there, but I went anyway. She was right."

"Oh, no!" If there wasn't any ghost town, was she going to have to figure out still another ending for the movie? Tory didn't think she could stand it.

Artie smiled smugly. "But I got it all figured out. There's an old shack—it could be full of ghosts for all

I know; it's practically falling down—and if we're careful to shoot around the power lines, I'm sure it will work. It's behind that ranch place. The rest of it looks sort of regular, but this shack, all by itself, looks like it could've been there for centuries, if you use the right angles.''

''I hope Lars thinks so, too,'' Tory said. Then she realized that Artie was waiting for something. ''That's great, Artie!''

Artie beamed. ''Yeah, Julie thinks so, too. I already told him.''

Chapter 11

Tory stared out across the desert while Julie read quickly through the typed pages of the film's new ending.

215 CU ALAN
   as he wrestles Jean Anne's drugged form into the passenger seat of the Jeep.
216 EXT. YUMA STREET NEAR HIGH-
      WAY—DAY
   Alan jerks away from the last stoplight in town and heads toward freeway on ramp. In b.g. see squad car pull away from curb and follow him.
217 EXT. HIGHWAY—DAY
   Alan is driving while Jean Anne slumps motionless in the seat beside him.
218 INSERT
   speedometer needle as it shows 80 mph.
219 EXT. HIGHWAY—DAY
   Alan is gunning it down the road. Suddenly

he looks in his rearview mirror and sees a police car chasing him with lights flashing. Alan hits the gas. He's not going to be stopped. We HEAR THE SIREN screaming behind him, but Alan doesn't slow down. Instead, he careens off the freeway onto a two-lane highway.

220 EXT. SECOND HIGHWAY—DAY

where the chase continues. Miles and miles of desert and no cars make this one of the great film chases. The squad car almost catches up, and then Alan pulls out into the oncoming lane to cut him off. Side by side they hit the dip of a RR crossing, both cars flying high off the ground before landing on the other side. Alan jams the engine into overdrive and edges ahead of the police car. Then he sees the sandy track he's looking for. He guns the Jeep and then slams on the brakes, sliding the four-wheel drive off the highway and into the desert. The squad car has no option but to stop.

221 INT. SQUAD CAR—DAY

The cop watches Alan's Jeep disappear over a sand dune. He picks up his mike.

COP

Car Forty-one to HQ. Air and four-wheel drive assist. Am twelve miles north of freeway on Highway Eighty-eight. Will wait here for backup.

OPERATOR (VO)

Backup will rendezvous. Ten-four.

The cop watches Alan's dust trail as it goes farther into the desert. He slams his hands against the steering wheel and settles back to wait.

222 INT. JEEP—DAY

Alan concentrates on his driving, not noticing that Jean Anne is coming to. Suddenly she grabs at the steering wheel.

ALAN

No! I'm taking care of everything now!

They fight for control of the Jeep, and it jumps off the sandy track.

223 EXT. JEEP—DAY

as the vehicle careens out of control. The Jeep bounces off a boulder and crashes in a ravine.

224 CU JEAN ANNE

her head against the dash, a trickle of blood from her temple.

225 EXT. JEEP—DAY

as Alan, thrown clear, picks himself up and walks to Jeep. He opens passenger door and pulls Jean Anne out.

ALAN

Jean Anne? Jean Anne!

226 CU JEAN ANNE

obviously with a broken neck.

227 EXT. JEEP

where Alan picks up her limp form and starts off across the sand.

ALAN
It's going to be beautiful, Jean Anne.
I've got it all planned.

JEAN ANNE (VO)
"Yet each man kills the thing he
loves . . ."

ALAN
No! No! We're going to be so happy.
Jean Anne, I'm going to make you
happy. You'll see.

PULL BACK
to see the ghost town ahead and Alan carrying Jean Anne's body over the dunes toward it.

JEAN ANNE (VO)
"By each let this be heard,
Some do it with a bitter look,
Some with a flattering word.
The coward does it with a kiss,
The brave man with a sword!"

"Not bad for a rush job, kiddo." Julie patted Tory's
arm awkwardly.

"I'm glad you're pleased, Julie. You were absolutely
right. This ending is much better."

"When you been in this business as long as I have,
kiddo . . . Listen, Tory, I want you to stay until we're
done shooting in this godforsaken burg." He held up
both hands. "I'll pay you, I'll pay you, but I gotta have
you here in case I need you."

"Oh, Julie." She couldn't keep her dismay from showing.

"It's only a couple more days, sweetheart. Besides, it's good for you to see how the real work is done." He dragged her toward the knot of cameras and equipment. "C'mon, they're gonna shoot the car stunts in a minute."

Tory let herself be guided to a spot with a clear view of what was going on. As long as she was here, she might as well stay till they finished. If the script needed more work, she wanted to be the one to do it. After all, her name would be up there on the screen; the better the picture was, the more in demand her work would be. She still had a lot to learn, but every script she wrote gave her more confidence in her ability. Keep at it, kid, she told herself with a grin—you'll win an Oscar yet!

She was lucky, she realized. She had a career she liked, and it paid well. What was Carrie going to do? She'd never had to earn a living. Tory hoped the office-manager job worked out.

Michael's Mustang pulled up behind the other cars, and Tory beckoned to him and Melissa. She was glad they'd arrived in time to see the stunts. It looked as if the shooting was about to start on schedule.

As the stunt drivers harnessed up and got their cars started, the three of them watched in fascination. Earlier, cameras had been strapped to the hood of the Jeep, and Lars had shot Jean Anne and Alan fighting for control of the vehicle, but the car had actually been going slowly, bumping along the highway out in the desert. Now the stunt drivers would do the real stuff—men who loved to risk their lives in death-defying feats, all recorded for posterity on film. Two cameras were set up so that they didn't interfere with each other's point of view. When the drivers were ready, the cameras started rolling.

Tory gasped as the cars raced along the highway. These drivers were doing in real life what she'd so easily written into the script. She could hardly bear to watch.

"Amazing!" Michael said at one point. "Are these cars specially modified for this kind of stuff?"

Tory shrugged. "I don't know. I just write the stunts; other people make them come true."

By the third time through, Melissa's attention had begun to flag. "Dad," she said, tugging at his sleeve, "what about the horses? When are we going?"

"In a minute," Michael told her, a trace of impatience in his voice.

"Guess what, Tory?" the little girl asked. "We're going horseback riding!"

"Wow, lucky you!" Tory smiled at the child. "That sure sounds like fun."

"I can't wait." Melissa looked hopefully at her father.

Tory heard John's voice calling across the sand, "What's the problem over there?"

"Car blew a tire," someone replied briefly. "And I want to check the steering before we start up again."

Dennis began rushing around. "This is a break, everybody."

Michael sighed. "I guess we'd better go," he told Tory. "Wish I could stay for more but . . . we'll see you later."

Tory watched as they got into the Mustang and then wandered over to where Sally sat enthroned under her umbrella.

"This is really exciting, isn't it? But it sure takes a long time."

Sally grinned. "Yes, you writers never think about the serious consequences of your words!" She picked up her can of grapefruit juice and sipped through the straw. "Have a seat, Tory. You look hot and tired."

"I am." Tory dragged a chair over and sat down. After a moment's pause, she blurted out, "Sally, are you married?"

"Yes. Why?" Sally sounded a bit surprised.

"Well, I just wondered, what does your husband think? I mean, you're away on location so much, for weeks at a time."

"Joe? That's no problem. We worked that out before we got married."

"Well, how?" Tory felt awkward asking these blunt questions, but she really wanted to know.

"Joe and I met ten years ago. We'd both been married before, you know, and we were both divorced; in fact I'd been divorced for about eight years and living on my own. Anyway, when we decided we wanted to get married, I sat him down and we had a serious talk. I told him I was willing to marry him—in fact, I wanted to—but I liked my job and I wasn't going to give it up to stay around the house. That was what wrecked my first marriage. And I didn't want to worry about him setting the oven on fire when I wasn't there. He'd just have to fend for himself and not bother me about it. And he said that suited him fine. He's an airline pilot and he's away a lot himself, and so he was happy with the whole arrangement."

She sipped at her juice again. "Of course," she went on reflectively, "neither of us had any kids, which made it easier—that's a decision I made a long time ago. And we were both older and knew what we wanted. But I was very tough about it. I said, 'What happens when you retire at age fifty-five?' He's a little older than I am. 'I don't want you underfoot all the time, complaining that you have no one to play with.' But he had that all worked out. He has this cabin where he goes fishing, and he plans to go up there and fish and maybe turn it into a resort for other fishermen.''

Tory was amazed at this outpouring. ''Wow, it sounds as if you have everything worked out so neatly.''

''Yes.'' Sally sounded a bit surprised herself. ''I don't really think about it too much, but I guess I do have the best of both worlds. I love my husband and I love my job. Of course, nothing in life is perfect. I've sometimes thought it might have been nice to have a family, but nobody can have everything, and I'm happy with what I've got.'' She glanced at Tory. ''Here I've been rattling on. How did we get onto this subject anyway? Are you thinking about getting married?''

''Oh, no,'' Tory said quickly. ''But my sister has just separated from her husband, and I can't figure out if I think she's doing the right thing. She's not like you,'' she went on more slowly. ''She got married at nineteen, she has two kids, and now she's thirty and she's never had a job in her life.''

''Why is she separating?'' Sally eyed her shrewdly.

''I guess she feels she's been in a trap, trying to live up to her husband's image of her as wife and mother. Now she says she has to find out who she is for herself.'' Tory looked at her and shrugged. ''I don't know . . .''

''Well, I don't know either. Nobody's got the answer to anyone else's problems. And I can see that with two children it's pretty hard to make the break. But I think it's better for kids to have one happy parent than two unhappy ones. And I guess if she's got the guts to strike out on her own, she'll probably manage okay. Maybe you're underestimating your sister.''

''Maybe so.''

After a pause, Sally said, ''Speaking of children, that little girl of Michael's is really a charmer. Does she live with him all the time?''

''Yes,'' Tory told her. ''Missy's mother is dead.''

''How sad,'' Sally said sympathetically. ''What happened?''

''Well,'' Tory replied slowly, ''Michael doesn't like anyone to talk about it, but his wife committed suicide when Missy was about a year old.''

''Good Lord.'' Sally gazed at Tory. ''Horrible for both of them.''

Tory realized she needed to talk about this. Michael didn't want her to, and she hadn't even told her parents about it, but Sally was such a down-to-earth, commonsense woman . . .

''Michael says Charlotte was a weak person,'' she began haltingly. ''They were graduate students in the same department when they met, and after Missy was born Charlotte couldn't handle going to school and taking care of a baby. So she decided to drop out of the graduate program and stay home, and then find something else to do when Missy was older. I guess Michael was kind of disappointed . . .'' Tory paused and then added, ''Anyway, she took an overdose one day when Missy was at the baby-sitter's, and Michael found her.''

Sally shook her head. ''Too bad. I'm sure that's not an easy memory for him to live with. But at least Missy was too young to remember it.''

"Yes," Tory agreed, "and Michael's doing such a great job bringing her up."

"Ye-es." Sally sounded cautious. "She's a delightful little girl, but not very childlike in some ways. She's so well behaved—almost as if she's afraid to let loose."

Startled, Tory said, "I hadn't thought about it, but maybe you're right. Michael does expect a lot of her."

"Well, sometimes fathers can be kind of hard on their kids." She smiled at Tory. "Anyway, Missy's certainly fond of you." She put one hand behind her ear. "But hark! Isn't that Dennis's worried voice I hear? Guess it's time to get back to work."

At the county sheriff's headquarters, Zack Fleming dropped heavily into the chair in front of the sheriff's desk. The two-story building, of no particular architectural style, seemed to hold the heat. Sheriff Dawson had the only air-conditioned office, which made it a lot easier to come in and report. Zack stared out the window; across the small parking lot the old white courthouse crowned a close-clipped sloping lawn. Then he closed his eyes and leaned back, waiting for Sheriff Dawson to finish reading the neatly typed pages.

"A bad business, Zack."

Zack had known he'd say that, but it gave him a certain pleasure to have his prediction confirmed. He sat up. "Yes, sir, it is."

"So where do we stand?" the chief asked.

Zack silently chalked up another point—he'd known Dawson would say that, too. "Well, sir, I'm still not sure whether all these incidents are the work of a single person or whether we have an imitator here. It's possible that the planting of the dead dog and the murder of the transvestite were performed by someone who saw a chance to take advantage of the coincidence of the stripper's death and harass these movie people.''

''Hmmm.'' Dawson's gravelly voice told Zack nothing.

''I'm convinced that there is some definite connection with the film company, but I'm damned if I know what it is. I've had some ideas. How do you like this for a far-out scenario? This Debra Scott, who strikes me as a real ruthless climber type, could be arranging this stuff as some sort of promotion gimmick—you know, 'the film comes true as they shoot it' type of stuff. I don't actually believe that. For one thing, I can't see her wielding a knife. But I'll tell you, that's the kind of wild thought I've been coming up with. I just don't know enough yet. I'm hoping the out-of-state info will give us something to work with when it comes in.''

Sheriff Dawson swiveled his chair around, making a steeple of his fingers. ''Sounds pretty damn unlikely, if you ask me. I had a call from this Kingman. He's mighty anxious to get these cases solved and out of the way—says he's worried the investigation will slow down his production schedule. I wonder, though . . . Maybe you've got something with this publicity angle. Kingman sounds to me like a guy who'd take any publicity he could get for his picture.''

The desert sun was setting as Tory walked into the production office at the Wagon Wheel Inn.

Julie hung up the phone and greeted her. ''Long day on location, huh?''

''Yes,'' Tory said, ''I just got your message. What's the problem?''

''It's about this ending—''

''Oh, Julie, no, not again!'' Tory wailed.

"Don't get me wrong, kiddo," he said hastily. "I think the whole scene works great. I just got a feeling that this voice-over poetry is a little too highbrow for our audience."

"It's not highbrow at all!" Tory protested. "It's just nice and spooky, and it gives you a way to show how crazed Alan is without messing up the action."

Julie turned up the air conditioning. "Well, I don't know . . ."

"Just record it," Tory urged. "You can always decide not to use it, but if you want it, it'll be there."

"Mr. Kingman?" Penny was getting ready to leave. "Captain Fleming called while you were on the phone. He wants you to call him back."

"Guess he's putting in for overtime," Tory said lightly. "He woke me up at the crack of dawn this morning to ask me a whole lot of questions. A movie company in town plus two local murders must be a lot for a small-town cop to handle."

Julie looked at her in surprise. "Yuma's a small town, but Zack Fleming ain't no hick, baby. I was on the phone to the sheriff this morning, and he told me that boy is the star of the show down here. He's a goddamn Phi Beta Kappa from Harvard, and this time next year he'll be a shoo-in for state attorney general. He's a mover, honey. Don't let that down-home act fool you."

"Zack Fleming?" Penny closed her purse with a snap. "Oh, his family's been here forever. His dad used to be the governor, until he got so sick. And everybody thought Zack's older brother Lucas was going to run for senator. He was just brilliant. But then he got killed while he was working for the drug enforcement people. Boy, there was stuff in all the papers about that. So now there's just Zack; he's the baby brother. He didn't used to be in politics at all, but now everybody thinks he's going to run the whole state. He's really dreamy-looking—I met him once at a barbecue. The girl who finally gets him is gonna be real lucky.'' She sighed, then put her hand on the doorknob. ''Is that all for today, Mr. Kingman? See you tomorrow, then.''

Tory stared out at the darkening sky while Julie picked up the phone and shuffled through his stack of messages. What's the matter with me? she thought. He must have thought I was a total idiot—the hotshot scriptwriter from L.A. trying to tell the country cop how to do his job. And now that some time had passed, Tory wondered why she had gotten so upset. Maybe she was scared at the idea of these murders coming so close to her own life, but that was no excuse. She was great at handling the Richards and Arties of this world, but when it came to a three-dimensional person who knew what he was doing with his life, she had made a complete fool of herself.

She sighed deeply and turned away from the window. ''I think I'll—'' She broke off as the door opened and John came in. He seemed a bit flustered when he saw her.

''I wanted to . . . uh, Julie, can I talk to you later on?''

''I'm just leaving,'' Tory said quickly. ''I'll see you both tomorrow.'' She let herself out, closing the door behind her.

Julie hung up the phone with a crash. ''Line's busy again. What can I do for you, John?''

John seemed to find it hard to begin. ''Oh, Christ, Julie, I don't know what to do. I thought this whole thing was over and done with long ago, but now it's all going to be dragged through the mud again, unless—''

"Whoa! Slow down. What's happened?"

Gradually Julie pieced the story together. He already knew that several years ago John had been involved in a sordid episode with an underage aspiring actress. He'd been arrested and indicted, but they'd finally disposed of the charges out of court and the case had never come to trial. As far as Julie knew, John had clung to the straight and narrow ever since. But today one of the Yuma sheriff's deputies had broadly hinted that unless John paid him off, the whole story would come to light again in the context of the recent murders.

"Shall I give him the money, Julie? God knows I don't want anything to jeopardize this picture, but I can't stand the idea of putting myself in this man's power. I swear to you, Julie, I haven't done anything since that first—" He gulped and brushed his eyes roughly with the back of his hand. "That first problem," he went on more quietly. "But I don't think I could bear going through all that publicity and—and that shame again. People whispering every time I went anywhere and turning their backs. I couldn't go through it again." John buried his head in his hands.

Julie laced his hands behind his head and leaned back. This reminded him of the old days in New York. He'd been in the garment business with his brother-in-law, and bored to death with lingerie, when he'd invested in a small porno film company. It had started out as a lark, but then he hadn't been able to stand the slipshod way the company was run. Before he knew it, he'd been managing the whole thing. In those days he'd had plenty of opportunity to deal with cops on the take.

Sitting forward, Julie put both elbows on the desk. "Lemme get this straight. This cop, this—what's his name?"

"Hurd. Deputy Hurd."

"This Hurd found out about your past problems from the L.A. police, and now he's threatening to blab it all over the place unless you come up with some money for his private pension fund. Is that it?"

John nodded mutely.

"Well, for a start, that don't make sense. If it came from a police source in L.A., there's no way he can keep it quiet, no matter how much you give him. It's stupid. And besides, what difference does it make? You haven't killed any of these people, right?" Without waiting for a reply, he went on. "This is ancient history. Nobody cares what gets printed in Yuma, and whatever they print, it can't hurt the picture. So tell him to go fuck himself."

John looked up hopefully. "You really think—"

"No." Julie stood and walked over to the window. "I'll tell you what you do. You get hold of this Zack Fleming and lay the whole thing on him. It'll give him something to worry about, and maybe it'll keep him off our backs."

Chapter 12

The cool weather they'd enjoyed for two days had broken, and heat mirages floated over the sand. It couldn't have been a worse day to shoot the desert scenes. But they'd finally wrapped up Kevin's trek to the old shack with Debra in his arms. Now they were shooting the aftermath of the crash.

Tory and Melissa wandered over to the makeup-wardrobe trailer in search of some air-conditioned relief. That morning Michael had snapped quite sharply at Melissa when the little girl knocked over her glass of milk. His cold sarcasm had seemed inappropriate to Tory—after all, a five-year-old wasn't equipped to deal with anger on that level. But then she'd decided that Michael had probably just had a little too much togetherness with his daughter for the moment. After all, he wasn't used to full-time child care. Tory knew he wanted to go to the library and do some research on the gold mines he'd seen the day before, and when she had offered to keep Melissa with her all day, Michael had been quick to accept.

As they entered the trailer, Richard looked up and smiled. "Well, if it isn't our two lovely damsels of the desert. Welcome to our happy home away from home."

Melissa giggled. She loved Richard's banter, and now he won her heart completely by asking, "How about a makeup job for this sweet young thing?" As Tory hesitated, he added quickly, "With my box of magic I can turn a little girl into a beautiful clown."

The child looked up at Tory. "Is it okay?" she whispered, her eyes imploring.

"Well . . ." Tory wondered what Michael would think. "Will this stuff come off pretty easily?" she asked Richard.

"Don't worry, Tory. I've made up many a child actor in my time," he reassured her.

"Okay," she said and was rewarded by Melissa's happy laugh.

The little girl gazed up at Richard. "Can you really make me look like a clown?" He nodded solemnly, and she turned to Tory. "You go outside till I'm done. I want to surprise you."

Tory laughed. "Okay, honey. I'll be waiting." She stepped outside into the heat and joined Rose, who was watching yet another take of the overturned Jeep and its stunned passengers.

"Poor Kevin," Tory said after a moment. "And poor Debra. It's bad enough standing here in the shade of the trailer. It must be awful lying on the sand out there."

"Yes." Rose smiled. "I often think how much easier my job is than theirs. Where's that nice young man of yours today? Not that I blame him for staying out of this heat."

"He's at the library," Tory answered. "He wanted

to find out more about the history of this area and decided that was the best place to do it.''

"He's a historian?" Rose sounded interested.

Tory laughed. "No, he's a research psychologist. He's working on simulating stress situations." At Rose's look of confusion, Tory went on, "Of course, I don't understand it completely, but I think he tries to figure out what kinds of things can make normal rats act crazy. He wouldn't like to hear me say it that way, but that's the idea.''

"I see," Rose said eagerly. "It's a kind of behaviorism turned inside out.''

Tory glanced at her in surprise. "Sounds as if you know a lot about it. You ought to talk to Michael.''

"Oh, I'd like to. It's a field where new things are being discovered all the time.''

Tory nodded. "That's what Michael always says. I'm sure he'd love to talk to someone who understands it better than I do. Do you know a lot of psychologists?''

"No, not really," Rose said hastily. "It's just an area I find interesting.''

Something in her tone sounded odd to Tory, but it was clear that Rose didn't want to pursue the subject. Then the older woman said, "Well, it's nice of you to take care of his little girl so he could go off by himself.''

With a brief laugh Tory replied, "Oh, well, Michael needed a break." And so did I, she realized with a little shock of surprise. It was odd—she'd been so pleased when Michael showed up unexpectedly in Yuma. She'd hoped that this time together away from their usual surroundings would deepen their relationship and help them become more closely connected. But now that he was here, they didn't seem to have much to say to each other. In fact, seeing Michael in a new setting had given Tory a different perspective on him, and she wasn't certain she liked everything she saw. He was as charming and sexy as ever, but his flashes of hostility were beginning to get to her. She never knew when something she said or did would trigger an icy response, and she was getting tired of trying to predict his reactions.

Dennis announced the lunch break, and everyone moved toward the mobile cafeteria. Tory smiled at Rose. "I think I'll have cottage cheese today. I can't face veal cordon bleu in this heat."

The door of the makeup trailer opened, and Missy's painted face peeked out at her. "Look, Tory! Richard says I can wear my clown makeup to lunch so everybody can see it!"

Richard appeared behind the child, and Tory told them both, "It looks great! We'll get Artie to take your picture after we eat."

They got their lunch trays and sat down with some of the others at one of the picnic tables set up outside the caterer's van. Through the general chorus of compliments on Melissa's makeup and complaints about the blistering heat, Troy could hear Lars talking to John.

"I had been hoping to finish completely this scene, so that after lunch we could move to the highway and the policeman." Lars sounded unusually annoyed.

"I'd hoped to myself," John said impatiently. "I certainly don't want to stay out here any longer than we have to. But we'll just redo those shots. Otherwise this ending will be a farce."

"Yes, yes, you are right." Lars took a long swallow of beer. "But my God. You will talk to Debra?"

"Yeah, I'll talk to her. It's only her shots. Kevin was

fine. He can leave; he's done for today. But, Lars, you were seeing her through the camera—did she look dead?''

''No,'' Lars said resignedly, ''she did not. One could see her breathing and her eyelids fluttering. One could expect her to get up and dance in a moment.''

''Well, it'll just have to be done. Artie!'' John raised his voice. ''Get down to the highway, find that actor who's playing the cop, and tell him we're running late. He can come up and have something to eat if he wants to.''

As Artie left, John strode off toward Debra's trailer, a little distance away. Tory didn't envy him that conversation. Everyone seemed cross and snappish, irritated that there was more to be done before they could move on. Only Rose seemed unruffled. She was telling Melissa a long story about two miniature poodles she had once owned. Tory stood up and walked away, needing to escape for a moment from the tension in the air.

She found Kevin standing at the edge of the parking area, staring after a car that was bumping down the track toward the highway. ''I'll bet you're glad to be finished for the day,'' she said cheerfully.

He turned, and she was shocked by his haggard expression. ''He's run away,'' he said hoarsely. ''God, what have I done to him?''

''Who has?''

''My son—he's run away,'' he said again, ''and it's all my fault. I'm never there when Greg needs me, and he said . . . He thinks I don't love him! But it's not true. I do love him; he's my son! I'm just not ready to have a teenager walk into my life. How can I make him understand? God, what a mess I've made of things!''

"Did he take your car?" Tory asked practically.

Kevin raised his head. "Yes, he did." He drew his breath in sharply.

Tory felt a stab of pity. Kevin's concern was obviously genuine, but he couldn't help expressing his emotions a little larger than life. "Well, then, he's probably going back to the motel. I'm sure he wouldn't just vanish with your car. The best thing you can do is go after him and talk to him. Make Greg see how much you care about him."

Impulsively she held out her keys, and he stared at her blankly. "Take my car, Kevin. What Greg needs right now is his father. He needs to hear you say you love him."

He grasped her hand in his. "You're right. Thank you, Tory."

She watched him drive off, wincing as her little Miata bounced over the rough terrain. It passed another car coming toward her. A moment later Julie stepped out in a cloud of dust.

"I saw Kevin driving your car. He all done for today?"

"Yes." The words rushed out before she had time to think. "Julie, you've got to give Kevin's son a job. It doesn't matter what it is. Just hire him to do something."

Julie gave her a shrewd glance. "You think that would help?"

"Yes, I do." Tory's voice was firm.

He gazed at her intently. "Okay, maybe you're right." He shrugged. "I'll make the kid a gofer."

Surprising herself as much as Julie, Tory flung her arms around him. "You're really a good guy, aren't you?"

"Don't tell anyone, kiddo, you'll ruin my image."

She watched him stomp off toward the picnic tables, a little smile on her lips. That made two good deeds already today—baby-sitting for Melissa and getting Greg Dean a job. At this rate she'd be Girl Scout of the Year.

When she walked back into the eye of the storm, a four-way argument was raging. Tory was thankful to see Rose hustling Melissa into the wardrobe-makeup trailer as snatches of angry conversation rose in the hot still air.

"Listen, asshole, I can't hold my breath for three hours while you screw around with your goddamn focus!" Debra's shrill voice cut across the others.

"You will be careful with your language to me." Lars sounded icily calm.

"I'll tell you what I'll be careful with—"

"Debra." John spoke in a warning tone.

"Don't Debra me! If you were any kind of director, you wouldn't let your damn cameraman run the show!"

"That's enough!" Julie's bellow silenced them long enough for him to go on. "Cut out this crap! I'm bringing this turkey in on time and on budget. So get out there and get this goddamn shot done right. I don't want to hear any more about it."

Julie's outburst had the desired effect. In short order, Debra was once again lying halfway out the open passenger door of the wrecked Jeep. Richard knelt beside her, carefully applying the trickle of fake blood to her temple and arranging her blond hair on the sand.

Everyone was so intent on getting it right this time that only Julie saw the pale blue sedan drive up. The door, with its black lettering—"Yuma County Sheriff Dept."—and its gold star, opened and Zack Fleming stepped out. Julie motioned him over. "We'll be with you in two shakes, Captain. If you could just stand still and not move around while they take the shot."

Debra's eyes, following Richard as he moved away, brushing his footprints out of the sand, focused on Zack standing next to Julie. When she caught his glance, she stared straight at him for a moment and then lowered her lashes suggestively.

"Ready, Debra?" John called.

With a return of her little-girl sweetness, Debra opened her eyes and stared at Zack. Arching her back ever so slightly, she cooed, "I'm ready."

Dennis called for quiet; the sound and camera rolled. "Okay, action."

It was over in less than a minute.

"That's a print!" John announced with relief.

Near the camera, Lars muttered, "Thank God!"

To Tory it looked as if someone had suddenly flipped a switch. The crew swarmed over the set, dismantling reflectors, coiling cables, packing sound and camera equipment. Everyone was anxious to get on to the shots down by the highway. She saw Zack's tall figure standing motionless in the midst of the activity.

No matter how difficult it is, you're going to apologize to him, she told herself firmly. She'd had absolutely no reason to act so high and mighty with him yesterday morning. He no doubt had enough on his mind without people like her making his job harder. The gray eyes in the strong tanned face watched her as she made her way toward him, but his expression gave her no hint of what he was thinking.

Debra was walking toward her trailer, a little way behind where Zack stood. She changed her course slightly, intercepting Tory. "I am completely exhausted,'' she announced in a pathetic tone. ''Tory, be a dear, would you? Just brush the sand off my back for me.'' She turned her back to Tory, giving Zack the full benefit of her spectacular front view, and raised her arms to hold her blond hair off her neck. ''Oh, thanks,'' she sighed. ''I've just got to lie down for a little while. No one understands how much this takes out of me.'' Debra glanced up and seemed to notice Zack for the first time. ''Oh, Captain, did you want to talk to me? I'll be in my trailer. It's nice and cool in there.'' She gave him a sweet little smile and moved off toward the trailer.

''Captain Fleming!''

Zack turned to see John hurrying up to him. ''You're Mr. Hartnell, aren't you? I got your message. You wanted to talk to me?''

''Yes.'' John sounded breathless. ''Come this way, would you? I want to tell you something a little disturbing.'' He drew Zack out of earshot, and after a few false starts spilled out the story of his encounter with Deputy Hurd. ''As you can imagine,'' he finished, ''I don't want this broadcast all over the world, but I also don't want to be in the position of bribing a police officer. So I felt the best thing was to tell you about it.''

Zack's face was grim. ''I'm glad you did, Mr. Hartnell. I'd prefer that you didn't discuss this with anyone else. But I can promise that you won't be hearing from Deputy Hurd again.'' Zack's thoughts were racing, and he seemed to forget that John still stood there.

''Well . . . thanks,'' John said awkwardly. He straightened his shoulders in relief and walked rapidly back to his crew.

Seeing Zack standing alone, Tory took a hesitant step

toward him, then halted. His strong profile gave him a look that was both attractive and forbidding. Oh, stop procrastinating, she told herself. Just walk up to him and get it over with. "Captain Fleming?"

He didn't respond. Tory felt a flush creeping up her neck, but she went on doggedly. "I just wanted—"

He glanced at her briefly. "I'm sorry. I'll have to talk to you later." He moved away with long strides toward his car.

Well. If he couldn't even be bothered to accept an apology—she looked after him, feeling absurdly let down. She wouldn't try it again.

Debra peered out the window of her trailer. Zack was leaning into his car, apparently talking on the radio. Her mouth twisted in annoyance. It didn't look as if he planned to join her.

Zack listened to the crackling voice on the box. Then he pushed the transmit button. "I'll be in shortly. I want to go over all the files on this business. Get them out for me so I can look at what each officer has been doing. I want the raw data, not just the summaries. Got that?"

"Ten-four, Captain."

Zack replaced the microphone, then looked around for Tory, wondering what she'd wanted to tell him. He wished he could find an opportunity to talk to her about something besides these murders. He wanted to get to know her better.

The door of Debra's trailer flew open with a bang, and clouds of smoke billowed out. Screaming hysterically, she stumbled down the steps. Cast and crew dropped what they were doing and raced toward her. Zack pushed through the excited group, and Debra clung to him in a panic.

"He tried to kill me!" she gasped, coughing and choking. "Someone tried to kill me!"

Jimbo snatched a fire extinguisher from the equipment truck. "There's another one in the van," he called to Bill. "You folks better move back. If the fuel tank goes . . ." He stepped solidly inside the trailer, the extinguisher shooting foam in front of him.

While Jimbo and the others put out the fire, Zack guided Debra to Sally's umbrella-shaded chair and sat her down. "Can you tell me what happened?"

Still grasping Zack's hand, Debra said brokenly, "I—I was lying down resting and—and I guess I fell asleep. The next think I knew, the trailer was full of smoke. Someone must be trying to kill me!"

"Did you see anyone around the trailer?"

"No! I told you, I was asleep. Someone must have snuck in and set my trailer on fire." She shuddered and raised her pretty tearstained face to him. "Who could want to kill me?"

A few crew members had gathered around. Zack motioned Sally closer. "Could you please stay with her? I'll be back in a few minutes." With her usual efficiency, Sally already had a cold soft drink and a damp cloth in her hands.

At the edge of the little crowd, Tory stood with Melissa, her arm around the child's shoulders. Melissa's eyes were huge as she stared at the last wisps of smoke filtering through the windows and doorway of Debra's trailer. "What happened, Tory? Is the trailer on fire?"

Tory shook her head. "The fire is out now, Missy," she said quietly. "I don't know how it got started."

They continued to watch as Zack approached the trailer. "You fellows did a fast job of putting it out," he said to Jimbo.

"There was a lot more smoke than flame. The area around the sink is pretty blackened up. The fire probably started in the trash bag."

Zack took the big flashlight from Jimbo and went inside to look around. Through the open window at the back, he heard Richard say snidely, "That bitch. I'll bet she set that fire herself. You'll notice it didn't do her any harm. Always looking for the spotlight, our little Debra."

When he came out, Zack nodded to Jimbo. "You guys are really on the ball. You did a good job in there. Now I'd like you to make sure no one goes inside or touches anything until the arson squad gets here."

"No problem," Jimbo told him. "I'll get one of the guys to keep an eye on it."

Julie came up mopping his brow. "God almighty, if it ain't one thing, it's another. Got any idea how it started?"

"I'm going to call in the arson squad. I'd like everyone to stay put until they can get here and take a look." Zack turned toward his car.

"Stay put?" Julie said. "We're already behind schedule! They're all ready to set up for the scene down at the highway. How 'bout if we stay put there?"

Zack considered for a moment. "That's fine. But no one is to leave the area. I want all of these people available when my men need to question them."

"No one's going anywhere till we get those shots," Julie said with determination.

"I'll want to talk to Ms. Scott in a minute. Would you ask her to wait for me inside?" He gestured toward the wardrobe-makeup trailer.

"Yeah, sure." Julie mopped his brow again. "Christ, I sure hope you get this cleared up soon."

Zack strode to his car, leaned through the window, and told the arson squad what had happened. He listened for a moment, then replied, "Right. That's it. And one more thing, Garcia. Check for a possible break-and-enter on the trailer."

Stepping into the makeup trailer, Zack closed the door firmly behind him. Debra had pushed Richard's makeup case out of the way and was leaning back against the arm of the couch, her long legs stretched out in front of her, her hair prettily disheveled. "Oh, Captain, I'm so glad you're here!"

Gazing at her speculatively, Zack said, "Now that you've had some time to think about it, Ms. Scott, is there anything you'd like to add—or change—in your account of the fire?"

Debra frowned. "I don't know what you mean. I told you what happened."

After a pause, Zack said quietly, "You fell asleep awfully fast, Ms. Scott."

"What kind of remark is that?" Debra sat up straight with a jerk.

In a conversational tone, Zack explained, "You know, we can usually tell exactly how a fire was set."

Debra glared at him and didn't utter a word.

After a moment he nodded. "Well, then, that's it for now. The arson squad will want to talk to you when they arrive. And you can call me at the station if you think of anything else you want to tell me."

Zack ushered her out of the trailer and walked with her to where Sally was preparing to move her chair and script book down to the new location at the highway. "Just wait here, Ms. Scott, until the arson squad says everyone can leave."

Before Debra could protest, he turned and headed back toward his car.

"Captain Fleming?" Tory walked over to intercept him, Melissa close beside her. When she was close enough, Tory asked, "Is it okay for us to leave? I don't think there's anything I can tell the arson investigators. I didn't see anything until Debra ran out of her trailer, and I'd like to get Melissa out of the sun."

He paused to consider and then said, "I don't see why not. They can always find you later if they need to. Sure, go ahead and leave." He looked over at the scattering of cars parked every which way. "I thought you had a Miata—I don't see it."

"Oh, damn!" Tory glanced apologetically at Melissa. I guess I'm a little more frazzled than I realized, she thought. "I completely forgot—I let Kevin take my Miata because his son took his car." She sighed and gave a little shrug. "Oh, well, we'll just have to wait and hitch a ride with whoever leaves here first. The arson squad will be done pretty soon, won't they?"

"It won't take long, but they haven't even gotten here yet." Zack looked at Tory and then down at the child holding her hand. "Tell you what—you can come with me; I'm leaving right now." He smiled at Melissa. "How about it—want to ride in a police car?"

The wide blue eyes shone with excitement. "Wow! Can I really? Can you turn on the siren?"

"I don't think we should do that," he told her, "unless we see some cowboys rustling cattle. But you can listen to the policemen talking to each other on the radio."

When they got to the squad car, the three of them squeezed into the front seat, and Zack gave Melissa a quick explanation of all the equipment on the dashboard. As soon as they had bumped over the sandy track and were tooling along the highway, Tory said, "I really appreciate this."

Melissa was mesmerized by the low voices coming through on the radio, and Zack smiled at Tory. "Just part of the regular service of the Sheriff's Department," he said lightly. "We aim to please." She returned his smile, and after a moment he went on more seriously, "I'm sorry I cut you off earlier. There was something I had to take care of. What was it you wanted to say to me?"

Flushing slightly, Tory said, "It wasn't important." But when his cool gray eyes rested on her briefly, she took a deep breath. "I just wanted to apologize for . . . well, for my attitude yesterday morning. I guess I took your questions the wrong way. I know you have to . . ." Floundering, she stared out the window.

"Don't worry," he said easily. "I think we both got started on the wrong foot somehow, so let's just step back and start over."

Tory looked at him gratefully. Then he grinned slowly. "Okay . . . but I never even thanked you for the great breakfast. I finished every bite."

His somewhat serious face softened in a laugh. "I like a woman with a healthy appetite."

When they pulled up in front of the motel, Tory said, "Thanks for the ride."

Tearing herself away from the police radio, Melissa looked up at him. "That was neat!"

"I'm glad you enjoyed it," Zack told her. "I did, too." With a wave to Tory, he drove off.

When he reached his office, Zack sorted through the reports that had been stacked neatly on his desk. Picking out all of Deputy Hurd's reports and notes, he read carefully through them. Then he spoke into the intercom. "Ask Deputy Hurd to come in here right away, Martha."

"You sent for me, Captain?" Hurd asked as he entered Zack's office a few moments later.

"Yes. Close the door and sit down." He looked directly at the beefy deputy. "I've had a report concerning your methods of investigation. I'd like to hear what you have to say for yourself." Hurd opened his mouth to protest, but before he could say a word, Zack said warningly, "I've got your whole file here, Hurd. And I've just gone over it very thoroughly." Then Zack told his deputy about John's allegations. "Did you know that Hartnell was picked up for 'endangering morals' in L.A.?"

Hurd met his eyes. "Yeah, I knew."

"Then why isn't it in this report?"

"Haven't had time to write it up yet," Hurd told him calmly.

"What do you have to say about this bribery accusation?"

"It ain't true." Hurd paused, as if thinking it over. "Maybe this Hartnell thinks I leaned on him too hard and he's trying to get back at me."

Zack looked at him a moment longer. Then he said evenly, "All right, Hurd. That's all."

After Hurd left, Zack opened the reports and started reading them again. A cold anger gripped him. A dishonest policeman was something he would not tolerate. He had to find a way to definitely clear or accuse his deputy. Police corruption was commonplace all over the country, but he'd be damned if he'd let it take hold here. His mouth set in a grim line.

Later that evening, after the crew had returned to the

motel, Zack knocked on Richard's door. There was no light showing through the cracks in the drapes, and Zack was surprised when Richard opened it. He must have been sitting in there alone in the gathering dusk.

Richard didn't look well. The reality of Georgette's murder the night before last was catching up to him. After the killing he had been able to operate fairly well on automatic pilot, and even now he could hold his own while he was on location and around the crew. But he'd been having nightmares, the kind you wake up in a cold sweat from, and they had taken their toll.

"Good evening. I understand Deputy Hurd interviewed you three days ago. When do you expect to see him again?"

Richard stared at Zack. Then his face sagged. "Oh, Christ."

In a way it was a relief to tell the story. Hurd couldn't prove anything. Richard had gotten rid of the cocaine he'd kept out of the shipment, and there was no evidence of their transaction. But Richard was afraid of Hurd.

He still had sufficient control to lie to Zack about where he'd gotten the cocaine—he said he'd brought it with him from L.A. In the end he signed a statement of what had happened between him and Hurd, and promised to let Zack know if Hurd got in touch with him again.

Back in his office, Zack tried to put Hurd out of his mind for the moment. There was nothing more he could do right now, though he did have the statement from Richard. He sipped his coffee and got out his notebook. He still had a killer to find.

Chapter 13

Tory settled into the booth of Joe's Steak House and looked around. The place didn't have much of a Wild West feel, but the red leather banquette was comfortable and the service was prompt. The waitress was just arriving with Melissa's Shirley Temple and the bottle of red wine Michael had ordered.

The restaurant was right next door to the Wagon Wheel Inn, and several crew members had assured Tory that the steaks were excellent. And she was in the mood for a good steak after a day on the desert and a long swim in the motel pool.

Michael said to Melissa, "How about some chicken with barbecue sauce, Missy?"

"Okay," the child replied. "Can I have french fries?"

"Sure." He gave the hovering waitress their order and then smiled at Tory across the table. "How was your day?"

Before Tory could answer, Melissa slurped up the last of her Shirley Temple and looked at her father hopefully. "Dad, nobody's using those games now. Can I play?"

Tory hadn't even noticed the video game machines against the back wall, but Melissa certainly had. The child's wistful expression was hard to resist, and Michael dug out a handful of quarters. He watched as his daughter ran across the room and without a moment's hesitation dropped in her money and grabbed the joystick. Then he returned his attention to Tory. "So how *was* your day?"

"Well, first of all, Missy was great—no problem at all. And I think she had a good time. But things got a little tense on the set. It was awfully hot out there, and then they had to reshoot Debra's dying scene several times." Tory paused and then added, "She's really pretty much of a bitch."

Michael looked at Tory in surprise. That was a harsh judgment coming from her. "Well, maybe the heat got to her."

For a moment Tory felt guilty, but then she remembered how Debra had snapped at Lars and John and the blatant way she'd flirted with Zack. "It was plenty hot, but she's still not a nice person. Anyway, after that all hell broke loose. Someone set fire to Debra's trailer, with her in it, and she was screaming bloody murder."

Michael put down his glass in astonishment. "Someone tried to kill Debra?"

"That's what it looked like. Personally, I wonder. Richard thinks she set the fire herself just to get some sympathy and attention."

"Maybe." Then Michael grinned sardonically. "But there's no fire in your script, is there? Someone must have gotten mixed up."

Appalled, Tory stared at him. She'd managed to keep

the whole ugly business out of her conscious mind all day. But now it all came flooding back. A defenseless animal and two human beings had been murdered. And today someone could have been burned to death. In a flash of anger, she snapped, "It's nothing to joke about, Michael."

He shrugged. "Sorry, I didn't mean to upset you. But, still, you did write the script."

"That's what's so horrible." Tory shook her head. "I don't know. Could the whole thing have started as a coincidence and then someone else followed along doing stuff from the script?"

"Oh, Tory." Michael sounded impatient.

She looked at him helplessly. "But it's all so much like the plot of the movie. It makes me wonder if I didn't cause some sort of mass hysteria just by thinking it up."

This time Michael didn't even try to control his annoyance. "Now, Tory, you're not stupid! There's no way your writing a script could have caused a mass reaction."

"Of course. I know that. But it's as if someone's out to get me—taking a story I made up and making it happen in real life. It's awful! I feel as if someone is trying to get inside my mind."

"Now you sound paranoid, as your Freudian friends like to say." Then he patted her hand. "But at least you do see that there's some sort of organizing principle behind it."

Tory looked down at the table. It was no use discussing these things with Michael. They always seemed to be at cross purposes; he twisted whatever she said to fit his own ideas and could never grasp what she was feeling. She was relieved to see the waitress arriving with their food. They waved Melissa back to the booth. Luckily, the little girl was brimming over with enthusiasm. Her excited chatter continued through most of the meal, and Tory didn't have to add much to the conversation.

"Mind if we join you?" Without waiting for an answer, Julie slid into the booth next to Tory. John, who followed Julie in, pulled up a chair and sank into it.

The waitress hurried over. "Can I get you gentlemen something?"

"God, yes!" Julie said. "Two double brandies, sweetheart."

John sighed. "Goodness, I'm glad to see you people. We are in desperate need of rational conversation with rational human beings." Tory looked at him inquiringly. "We've been talking to Debra. Need I say more?"

"That dumb bitch—excuse my French." Julie glanced at Melissa as his pudgy fingers scooped up the cold french fries from Tory's plate and stuffed them into his mouth. "Would you believe," he went on indistinctly, "she's sitting up there in her room pretending she's afraid to go to the bathroom without an armed escort. And talk about a motor mouth! There's no way to shut her up." Grabbing the brandy from the waitress's hand, Julie downed a healthy swig. "She couldn't con the cops into giving her round-the-clock protection—I mean, they're no dummies. So now she tells me if I don't hire her a guard, she'll walk off the picture. I ask you—armed guards. I told her, this ain't the *3:10 to Yuma*, chickie."

Tory couldn't help it—she burst out laughing. "Oh, Julie, you're priceless!"

Michael looked slightly puzzled. "The cops don't think Debra needs protection, but she thinks she does?"

John shook his head. "Debra obviously realizes that all of us, including the police, think she set that fire herself. But of course she can't admit it. She's backed herself into a corner with her little performance. Now she's got to follow through, and she's very angry that no one is helping her out. At least, that's how I read it."

"Makes me wonder if I'm losing my marbles." Julie passed a hand through his thinning hair. "I shoulda spotted that broad for trouble the minute I laid eyes on her. I'll tell ya, the next time I even think about hiring another one of these prima donnas, just ship me off to the funny farm. At least I couldn't get into this kind of mess doing basket weaving." He polished off his brandy and signaled to the waitress. "The thing that makes me so goddamn mad is she's got me by the short hairs, and she knows it. If she walks now, with her other scenes left to shoot, the whole picture's down the tubes. I sure as hell can't replace her at this late date. Might as well kiss the whole thing good-bye."

"Well, Julie," John said resignedly, "we can rearrange the schedule and get Debra's scenes out of the way tomorrow and the next day. That way you'll only have to get a guard for two days, and then we'll be finished with her."

"I'll tell you how I'd like to be finished with her— I'd like to wring her cute little neck. Now I gotta scrounge around for some ex-cop who probably got canned for drinking on the job, and pay him to hold her hand. It ain't even the money—although God knows we're over budget as is—it's the goddamn principle. I can't stand to see her get away with this. It's blackmail is what it is.''

Michael nodded sympathetically, and John heaved a sigh. ''I'm not looking forward to the next two days,'' he said wearily. ''She was impossible to work with before. Can you imagine what she's going to be like now? I can hardly stand the thought of it.''

Tory had been staring into space, her fingers tapping idly on the table. Now she looked at John. ''Maybe you won't have to.''

''What?''

Julie leaned forward. ''Got an idea, kid?''

''I think so.'' Tory spoke eagerly. ''We've only got the stuff in the bar with the other waitress and the shopping scene with the girlfriend next door. Right?''

John nodded.

''Well, we can do those scenes without using Debra at all. How about if we move most of the bar sequence to the dressing room area?''

Julie frowned. ''Yeah? So what?''

''Don't you see? You shoot her from the back. It'll be a real nice sexy little scene of her changing from her street clothes to her uniform while the other waitress talks to her. That actress who played the stripper could do Jean Anne fine if you get her a wig. She's the right build, and we won't ever see her face.''

Julie grinned and slapped the table. ''Son of a bitch!''

''Then, we can do the shopping scene on the phone. You have plenty of footage of Debra talking on the phone in Jean Anne's apartment—that'll be for intercuts. Put the girlfriend in an outdoor phone booth so there's something going on in the background. You'll even save money doing it this way.''

''I love it!'' Julie grabbed Tory's hand and kissed it.

"You're a genius, sweetheart. I knew there was a reason I told you to stick around."

"I think you're right, Tory. We can finish those scenes without using Debra at all. And this means"— John grinned at Julie—"that we're finished with her altogether. My dear girl, I do believe you've saved us from a fate worse than death. Julie, the three of us had better take a look at the script right away and make sure this is going to work."

"You betcha. And then I'll have a talk with her first thing tomorrow morning—no need to listen to her screaming tonight. It'll be my pleasure, believe me. Then I'll get Artie to ship her out as quick as he can. Boy, I can't wait to get that broad out of our hair—I love it! Come on, Tory."

Julie started to shove himself out of the booth and then felt John giving him a steady frown. Suddenly he realized that Michael and Melissa were still sitting at the table. Hastily, Julie began to make amends. "Look, I don't want to break up your evening . . ."

Michael smiled. "No problem at all. I can see that you all have a busy night ahead." He looked at Tory. "Don't worry, we'll be fine. You go on and get your work done. I'm sure you want to get rid of your leading lady once and for all."

John, Julie, and Tory trooped out of the restaurant and along the open walkway toward the production office. "Nice fellow you've got there," John told Tory. "He certainly was a sport about us dragging you away to work this evening. I'm sure you both had other plans."

"Oh, well, Michael understands." Tory gave John a brief smile, but she was puzzled by Michael's genial reaction to the evening's disruption. It was almost as if he wanted to get rid of her. No, that was silly. But why did she feel so ambivalent toward him lately?

Unbidden, the face of Zack Fleming sprang into Tory's mind. She knew she was blushing, but fortunately John and Julie were too engrossed in conversation to notice. Zack Fleming—she didn't even know him. And his appearance of being interested in everything she had to say just showed that he was good at his job. But he'd taken time to entertain Melissa, and surely that wasn't part of his work. Stop fantasizing, Tory told herself severely. You're just hoping he'll be able to solve these murders quickly and put everything back to normal.

But as Julie unlocked the production office door and the three of them went inside, the image of Zack's steady gray eyes refused to fade.

Debra stepped out of the steamy shower and wrapped her golden hair in a towel. Using the two other bath towels, she gently patted her body dry. The mirror wasn't full length, but it was serviceable. She turned her back to it and over her shoulder studied her round, rosy bottom for telltale dimples. Thank God, no signs of cellulite yet. Still, a girl was never too young to start taking care of herself. She turned to examine her profile. Good flat tummy and high, firm ass, but were her breasts beginning to droop the tiniest bit? Pouring a generous amount of lotion into her palm, she began to slather it on her arms and chest. This dry heat was death to sensitive skin like hers.

As she ran her hands around her small waist and down her well-defined hips, Debra thought that those exercise classes she'd taken in L.A. had been well worth the money. She had excellent tone, good muscle control, and not one ripple of fat. She'd get right back into the classes as soon as she got home. Debra smiled as she thought of Joe, the lithe young man who ran the classes. She was sure he swung both ways, but sometimes that made things all the more interesting. Yes, she'd definitely start exercising again right away.

After blowing her tangled curls dry, Debra settled down with a bottle of nail polish and a wad of cotton to give herself a pedicure. When she'd finished, she sat fanning the polish dry and laughing along with a "M*A*S*H" rerun on the local channel. She'd seen this episode at least twice before, but she still loved it. Debra decided she wouldn't mind at all if Julie provided Alan Alda as her armed guard. In fact, he wouldn't even have to stay outside her door in the cold night!

A commercial had just come on when the phone rang. Probably that pig Julie whining that he couldn't find a guard, she thought. She licked her lips in anticipation. No way was he getting off the hook now; she'd make him pay through the nose for all those insults she'd had to ignore on the set of this ridiculous film. All she had to do was threaten to walk off the picture and he'd climb right down off his high horse. That fire had been a stroke of genius, if she did say so herself.

"Hello?"

"Ms. Scott?"

It was a man's voice—one she'd never heard before. "Yes?"

"This is Sergeant Kelly from Captain Fleming's office. I'm terribly sorry to disturb you this late at night—"

Debra's voice took on a breathy quality as she cut in eagerly, "Oh, that's all right. I'm always ready to help the captain."

"Well, ma'am, he asked me to phone you and see if you would be able to meet him. He said it's rather confidential, but there are a few things he wanted to talk over with you. He would've called himself, but he's out of the office finishing up some routine business."

"Yes?" Debra smiled at herself in the mirror. She could just imagine what sort of conversation that cute Captain Fleming had in mind at this time of night. So he wasn't the cold fish he'd pretended to be; he'd just wanted to keep things between the two of them. Her thoughts raced on. The word was Zack Fleming was about to get into politics, maybe even go to Washington, and he was a very eligible bachelor. Plenty of political men had found that a film star wife was an asset to their careers—look at Nancy Reagan, for instance.

"Captain Fleming was hoping you could meet him in half an hour at the Territorial Prison."

"Well, okay—"

The voice cut in. "You've got a car, right? Just go up Fourth Avenue and turn right on Third Street. Stay on Third; it curves around and becomes Giss Parkway. You'll turn left for the prison after you go under the freeway. There are lots of signs—you can't miss it."

"Fine. Tell Captain Fleming I'll be there." Debra hung up the phone with a self-satisfied smirk. Things were looking up out here in the sticks.

What a good thing she'd already washed and dried her hair. Without Richard's work with the hot rollers, it was an enticing silken mane that framed her face with wild promise. Crossing to the dressing table, Debra quickly pulled on a pair of black lace bikini panties and opened her makeup case. Just the merest touch of silver-gray eye shadow to enhance her enormous blue eyes, and a wisp of blusher to bring out the cheekbones.

Leaning closer to the mirror, she carefully stroked on charcoal mascara. Too bad her eyelashes weren't longer and thicker—even having them dyed every month didn't help as much as she'd hoped, but false eyelashes were definitely tacky.

What to wear? It was a balmy night—maybe the turquoise body suit and the matching silk wraparound skirt. No—all those ties and straps were too cumbersome. What about the strapless black? She'd paid a goddamn fortune for it, but its deceptively simple elegance was worth it. She stepped into the tube of silk jersey and tugged it up over her hips. Settling the elastic at her waist, she shook the slithery skirt so the long slit ran straight up her thigh. Another band of elastic ran around the top of the dress. Pulling it up, she craned her neck to make sure the back was even. Then, facing the mirror, she bent forward so that her full breasts filled the fabric as she adjusted the elastic low across her bosom.

Debra slipped on her high-heeled sandals and moved away from the mirror to get the full effect. How about jewelry? She loved the gold Pisces pendant, but maybe it was better to keep the neckline uncluttered. No, just the big silver bracelet—not everyone could carry off these big chunky pieces, she thought complacently. Stepping back to the dressing table, she dabbed her finger in the pot of lip gloss and smoothed a slick film over her full lips. Then she picked up the distinctive lacquer-red atomizer of Opium and sprayed a fine mist of scent over her throat and chest. She didn't neglect to send a waft of spray over her hair—everyone knew that hair held the fragrance longer than any part of the body. She gave herself an approving smile, picked up her bag, and quietly let herself out of her room.

As Debra closed the door behind her, she glanced quickly along the open walkways. There was no sign of anyone from the movie crowd—only a couple of salesman types coming back to their room with a full bucket of ice from the machine by the pool. She walked the other way, around to the far side of the building where another staircase led down to the parking lot. She hadn't used her car that day. It was still parked in the last slot near the street, where she'd hoped the line of trees would keep the worst of the sun off it. The rented blue Malibu started easily, and she pulled out into Arizona Avenue, congratulating herself on having escaped unseen by anyone she knew. Let Julie think she was still locked in her room crying her eyes out.

Traffic was light even on Fourth Avenue, Yuma's main drag. Stopping at a signal, Debra glanced curiously at a group of boys hovering in the doorway of a squat stucco building with darkened windows. The painted sign told her this was the Twilight Zone, and a few phosphorescent stars and moon shapes suggested a teen hangout. The light changed and she continued north. The line of gas stations and restaurants petered out as she turned right on Third Street, but the signs at the bottom of the hill were plainly visible. Around the curve, and there on the left was the sign—"Yuma Territorial Prison." The road climbed up again and then ended in a deserted parking lot, and Debra got out and looked around.

To her left ran the rough stone of the prison walls, while straight ahead was some sort of pavilion atop a high, rocky base. But the whole place was in darkness. Only a single bulb mounted on an outside corner of the prison wall was lit. Debra stared around uncertainly. Was this the right place? But she was sure she'd followed the directions. Then she smiled slowly. Captain Fleming certainly was a fast mover. He wasn't even making a pretense of this being business. Debra took a few steps to the right and saw that she was on a bluff with the gleaming Colorado snaking lazily below her. The handsome captain had lured her to the local lovers' lookout point, she was sure. Only tonight they seemed to have it all to themselves. Had he managed that as well? A shiver of delightful anticipation ran through her. An old abandoned prison overlooking a winding river—she had really underestimated his sense of the romantic. Now where could that devil be?

Debra started along the wide open path that led into the prison grounds. Then she heard a voice from high on her right. "Ms. Scott?" he called softly.

Of course. He was up on that platform thing. There'd be a terrific view from that spot.

"Yes, Captain."

"Come on up and join me. Just follow the rail to the steps. It's quite spectacular up here."

Oh, yes, she thought. "Spectacular" will be just the word for it. Debra clutched the handrail and climbed to the observation platform, her heels echoing sharply in the silent desert night. She stopped and peered around in the dark.

Suddenly she felt his hands on her shoulders as he slipped up behind her. "Isn't the desert beautiful at night?" he said softly in her ear.

His voice wasn't as she'd remembered. But when Debra leaned back against him, his body was as strong and warm as she'd imagined. They stood there for a moment gazing out at the river and the few twinkling lights, his arms holding her close. Then Debra turned her head and looked up at him. She stiffened in alarm.

''You're not—''

''No. I'm not.'' A length of braided leather dangled from his left hand. His right hand grabbed the other end and pulled it tight around her neck. Before she could cry out, the leather had sunk deep into her tender flesh, cutting off her breath. She clawed at her own neck, desperately trying to tear off the deadly noose, her long nails gouging ugly furrows in her skin. Her stiletto heels kicked helplessly at his ankles. Finally her choking subsided and her body hung limp, held up only by the cruel thong around her neck. He waited a few moments longer, until he was sure she was dead, then let go. Debra's body slumped into a heap on the platform.

The man kicked at Debra's dainty clutch bag lying on the platform and sent it skittering off into the darkness toward the river. Without another glance at the body, he headed quickly for the steps.

Chapter 14

Jim Santiago, the state park ranger in charge of the Yuma Territorial Prison for that day, arrived promptly at 7:45 A.M. The prison, now a museum, was open every day except Christmas from eight o'clock until five-thirty.

Jim parked his cream-colored sedan at the far end of the lot. He didn't like to take up a closer space that a visitor might use. Getting out of his car and adjusting the jacket of his dark green uniform, he strode toward the entrance. As he passed the blue Malibu parked near the path, he glanced inside it.

The car was empty and unlocked. Santiago shook his head. Some tourists really liked to get an early start. But there was no one waiting at the museum entrance or sitting at the picnic table near the vending machines in the comfort station.

Jim looked around, slightly perplexed. Walking over to the comfort station, he pushed open the doors to both rest rooms. He'd wondered if maybe a late-night reveler had ended up sleeping it off on the floor in here; it had happened a couple of times before, and he didn't enjoy dealing with other people's hangovers. But the place seemed deserted except for him.

Shrugging his shoulders, he walked over and unlocked the heavy iron gates set in the stone archway. As always, the dim interior of the museum was cool and quiet. Even at the height of the tourist season, the century-old prison was a restful place to work. He gazed around affectionately at the glass cases with their assortment of old documents and iron manacles and more prosaic items like cooking pots. It wasn't a big museum, but the stuff in it was really interesting, he thought. Kids especially loved reading the lists of prisoners on the wall, and the details of how old they were, what they'd done wrong, and how much time they'd served. His own kids liked to imagine themselves capturing the notorious desperadoes who'd done time in Yuma.

Stepping around behind his counter at the entrance, Jim began to get set up for the day. Unlike some of his colleagues who arrived breathless a minute or two after eight and then hurried around looking for change and information sheets while the visitors straggled in, Jim preferred to get organized beforehand. From a cabinet he pulled out a bunch of maps of Yuma's historic sites and stacked them neatly at one end of the counter. The postcards and booklets he arranged at the other end. These cost money and he wanted to be able to keep an eye on them. He opened the cash register and counted the bills and change, making sure his count matched the tally from the end of the day before.

Once his counter was just the way he liked it, he walked through the one-room museum and unlocked the wooden door at the back that opened onto the interior courtyard of the prison. The admission fee allowed a visitor not only to view all the exhibits in the museum but also to wander around the courtyard and to peer through the iron grating of the cells. Of course the cell doors were kept locked and there was little even the youngest tourists could do to get themselves into trouble out there. Jim stepped into the courtyard and shaded his eyes against the already blazing sun. Then he walked back to his counter. He was ready for the day.

In his room at the Wagon Wheel Inn, Richard woke up to the ringing of the phone. He looked at his clock and cursed. No one was supposed to be on the set until eleven this morning. Surely they hadn't changed the call again! He rolled over and grabbed the phone on the sixth ring.

"Hello?" The anger in his sleepy voice came through loud and clear.

"Good morning, Richard." The voice on the other end was an oily threat. "We got your delivery. It was a little short."

Alert now, his heart thumping, Richard sat up on the edge of his bed. "Right. I wanted to tell you about that, but dropping you a little note didn't seem quite the right touch."

There was a heavy silence on the other end of the line. Then the voice said, "So? Explain."

"Well, you see," Richard began, now warming to his theme, "I got the items here without a hitch. But as I was eviscerating the first piñata—by the way, I don't know if you're aware that your merchandise came packed in fifteen truly incredible piñatas, and if you think it doesn't take some fancy talking to get those across, you just haven't tried it. Anyway, where was I? Oh, yes. As I was relieving the first of the little darlings of its burden, the package broke. If I'd known I'd be doing this kind of surgery I would have taken a course in it. However—''

"Stick to the subject, Richard.'' The voice didn't seem to appreciate Richard's witty sarcasm.

"Well, there it was. Spread all over the fabulous olive carpet in my glamorous abode. Who would have guessed we'd have a snowfall down here in Yuma? Not quite the thing for the maid if you know what I mean. There simply was no help for it. I scraped up what I could and sent it on to you. The rest went down the drain.'' Richard made a dramatic pause and then continued. "Yes. Sad but true, I had to blot it up with a wet washcloth. There I was down on my knees like the proverbial washerwoman. And all for the love of the company.'' Richard smiled into the phone.

There was a long silence. Then the voice spoke, sounding depressed. "I was afraid you might say something like that, Richard. But those bags can hardly be cut with a surgical knife. I really wish you hadn't decided to play games with us, Richard. I had such hopes for you.''

"But wait a minute!'' Richard's cockiness had given way to genuine concern.

The man gave him no chance to go on. "Sorry, Richard. We won't be able to use you anymore. We don't like sticky fingers. But we'll be in touch.'' The phone clicked off, leaving Richard staring at the instrument white-faced and open-mouthed. Slowly he hung up his own receiver.

He sat at the edge of his bed in a sort of trance for almost a full minute. There was no mistaking the gravity of the threat that had just been delivered to him. He remembered his friend's description of what had happened to another man who "disappointed" the big boys by blabbing about his hotshot connections. "They treat the problem at its source," the friend had told Richard. "He talked too much, so they sent some fellows around to cut out his tongue." Richard remembered the friend's laugh as he went on, "It sure worked. He hasn't said a word since!"

"Sticky fingers." Richard looked down at his slender artistic hands. Oh, my God! He raced into the bathroom and made it just in time. Then, when he couldn't keep the thoughts out of his mind, he threw up again. What a fool he'd been. And all for nothing—he'd flushed the stuff away in a panic after Deputy Hurd had threatened him. Now there was no way of stopping the men from the "company."

Richard ran back into the bedroom and started yanking open the dresser drawers. The only thing he could do was disappear. As he jammed clothes into his suitcase, he realized he would lose his union card along with his identity. No more credits on the silver screen. But then, there was more at stake than that. Determined not to be sick again, Richard shuddered and forcefully shoved the thoughts out of his mind. Just get away, his instinct for self-preservation told him. Just disappear and change so completely that they'll never find you. At least he could do that. His talent with makeup and mimicry would stand him in good stead.

Not even bothering to shower or shave, Richard hurriedly splashed his face with water and gave his teeth a swipe. He could almost literally feel them breathing down his neck. Pulling on some inconspicuous chinos and a T-shirt and tossing his room key on the dresser,

Richard picked up his bag and makeup case and let himself out of his room.

He looked around furtively, slithered down the steps, and trotted out to the street. He could probably hitch a ride to the bus station. There he'd buy a couple of tickets, to different destinations. Patting the money belt safely tucked beneath his shirt, Richard permitted himself a slight smile. Then he adjusted his sunglasses and started walking along Fourth Avenue.

The dark-haired girl who picked him up was a nonstop chatterer. Her dad owned a place called Quicker Liquor in Winterhaven, just across the river, and she was on her way to work there.

"Of course we sell other things too—Kleenex, gum, milk, bread, cold cuts, cheese—all that kind of stuff. It was my dad's idea. It's sort of a mini-market. He's real smart, but I tell you, living in a town of eight hundred people was enough to drive me crazy. I mean, everybody knows everybody else's business. It's nicer living in Yuma. It's so big and people don't care what you do. I mean, it's got a lot going for it."

Richard sat in the passenger seat and listened to the girl rattle on. Yuma, the big city—God, was this what he was going to be reduced to? How could he have been so stupid; what had happened to his brain? Why couldn't he have just made the deal and taken the money and gone on with things? Now he'd fucked up his whole life. Now the biggest thing happening for him was some dumb twit going on about how grand things were in the big city of Yuma.

"Where you from?" The girl's question brought Richard up with a start.

"L.A.," he said shortly.

She turned to face him, narrowly missing a slowing

truck in front of her. "Wow! L.A. is some place, right? I've always wanted to go there!" She pulled over to the curb, regret written all over her face. "Well, this is where I let you out."

Richard opened the car door. He had no intention of being shanghaied home to dad and the Quicker Liquor. "Thanks."

"That's okay. Just go along First Street here and you'll hit the bus station in about a block. And say hi to L.A. for me."

"Yeah." He slammed the car door and turned away, makeup case in one hand and suitcase in the other. As usual, it was already hotter than hell, and the soles of his feet were burning through the thin leather of his loafers. He trudged along doggedly, but after a few hundred yards he had to stop and rest. Rattling up the street behind him was an ancient yellow school bus, its side emblazoned with the words "Yuma County School District." Its windows were rolled down all the way and as it passed, a horde of little kids leaned out and screamed at him. "Hey, mister!"

"Look out for flying elephants, mister!"

They shrieked with laughter as the bus rumbled on. Richard looked after it. Ah, the innocence of youth. Then he picked up his bags again. Stupid brats. He'd always hated kids. Looking ahead, he sighed and trudged on—the bus station wasn't much farther.

At the Yuma Territorial Prison, the school bus driver yanked on the hand brake and shut off the engine. He sat mopping his forehead as thirty-two third graders tumbled out the door. As an earnest young teacher's aide tried to muster the children into a neat double file, their teacher stopped at the bus door.

"We'll be about an hour or so, Jack," she said with a smile. Miss Harvey never rushed, but she always seemed to be in control of things.

He grinned back. "Take your time. I'm just going to sit and have a Coke."

On the grass in front of the museum, Miss Harvey clapped her hands for order. "Okay, boys and girls. Today we are visiting the Yuma Territorial Prison. It was built in 1875, more than one hundred years ago. Some of the most famous outlaws of the West were put in jail here."

"You mean like Jesse James, Miss Harvey?"

The teacher nodded with a smile. "That's right, Tommy. Now, before we go inside, you can all take a look around here. That building over there is the old guard tower. If you climb up and look out, you'll be able to see the Colorado River where ferryboats used to bring supplies here from the ocean."

She held up a hand. "See those big iron gates? When I blow my whistle, I want you all to line up over there so we can go inside."

The children raced off in all directions, seeming less than thrilled with the chance to see the Colorado. A few shy ones hung around Miss Harvey, while the bolder spirits began a rambunctious game of shoot-'em-up around the comfort station. A group of boys made their way to the steps of the guard tower, arguing loudly about who would be Jesse James and who had to settle for being the sheriff.

"Bang, bang! You'll never capture me!" A red-haired boy raced up the steps, followed by three of his friends in a posse. But at the top of the stairs they all stopped.

"Look, that lady's asleep."

They stared for a moment, and then the redhead couldn't resist. "I can see her underpants," he whispered loudly. The others giggled. Then one of them turned and walked back down the steps.

"What's the matter, Benjy?" Miss Harvey's brisk voice captured his attention. "Did you see the river from up there?"

"I don't like it there," he mumbled.

"Why not?"

"There's a lady sleeping. She looks funny."

With a puzzled frown, Miss Harvey marched up the stairs. She could hear the boys' voices above her. "I dare you." "Double dare!"

At the top of the steps she stopped abruptly and caught her breath. A woman lay crumpled at the far end of the platform. The redhead was reluctantly inching toward the woman, his friends repeating, "Dare you to wake her up, Hughie!"

"That's enough of that, boys," Miss Harvey said automatically, her eyes fastened on the still figure. "You go on down and wait for me."

She walked toward the huddled form. The woman's body was oddly twisted—surely no one could sleep in that awkward position. Stepping around the woman, she bent down, then straightened with a gasp. She could see the ends of the leather strip at the back of the neck, and the swollen, contorted face under the tumble of blond hair.

Knowing she should feel for a pulse, Miss Harvey stood motionless, her face gray with shock, unable to force her hands to touch that dreadful object. She leaned against the railing for a moment and then, steeling herself, walked unsteadily to the top of the stairs.

"Miss Adams!"

The aide looked up at her. "Yes?"

"Tell the park ranger to come out here immediately. And"—she swallowed convulsively—"don't let any of the children come up these stairs!"

A few minutes later a blue and white squad car roared into the parking lot with lights flashing. The two uniformed city policemen found Jim Santiago waiting for them on the path leading into the prison grounds. They talked with him briefly and then went to view the body.

"Nothing we can do here." The older policeman stood up and looked at his partner. "I'll radio in for the meat wagon, and I guess we better get the fingerprint kit out here." He walked off heavily toward the squad car.

The younger policeman looked around for a purse. But he couldn't find one. He turned to Santiago. "Who is she? Ever seen her before?"

Jim shook his head. "No, I've never seen her in my life. I didn't even know she was here—I mean, of course I didn't; if I had, I'd have called you."

The policeman sighed. "Yeah." He pulled out his notebook. "First time I've seen anything like this. I guess somebody got pretty mad at this girl. What was she doing here anyway?"

"I have no idea. But you know, I think that must be her car in the parking lot."

The policeman looked interested. "What car? How do you know?"

"When I arrived this morning to open up, a car was in the lot. But there was no one here—no tourists or anyone. So I figured someone must have gone home with a friend or something last night. But now I think it must be her car." He gestured vaguely toward the body, keeping his face turned away from the grotesquely bloated features.

"Which car is it?"

"The blue Malibu, right by the entrance."

"Show me."

In the parking lot the two policemen looked over the Malibu. "This is from Dave at Yuma City Rentals, isn't it, Ted?"

"Yeah." The older officer wrote down the license number. "I'll give him a call and see if we can get a line on her that way." He steered Santiago in the direction of the museum. "Let's get out of this sun, and you can tell us who found her."

"Well . . ." Santiago collected his thoughts. "Actually it was a couple of the children. We have a school group here today; I'm sure you noticed the school bus. They told their teacher they'd seen a woman asleep up there, and she went up to see and realized right away that the woman was dead. So of course she called me and I called you." He wiped his forehead. "I knew I shouldn't let anyone leave, but it didn't seem right to make the kids wait out here in the hot sun. So we took them inside. They're out in the courtyard now with the assistant teacher and the bus driver; his name is Jack something. Miss Harvey—that's the teacher—is in my office. She was feeling pretty rocky. I'm sure you can understand; this thing makes me feel a little queasy myself."

"Okay," the older cop said. "Howard, you go on and talk to this teacher. I'll get on the phone."

When Ted joined Howard in the park ranger's office a few minutes later, Miss Harvey, still pale, was seated in the visitor's chair.

"Ted," his younger colleague said, "this is the

teacher, Miss Harvey, who found the body. I've taken her statement, and she can't tell us anything more. She's anxious to get the kids out of here and back to school, and I told her I thought that was okay.''

She smiled at Ted rather wanly. ''Of course I'll be happy to help any way I can, if you think of other questions you want to ask me, but I feel I've told you everything I know. And I do want to get the children away before they become upset or frightened. This was a gruesome experience for them.''

''Of course. And I don't expect I'll have to talk to any of the kids myself. But you could help us if you will. We didn't find the woman's purse up there, and it's possible that one of the children may have picked up something from the floor—keys, a matchbook, anything—without knowing it was important. You'd have a better chance of finding out than we would.''

She nodded. ''I'll certainly ask them about it, but I'd rather not do it here.''

''Sure. Just give us a call if anything turns up.''

Miss Harvey stood up and squared her shoulders. ''This thing has affected me more than I'd realized.'' She walked out of the office and soon they could hear her marshaling the third graders and leading them out to the bus.

''She's plenty shook,'' Ted commented. ''I got Dave on the line, and he said that car is one of several he rented to this movie outfit, Royal Productions. They're all staying at the Wagon Wheel, and the boss is some guy named Julie Kingman. Why don't you give him a call?'' He tapped his pencil on the desk. ''Never heard of a guy being named Julie before.''

Howard dialed the Wagon Wheel number. ''Hi, sweetie, guess who?'' He winked at Ted as he listened to the pleased surprise of the switchboard operator on the other end.

"Howard! Hi, how are you? Where are you, at the office?"

"No, but I'm workin' on something. Lucky it just happened I had to call you. Are we still on for tonight?"

"Of course. What do you think?"

"Good. Now, listen, I need to get hold of a guy named Kingman, Julie Kingman, who's staying there. Can you ring him for me?"

"Yeah, sure. I'll try his room, but he might be in the production office, so just hold on."

A few clicks, and then a ringing sound were followed by more clicks and two more rings. "Hello? Royal Productions."

"This is Howard Bell of the Yuma Police Department. Can I speak to Mr. Kingman, please?"

Julie's voice boomed over the wire. "Yeah? This is Julie Kingman. What can I do for ya?"

"Mr. Kingman, I understand your company has rented a blue Malibu, license number nine seven eight GGY. Can you tell me who has been using that car?"

"What is this, somebody got a parking ticket? Hang on." Howard heard Julie yelling, "Artie? Who's been using the rented blue Malibu?" After a pause through which Howard heard an indistinct voice in the background, Julie muttered, "Aw, Jesus, what's she been up to now?" Then he spoke into the phone. "Officer, that car is assigned to Debra Scott, an actress on the picture. What's the problem?"

"Can you tell me what Ms. Scott looks like, please?"

"Well, she's a blonde with blue eyes, and she's, you

know, well built, like they say.'' Julie sounded puzzled but cautious.

''Mr. Kingman, I'm sorry to have to tell you this, but we've found a body, and I'm afraid it must be Ms. Scott.''

''Holy shit. What happened? She smash up the car or something?''

''I'm afraid it's a little more complicated, Mr. Kingman. She's been murdered.'' After a silence, Howard went on. ''We'd like you to come down and identify her for us, make sure that's who is it, you know.''

''Yeah. Okay.'' Julie's voice was hollow with shock, but he managed to take in Howard's directions to the morgue. They agreed to meet there in half an hour, and Julie laid the receiver gently in its cradle.

He sat staring blankly into space. ''Are you all right, Mr. Kingman?'' Penny's timid voice asked the question twice before he responded.

''Huh? Yeah, I guess so,'' he replied heavily. ''Look, I guess I better tell you.'' Julie included Artie in his look. ''The cops think Debra's been murdered.''

''Oh, my God!'' Penny burst into tears.

Artie grabbed the edge of the table. ''You're kidding!'' he whispered hoarsely.

''Not this time I ain't. I gotta go down to the morgue and make sure it's her, but those cops sounded like there wasn't no mistake.'' He sighed. ''Christ, what a mess. You better get hold of everybody and cancel the shooting for today. I'll call ya when I find out what's going on.'' Julie heaved himself out of the chair. ''And for God's sake keep a lid on it.'' He glared at both of them. ''The last thing we need is for everybody to go into a panic. Just tell 'em I canceled today, and you don't know why.''

* * *

Debra's body lay on a high white table in the morgue. Ted took Julie's arm. "I want to warn you, she's not a very pretty sight."

Julie nodded. Then, as the attendant pulled back the sheet that covered Debra's face, he gulped hard. He turned away, his face shiny with sweat, and muttered, "That's her."

Later, in the police station with a cup of coffee in front of him, Julie shook his head. "I still can't believe it." His skin had not yet regained its natural healthy color.

"Gee, with all the gruesome stuff you guys put in movies, I'd think you'd be kind of used to it," Howard said casually.

"It ain't very gruesome when you can wash it off," Julie said slowly. "The real thing is a lot worse. Jesus, you know, she just died on screen yesterday." For once he sounded awed by a turn of events he couldn't control. "I didn't like the kid, but what a way to go."

The two policemen asked for Debra's home address and the names of relatives to be notified.

"I don't know. We probably got some of that information back at the office, but your best bet would be to call her agent in L.A., Morty Silver. He knew her a lot better than I did." Suddenly his expression changed. "Hey, where's that Captain Fleming? I thought he was the one that handled all this stuff."

Ted looked surprised. "How do you know Captain Fleming?"

"For God's sake! He's been hanging around asking questions about these other killings you guys had here, the ones that looked kinda like the movie we're making. I'd've thought he'd be in on this."

"Well, Mr. Kingman, Ms. Scott's body was found inside the city limits, so that makes it our case, not the sheriff's. But if Captain Fleming has been involved, we'll give him a call."

Julie looked at his watch. It was just past eleven. He hoped Artie had told everyone the shooting was off while avoiding any questions. "Could I use your phone for a minute?" he asked.

Ted motioned to the desk in the next cubicle. "Sure. Use that one. And, Howard, after Mr. Kingman's finished his call, maybe you'd better go back with him . . ." Julie didn't wait to hear the rest. He was afraid he'd hear it all soon enough. Too bad about Debra, but he sure as hell didn't need more cops scaring the hell out of everybody.

He dialed the office and asked for his nephew. "Artie? Did ya get hold of everybody?"

Artie's voice was full of self-importance. "Well, sure, but—"

"Good. Hope you managed to keep your yap shut, though what good that's going to do now, I dunno. Okay. I'll be back pretty quick, I think."

Julie was about to hang up, but Artie's voice stopped him. "Julie? There's a problem about Richard."

"Richard! What the hell? Look, Artie, just take care of it till I get there, can't ya?"

"But, Julie, he's missing. No one knows where he is, and he didn't show up for the call. I figured if I couldn't get to him before eleven, he'd be here at the office. But he isn't. And Richard's always on time. What do you want me to do?"

"Don't *do* anything." Julie hung up, wondering what he'd done to deserve all this. Now Richard, for God's sake. Well, he'd have to handle this himself; he was a fool to let Artie try to do anything. Still, it was pretty strange. Whatever his other faults, Richard was a professional and a damn good makeup man.

Ted and Howard looked up as Julie came back into their office. "All set?" Howard asked.

"Yeah, I'm all set," Julie said wearily. "I just hope you guys aren't gonna come up with another body." Ted and Howard stared at him. "My makeup man is missing now."

"What's his name?" Ted pulled out his notebook.

"Richard Reed." Julie shrugged. "It's probably nothing. He coulda heard from somebody else that shooting was canceled and took off for the day. Still, it ain't like Richard not to stop in and get the gossip." Julie shook his head sighed. "Well, let's go."

Ted extended his hand. "Thank you for coming down, Mr. Kingman. Howard here will go back to the motel with you now, and I'll be along later." He turned to his partner. "I'll give Fleming a call and fill him in; then I'll catch up with you. In the meantime you may as well start interviewing the movie people and see who talked to her last—you know, the usual."

As Julie and Howard left the office, Ted picked up the phone and began to dial.

Chapter 15

Zack stretched luxuriously before getting up and putting on his robe. It was the first decent stretch of sleep he'd had for almost a week. The phone rang and he padded over to answer it. At least whoever was calling had been kind enough to wait till he was awake.

"Yes?"

"Captain, this is Ted Franks, over at City Police. Sorry to roust you out—"

"That's okay. I was awake."

"Boy, I guess the sheriff's office keeps easier hours than us poor slobs."

Zack stifled a yawn. "Yeah, sure. I didn't see your guys out with the blowtorches cutting bodies out of cars this morning at three o'clock."

"Heard about that one. Bad, huh?"

"You said it. And they always seem to have these big smashups just off the interstate on county roads. Well, what's up?"

"We picked up a stiff this morning. A young woman got herself garroted up at the Territorial Prison. We think she may belong to you.'' Ted went on to give Zack the information he had on Debra's death and what he'd learned from the preliminary investigation. He wound up with ''Anyway, since you're already checking these folk out on those other killings, you'll probably want to be in on this one, too.''

Zack said thoughtfully, ''Yeah, there sure could be a connection. I'll call my office and have them send someone out to join you at the motel. Then we'll take it from there.''

''Fine. Oh, and one other thing. A Richard Reed, the makeup man on the movie, may or may not have disappeared. It's not clear yet.''

''Okay. I'll have my boys check on that, too. Thanks for the information, Ted.'' Zack hung up the phone and stood there silently for almost a full minute. Another murder connected with this damn movie—and this time he felt partly to blame. He was sure that Debra had set the trailer on fire herself, and the arson squad agreed with him. Her hysterics and fear had been more synthetic than real. But one thing was certain: If he'd put a man on her yesterday as she'd wanted him to do, she wouldn't be a corpse this morning.

He shook himself. He'd better call the office and get things started.

When he reached Lieutenant Martinez, who'd been working with him on the other murders, he told him what had happened. ''Take a couple of deputies and get on over there, Pete. See what you can dig up about this Richard Reed at the same time. And listen. Don't let any of the movie people leave the motel. Tell them to stay put until we know what we're dealing with. I sure don't want any more deaths.''

''Right, Zack.''

"I'm going to go over what's happened up to now and try and make some sense out of this whole business. Get back to me at the office when you've got something concrete."

After hanging up, Zack walked into the kitchen of the old family home. Since the late 1800's successive generations of Flemings had owned the land and lived in the rambling old house. Its thick adobe walls kept it cool even in summer, and its large, high-ceilinged rooms were both charming and comfortable. A long living-dining room ran across the front of the house, and an old oxbow still hung above the fieldstone fireplace where someone had put it years ago. Beyond the dining room end was the sunny kitchen, and next to it were two bedrooms and a big old-fashioned bathroom. There were two large bedrooms and a bath upstairs, but Zack rarely went up there. He had converted one of the downstairs bedrooms into an office, but he spent most of his time in the living room and at the heavy oak table in the kitchen.

Putting the kettle on to boil, Zack measured dark coffee beans into the grinder. He didn't mind drinking the office coffee, though it was the subject of much bitter complaining by most of the men, but he liked to start his day with a cup of really good coffee. He often thought that if he ever got married, his wife would have a lot to put up with one way and another.

He was still feeling a sense of responsibility for Debra's death. Why hadn't he listened to himself more carefully? He'd been sure the other killings were somehow following the script of the movie. So why hadn't he believed that the heroine had to die?

Still worrying this idea, Zack walked into the bathroom and turned on the shower. As he stepped in, another thought struck him. Why had the killer changed his MO? Assuming that it was the same killer, why had Debra been strangled rather than knifed? Maybe his earlier idea of a second killer imitating a freak crime had been right after all. Or maybe the whole series of crimes had been leading up to someone's primary aim of killing Debra. The incident of the dead dog did seem to point to her, and garroting with a length of leather was a particularly brutal method—that argued a special degree of hatred and rage.

Of course the leather thong seemed to point directly at Gary Barton, the guy Tory called Straight Arrow. He'd have to find out where Barton had been last night. But surely Barton wouldn't have left such an obvious clue. Why hadn't the killer taken the thong away with him?

Standing under the hard spray of water, Zack thought back over recent events. He had seen Debra's film death yesterday; she was killed in a car crash on the desert. And he knew there had been two other deaths in the script. One of them was the heroine's co-worker, who was strangled in an alley. Something was out of kilter.

Turning off the water and shrugging on his terry-cloth robe, he went back to the kitchen. The kettle was steaming, and he poured boiling water through the paper filter into the coffee pot. Better get back to routine. The inconsistencies between the script and what had actually happened still nagged at his brain, but he pushed the problem away to think about later. Routine police work was often boring, but he'd found that it sometimes helped him clarify the issues enough to lay a basis for answering the final questions in a case.

Zack poured some more water through the filter and went to get a tape recorder and some notes from his desk. He settled down at the kitchen table with a large glass of orange juice and a bowl of cornflakes, then spread the notes out in front of him. He would start at the beginning and go through all the possible suspects one at a time; then he'd have something to work with.

Deciding to start with Richard, Zack turned on the tape recorder. "Richard Reed," he said into the microphone. "I don't buy him as a killer type, but he's plenty nosy. If he is missing, it's possible he stumbled onto something and the killer had to get rid of him. I could see Reed as a blackmailer. If he turns up dead, too, that might be the reason. Of course, as far as I know now, he could have killed Debra Scott and run away. But he's got good alibis for the other killings—the stripper at Hank's and the transvestite at the party."

Turning off the machine, Zack gulped the last of his juice thoughtfully. Of course, Richard couldn't have engineered the dead dog in Debra's room, either; he was too busy in his room having the cocaine party that Hurd broke in on. There could be more to that whole business than Richard admitted. He could have skipped for reasons that had nothing to do with the murders.

He spoke into the machine again. "The other thing is that Reed seems to have the wrong psychology for a killer. He's openly nasty to people he doesn't like. I think he handles his hostilities fine that way. He doesn't need to kill."

Shutting off the recorder, Zack stood and carried his dishes to the sink. He turned on the flame under the big black skillet and slung in some butter. When it was sizzling, he carefully cracked two eggs and dropped them into the frying pan. He cut two slices of the whole wheat bread his housekeeper Juanita had baked the day before and dropped them into the toaster. Pouring a mug of coffee, he went on to consider the next possible suspect on his list—Gary Barton.

Standing at the stove, Zack recalled that Barton had a good alibi for the transvestite's murder. On the other hand, alibis were always suspect, and Zack respected Tory's opinion—she really was scared of this guy. He had to admit that Barton was peculiar, and his comments to Tory could certainly be construed as threatening—although of course "evil woman" could well have referred to Debra. He couldn't ignore the fact that Debra had been strangled with a piece of leather like the one Barton always carried around. But Zack couldn't help feeling that the killer was someone more intimately connected with the film than Barton, who just hung around the edges. Poor guy probably secretly longed for bright lights and glamour and couldn't admit it to himself. Besides, as far as Zack knew, Barton hadn't shown up at the film locations since Pete Martinez had talked to him and gotten his alibi. Possibly he'd been scared off completely.

Zack flipped his eggs carefully, smiling as he accomplished this without breaking either yolk. His smile faded as he recalled Tory's comments about his rejecting the idea of a local killer and pinning the whole thing on the movie group.

He carried his eggs and toast to the table and applied butter with a liberal hand. Then he wiped his fingers and flipped on the tape recorder. "A guy named Gary Barton has been hanging around some of the movie locations while they've been shooting. He's always fooling with a braided leather bolo—could be the one that was used to strangle Debra Scott. He's got alibis on the other killings, and somehow I don't think he's a realistic possibility. But check him out anyway."

Leaving the tape running, Zack crunched a large mouthful, then said, "Kevin Dean. I can't figure a motive for this guy unless he hatched an elaborate plot to get rid of Debra Scott. But that doesn't make sense. She wasn't that important to him, and besides, he blew up at her on the set the other day because of some problem with his kid, but he worked that out afterward. Dean certainly had a strained working relationship with Debra, but he's a guy who blows his top. This whole business seems too complicated and involved for someone with his mentality. Still, we'll check on where he was last night."

Stopping the tape, Zack mopped his plate with the last corner of toast. Then he cleared the table and picked up the recorder. In the bedroom, he turned it on again. "John Hartnell. From what I gather, he's pinning his hopes of a comeback on this film. He could have felt Debra Scott was ruining the picture—they were definitely not on cordial terms, and he thought she was a rotten actress—but would he really have sabotaged the whole movie by killing her?" Zack stopped and thought. "He's got a background, but it involved young girls, which would let Debra out. And he's kind of namby-pamby—not the type you can imagine taking this kind of definitive action. On the other hand, his only solid alibi is for the stripper's murder, which of course could have been a coincidence that gave the killer the idea for the other stuff. And he has the kind of repressed personality that fits with this bizarre series of incidents."

Zack checked his notes. "Rose Murphy. The only reason she's on this list is that she rarely socializes after working hours. Nobody seems to know much about her, although they all seem to like her. She's definitely a loner, and she's kind of hard to pin down. The info we got from L.A. shows that she spends most of her money to support a retarded kid in some private institution down in San Diego County. Suspicion is that it's her kid, maybe illegitimate or something, but no one she works with seems aware of his existence. Pretty hard to imagine her doing anything more violent than squashing a bug. I think she's kind of a sad story, but there's no reason to suspect she had it in for Debra or anybody else—unless they found out about the kid and started squeezing her. Still, would she have gone to such elaborate lengths—and killed three people?''

Zack knotted his uniform tie, then carried the machine back to the kitchen and poured another cup of coffee. ''There's a whole bunch of other people involved in this film company, and we've got to check them all out for alibis last night, but based on what we've got so far, I don't see any of them as serious contenders. I've saved my best bet for last.'' He swallowed a scalding mouthful. ''Julie Kingman. First the motive. He seems like a nice guy, but our info shows he's heavily in debt: this picture could make or break him, although I think he's kept this quiet. No one in the cast and crew seems aware of it. And he carries large insurance policies on the principals in the cast. This seems to be standard procedure, but it means that he'll benefit financially from Debra Scott's death. I don't know the intricacies of film financing, but I'd guess that an extra infusion of cash might tide him over until the picture is released. Also, he's a guy who knows all the angles. Having the leading lady of a murder film killed on location might be turned into a major publicity gimmick that would help him at the box office if he gets the picture out fast.

"Next, opportunity. No one ever knows where Kingman is unless he's making a scene somewhere. He's in and out of every location, the office, you name it—it's hard to keep track of his movements. The others say they're sure he was around when the first two murders took place, but he doesn't have a real alibi for any of them."

Zack paused, then went on. "Based on what we've got, he's the most likely suspect. But my gut feeling is he's a pussycat. Under that bark there's not much bite. I don't like it, but I can't suggest anything better."

Zack clicked off the tape recorder. There was nothing more he could do till he got to the office. And he still felt he didn't really have a handle on what was happening. There was something going on that he hadn't yet grasped. Oddly dissatisfied, he collected his paraphernalia and went out to his car.

Just about everyone from the cast and crew of *Cry for Help* was clustered around the pool. Once the police had arrived at the motel, Artie hadn't been able to quell people's curiosity, and news of Debra's murder had spread rapidly. Shock and horror were evident on every face, and there was fear, too. The first two murder victims had been strangers to this tightly knit group. And while murder was always distressing to hear about, those two killings hadn't hit very close to home.

But this one did—Debra was one of their own. Although she hadn't exactly been a favorite, she had been someone they'd known. Working together on location always produced a special kind of intimacy. Members of the cast and crew were now trying to cope with Debra's death. Already they missed her feisty vitality. And mingled with their grief was an unspoken question: Would one of them be next?

Each in turn was being interviewed by the police in the production office, and those outside spoke in subdued tones. While she waited, Tory looked over at Melissa splashing in the kiddie pool with three other children. Michael had wanted to remove his daughter from the charged atmosphere surrounding the movie group, and he was now chatting with a woman who appeared to be the other kids' mother.

Sally Manganaro came out of the production office and dropped into the chair next to Tory's. Turning to her, Tory asked, "What did the police say?"

"Well, they wanted to know where I was last night from about ten o'clock on. I guess that's the last time anyone admits seeing Debra, and I gather they think she was killed around midnight." Sally was matter-of-fact as usual, but her face looked drawn and tired. "It's really awful, isn't it? I know we all thought Debra was a nuisance, but she certainly didn't deserve this."

"No, she didn't." Tory's agreement was fervent. "I feel terrible about it. I keep thinking that last night, while I was helping John and Julie write her out of the rest of the shooting, she was getting killed. It's stupid, but I can't help feeling as if I'm to blame."

Sally nodded. "I think we all feel that way. She was hard to get along with, and we all made jokes and sarcastic remarks about her. I guess we're all feeling bad about that, now that it's too late."

Tory glanced around the group. "That reminds me, I haven't seen Richard this morning. He certainly was vocal about Debra's faults, but I can't believe he—or any of us—really wished her dead. He must be feeling lousy."

Sally regarded her in surprise. "Didn't you know? Richard seems to have disappeared. He never showed up for the call this morning and no one can find him. For a while they thought he might have been killed, too, but then they went into his room and saw that all his stuff is gone. So it looks as if he just skipped."

"But, Sally"—Tory sounded really upset—"why would he do that? He couldn't have had anything to do with Debra—"

"I doubt it." Sally spoke decisively. "You never know what Richard's up to, but he knows how to look out for himself. I've worked with him enough times. If he knew anything about the murder, he'd have hot-footed it to the police. I think he's disappeared for his own reasons—reasons that have nothing to do with the murder. Still, it kind of gives me the willies. I keep wondering what's going to happen next."

"I wish I'd never come down here."

Tory's low voice held such force that Sally looked at her in astonishment. But her reply was forestalled by Penny, who approached and said, "The police are ready for you now, Tory."

To Tory, the interview felt as if it dragged on for hours. Lieutenant Martinez was polite enough, and it was clear to him that Tory had nothing to add to what he already knew. But answering his questions made Tory feel that the distance she'd tried to put between herself and the fact of Debra's murder had been irrevocably bridged. The full horror of the event seemed to close in on her again, and she emerged from the interview pale and trembling.

Michael was waiting for her, and Tory blurted out, "Oh, Michael, this is all so horrible!"

He patted her shoulder. "Now, honey, it's all over.

Come on, let's go inside and get something to eat"—
he glanced around the courtyard—"away from these
ghouls."

"I don't think I can eat anything—"

"Well, I'm hungry," he interrupted her. "And you
really ought to have something."

"But what about Missy?"

"She's fine," Michael assured her. "She's found
some new friends, and their mom's going to be by the
pool all day."

Tory allowed herself to be led into the coffee shop,
but when they were seated in a corner booth, she burst
out again, "Michael, I still can't believe it!"

"Just stop thinking about it for a while and have
something to eat. You'll feel a lot better."

"I can't eat anything. And I can't stop thinking about
it!" Tory's voice rose, and Michael gave her a warning
look as the waitress approached. When she'd taken his
order and left, Tory went on more quietly, "It is just
so hard to believe that someone I know and work with
is capable of murder. It must be someone connected
with the picture—I'm convinced of that now—but I can't
convince myself that one of them is a homicidal ma-
niac."

"That's a meaningless phrase," he said almost automatically. "But, Tory, don't you see that this whole
thing proves what I've been trying to explain to you all
this time? The fact that you can't spot this so-called
insanity shows that it doesn't exist. You're an intelligent
person, Tory. Use your head. 'Sane' and 'insane' are
useless categories. Do you know why? Because they
don't explain anything. You can only look at individual
actions and determine the stresses or motivations that
caused them to occur. And when you find the causes

of these actions, you can see that they are the normal responses of normal individuals.''

She stared at him dumbfounded. ''You can't really believe that. Whatever someone's reasons were for killing Debra, that person is insane. There are no reasons that make it all right to kill someone.'' She stopped, unable to find the right words to express what was so obviously true.

He pounced immediately. ''No reasons? Of course there are reasons. How about war? Do you think every soldier who fires a gun is insane?''

''Well, no, of course not, but—''

''They pin medals on those guys. They're heroes, not 'insane.' Society decides when killing is acceptable and when it's not. This is a historical process. Centuries ago it was considered sane and normal to kill a man who insulted you. Now society has decided it's only normal to kill so-called enemies of one's country. But a hundred years from now, it may be fashionable to kill anyone who doesn't have twenty-twenty vision. Who knows? It's arbitrary. But the funny thing is, Tory, this same society that disapproves of killing wants to bring back gas chambers and electric chairs to dispose of the people who disagree with its accepted ideas.'' He sat back and waited for her to respond.

Tory stared at him and shook her head. What could she say?

''And what does society do, Tory, with the people it doesn't electrocute? It labels them 'insane' and locks them up in so-called psychotic wards and throws away the key. It destroys them, slowly but surely. It turns them into vegetables, and then it says, 'See? They were insane after all.' ''

There was a silence between them. Then Tory looked

down at the table. In a low voice she said, "Michael, I can't answer all those big questions about war and the death penalty. I know those are serious issues. But we're not talking about society—we're talking about people killing other people."

"Well, fine, then, let's talk about one person murdering another." Michael wore his patient expression, as if explaining an obvious concept to a particularly dull student. "Let's consider the wife who finally turns on her husband after he's beaten her for years—a normal response, wouldn't you say? Or what about the hardworking husband who comes home to find his wife in bed with someone else and kills her? Plenty of people view that as normal behavior in a stressful situation."

Michael couldn't really believe what he was saying, Tory thought. He couldn't possibly think that murder was an acceptable solution to a problem. But it was always so difficult to counter his seemingly logical reasoning. At last she said, "Well, there's one kind of murder that even you can't find excuses for—the cold-blooded killing of a child. I mean, what if Missy were . . ."

Tory stopped herself as she heard what she was saying. She had let herself get sucked into arguing from his premises. Murdering a child might be the worst, but no murder was acceptable. Michael was good at shifting the discussion into abstract generalizations that could be twisted to suit his point of view. But this was real life.

"Michael, we're talking about Debra, someone we both knew. She had as much right to live her life as anyone else does, and whoever killed her is, by my definition, crazy."

She looked up and caught his triumphant look. "But,

Tory, you're the one who thought up Debra's murder. You wrote the script. All these killings are just carrying out the ideas that came from your mind. And you're not insane, are you?''

Refusing to be baited, Tory said patiently, ''I don't think so. But I didn't kill anyone. I just made up a story. It's fiction. It's far removed from someone actually dying. I don't know—maybe the dividing line is that sane people can distinguish between fantasy and reality, and insane people can't. Surely you can see what I mean?''

Her words went unheeded. Michael said calmly, ''You're just hiding behind labels again, Tory.''

Her control snapped. ''I can't stand you when you're like this! You're just making a game of the whole thing, and it's too serious and too sad to be made fun of. A real human being has been killed, Michael. It's not an intellectual exercise or one of your dumb experiments!'' Tory stood abruptly and walked rapidly out of the coffee shop. Michael stared after her.

Chapter 16

Zack tossed the sheaf of neatly typed reports onto his desk. He leaned back in the old swivel chair and propped his feet on an open drawer. The information his men had gathered on everyone's whereabouts last night didn't get him very far. He ticked them off in his mind.

The last people who admitted seeing Debra were John Hartnell and Julie Kingman. They'd been talking—arguing was probably more like it—in her room. She'd asked for an armed guard, and John and Julie had tried unsuccessfully to dissuade her. Then apparently she'd threatened to walk off the film, and the two men had left in disgust. This was about eight o'clock, as near as they could figure. They said she'd put on an act of being frightened and nervous and she'd made a big deal about locking the door behind them.

She'd gotten a phone call around eleven; the night switchboard operator remembered that it was a man, but he didn't know anything more. And she hadn't made any calls herself. It looked as though the phone call had lured her out of the motel. But why would she have left if she wanted everyone to think she was afraid? Of course, she might not have left by herself. Maybe someone was with her.

Zack sighed. This whole line of inquiry was fruitless. He didn't have enough information to go on. The only sure thing was that her car had been driven to the parking lot of the old prison, but they'd known that when they started.

The rest of the reports were equally vague and inconclusive. Only two people had sturdy alibis for the period between 11:00 P.M. and 1:00 A.M.—Tory and John Hartnell. John and Julie had joined Tory and Michael in the restaurant of the motel after leaving Debra's room. They'd talked over their problems and decided to change the script so they wouldn't have to use Debra any more. Tory, John, and Julie had gone to the production office, maybe around 8:30, and had stayed there till about 10:30. They'd all discussed the revisions, and decided they should find out from Lars if he would need extra equipment. He hadn't been in his room, and Tory and John had gone to look for him in the bar, leaving Julie alone in the office.

In the bar, Tory and John had talked briefly with Lars, who had then left to go to his room. They went back to the office and found that Julie was no longer there. The two of them worked a while longer on the script. Then they decided to call it a night and celebrate with a drink. They'd been in the bar till almost 1:00. The bartender had had an interesting discussion with them about movie-making.

That took care of them. A number of the crew members had been together at the Rumpus Room until closing time, but they hadn't been seriously considered as suspects in any event. Unfortunately, it had been one of those nights when most people had gone off on their own. Zack ran down the list.

Rose Murphy and Sally Manganaro had had dinner together in the motel. Afterward Rose said she went back to her room, read for a little while, and then went to sleep. Sally, too, had gone to her room; she said she'd washed out some clothes and then watched the late movie on TV. They both said they hadn't seen or talked to anyone after returning to their rooms. There was no way to verify or disprove their stories.

Lars Swenson, too, said he'd gone up to his room after talking with Tory and John and had gone to bed soon after. It was all very unsatisfying, Zack thought resignedly.

Kevin Dean and his son Gregory had gone together to a night spot called Skinny Minnie's in another motel, a little after nine-thirty. Kevin said he'd quickly decided he wasn't interested and he'd left Greg there and gone for a drive. He claimed to have stopped somewhere on a side road off 80 East and sat on the sand looking at the stars. Kevin had told Lieutenant Martinez that he'd had a lot to think about. Who knew? Maybe he had. It was a pretty weak story for anyone to invent, which argued for it's being true.

Gregory Dean said he'd stayed at Skinny Minnie's until one o'clock when it closed and then had walked back to the Wagon Wheel. His father was asleep when he got in.

Kevin and Greg had both been somewhat evasive at first about where they'd been; Greg had of course had to use a phony ID to get into Skinny Minnie's, since he was underage. Zack hoped Martinez had expressed his disapproval strongly enough to both father and son so they wouldn't try that in Yuma again.

The Deans had seen Arthur Silverstein when they first arrived at the club. But later, when the place was really mobbed, the Dean boy and Silverstein could not remember seeing each other. Artie had spent most of his time dancing with a girl named Yvonne—he hadn't caught her last name. She left around midnight, and he hung around another half hour or so and then went to look for more action elsewhere. He'd sounded aggrieved that all the bars closed at one o'clock, but someone had been kind enough to tell him that Winterhaven, a couple of miles away, was across the California line and thus not subject to Arizona liquor laws. Red's Place had made a big impression on him. Reading between the lines, Zack gathered that the crowd at Red's hadn't exactly taken Artie to its heart. Artie hadn't stayed long; he thought he'd gotten home about one-thirty.

Moving on, Zack considered Dennis Sullivan, the young man who'd been at the party when the transvestite was murdered. He'd been quick to tell them he had not been with Richard Reed last night. According to him, Richard had invited him to go barhopping, but Dennis had claimed to have other plans. He'd left the motel right away and taken himself to dinner at the Ol' Trails restaurant. Then he'd gone on up Fourth to the Plaza II to see a movie. After that he'd stopped for some ice cream and returned to the motel. It sounded as if Dennis had been anxious to avoid Richard without offending him. Zack could see why he might be a little wary of Richard's sharp tongue.

About Richard himself there was little information as yet. A couple of deputies would visit every bar and dive in town with Richard's photo to try to trace his movements. But none of the movie people admitted seeing him since they'd arrived back at the motel after yesterday's shooting. It was possible that Richard had allowed himself to get picked up and taken home by some local fellow and then found himself in the middle of a lovers' quarrel. Some of Zack's men were checking that possibility as well.

However, Zack thought Richard had been playing the game too long to get caught up in that kind of thing. And it didn't explain why his bed at the motel had been slept in and all his stuff was missing. No, it seemed more likely that he'd skipped. And in a hurry. That call he'd gotten this morning might have been the provocation. Well, if he'd taken public transportation out of town, they'd soon know where he'd gone.

That left Julie Kingman. His alibi stopped when Tory and John left him alone in the production office at ten-thirty. There was plenty of time for him to kill Debra. Of course, he couldn't have been the man who called her at eleven, unless he'd gone somewhere and used a pay phone—calls between rooms didn't go through the switchboard—but that call wasn't necessarily the reason Debra left her room. All it proved was that she was in her room at eleven to receive it. And certainly she wouldn't have been afraid to leave with Julie or to meet him somewhere. Almost any excuse Julie made up would have sounded plausible to Debra so long as he made her think he was capitulating to her demands. And maybe he'd decided she was worth more to him dead than alive.

Nonetheless, Julie struck Zack as a smart fellow. Once he'd found a way to write her out of the script, he wouldn't have been stupid enough to kill her. More likely he'd been eagerly awaiting his chance to tell her she wasn't needed anymore—and to do it in front of an audience.

Oh, hell, Zack thought. They'd all had the opportunity except Tory and John. And they'd all had some sort of motive. The answer had to be in that damned script. He was sure the key was there somewhere, if only he knew what he was looking for. It was possible that Tory had some sort of knowledge that she hadn't thought important enough to relay—or that he'd been too stupid to ask for, he thought wryly. Well, he'd go and talk to her again. Maybe someone had helped her plan the murder scenes in the story or had given her suggestions or comments. She was plenty bright and would see what he was driving at. Her only problem was that she couldn't see any of her colleagues as a murderer. And Zack couldn't blame her for that.

He wished he could get to know Tory better. She certainly wasn't much like the rest of the movie people, as far as he could see. They all seemed to be playing roles even off camera—Rose the mother hen, Julie the bellowing producer, Richard the bitter homosexual. They all had images to live up to. And he couldn't help feeling they were all self-centered.

Tory wasn't like that. She was smart and self-sufficient, and yet she seemed to really care about other people. And she was awfully attractive. He loved the way her dark eyes lit up with enthusiasm . . . Zack let his feet fall to the floor with a thump. What was he doing building castles in the air? Tory had a boy-friend—that Michael Canfield. And he cared about her enough to come all the way from L.A. to be with her. Zack wondered how serious the relationship really was. But serious or not, as soon as this film was finished, she'd be off, back to L.A. He shook his head—she wasn't likely to find herself in Yuma again in the near future.

Standing up, Zack stretched and reached for his sunglasses, intending to talk to her about the script. He hesitated, his hand on the knob. Who was he kidding? And what made him think she'd be happy to see him? Oh, well. He had no other leads to pursue at this moment, so he might as well follow his inclinations. He yanked the door open and strode out.

At the Wagon Wheel Inn the entire movie company was trapped in a suspended state of unknowing. In addition to their distress about the murder in their midst, they had no idea what was going to happen to the film. Naturally, Julie had been on the phone most of the day, but no one knew what decisions, if any, he'd come to. Was he looking for Richard or was he trying to hire a new makeup man? Would they resume shooting tomorrow or was the film on indefinite hold? Had the police released Debra's body and, if so, who was making arrangements for a funeral? They realized they didn't even know if she had a family.

Talked out, they had dispersed, some going to their rooms, others into the bar. But no one wanted to stray too far from the group of familiar faces, even though they wondered if one of those faces masked a killer.

Tory couldn't seem to settle down. She'd spent a little time at the kiddie pool with Melissa and her new friends, but the high-pitched childish voices grated on her nerves. Michael had joined her on the patio, but Tory, unable to bear a continuation of their earlier discussion, fished her paperback out of the bag beside her chair.

Suddenly she snapped the book shut in frustration.

''That's the fifth time I've read this paragraph, and I still don't know what it's about.'' She rubbed her eyes wearily. ''I just can't seem to concentrate on anything. Maybe I'll go and lie down for a while.''

Michael raised his glance from the journal he was scanning. ''Good idea—you seem pretty tense. A nap is probably what you need. Here.'' He dug into the pocket of his jeans. ''Why don't you take one of my tranquilizers? It'll help you relax.''

Tory shook her head. ''No, thanks. You know I don't like taking those things. I'll just stretch out for a bit.'' She gathered her belongings and walked slowly toward the stairway.

Michael looked after her thoughtfully. Then he stood up and moved briskly toward the coffee shop inside the motel.

''Can I get a pot of hot tea to take up to my room?'' Michael smiled absently at the girl behind the counter. As she turned away, he thought again that Tory would never be able to understand. He'd tried to explain it to her as many ways as he could, but she refused to take that first step toward rational and enlightened thinking. He had gone to a lot of trouble to set up a well-designed experiment to prove his point to her, but . . .

''I'm not supposed to do this, but I gave you a real cup and saucer.'' The waitress smiled conspiratorially at him. ''Don't you just hate those Styrofoam ones? I know you're the type who'll bring it back.''

''Thanks.'' Michael paid for the tea. ''And could I have a whole bunch of extra sugars? I've got a sweet tooth.''

The girl blushed as she dropped a handful of sugar packets on the tray. ''Now, be sure to pick up the pot by the handle. I wouldn't want you to burn yourself.''

He carried the tray carefully through the swinging glass doors. His shoulders were slumped in disappointment. He had tested Tory and she had failed. He was every bit as upset as he always was when his rats failed to perform the way he hoped.

But the thing was, Tory wasn't stupid. She was just too stubborn to change her frame of reference. She was gnawing away at the problem, and Michael could see she wasn't far from figuring it out. As soon as she did, she'd be off to tell her newfound friend in the police, what was his name? She'd think it was her duty.

He stopped under the outside stairway and balanced the tray carefully on a large standing ashtray. Taking the flat metal pill-box from his pocket, he opened it and dumped its contents into the cup that waited on the tray. Lifting the tray, he headed up the stairs.

Michael tapped softly on Tory's motel room door, and a moment later she came to open it. She had drawn the drapes against the late-afternoon sun, and the room was dim and quiet. Over her shoulder he could see her sundress crumpled on the far bed and her sandals overturned where she'd kicked them off.

"I've brought you some tea," he said as he walked past her and put the tray on the beside table. "Get back into bed and I'll pour it for you."

Tory didn't really want any tea, but she recognized that Michael was trying to make amends. Still clutching her robe around her, she slid under the sheet and pushed herself back against the pillows.

Michael had already poured steaming tea into the cup. As he picked up a couple of sugar packets and tore off the ends, he said, "I know you don't like sweet tea, but I think you need some sugar in your system." He smiled at her. "I don't want to hear any protests.

You haven't eaten anything today, and you'll wake up with low blood sugar and a terrible headache if you don't have something now.'' He dumped the last of the sugar into the cup and stirred vigorously. Then he handed the cup to her and sat on the edge of the bed. ''Drink it down.''

Tory sipped at the tea and made a face. ''This is revolting. It tastes like syrup.''

''I know, but it's good for you. Pretend it's medicine.'' He sat watching her as she obediently drank the sweet liquid. ''Want some more?''

''No, that was plenty.'' She put the cup down on the bedside table.

She slid down beneath the sheet, and Michael leaned over to kiss her cheek. ''Sleep well, Tory.'' His hand moved lingeringly over her body, and he felt a pang of sadness. He'd be sorry never to hold that exciting warmth in his arms again. Then he stood and walked silently to the door.

Letting himself out, he hung the ''Do Not Disturb'' sign on the outside knob and shook his head regretfully. He had thought he'd found the perfect mate, but he had been mistaken.

Tory closed her eyes, but she couldn't relax. Her body lay rigid in the bed, and her mind went around in circles like a rat in a cage. She thought over the sequence of events for the thousandth time. The stripper's death had been the beginning. And that had to hold the secret. But it was a paradox. The members of the cast and crew who knew about the stripper murder scene Tory had dictated on her way to Yuma were all on the set that night and couldn't possibly have committed a murder in a different bar. But that meant that the only people who could have killed the girl didn't know about the new scene.

It didn't make sense. Was there someone nobody had thought of—someone who knew about the scene but who wasn't on the set?

Sleep began to overtake her. Of course there was someone, she thought hazily, but she couldn't quite . . .

Michael strolled toward the kiddie pool. Missy climbed out of the water and pushed her dripping hair out of her eyes. "Hi, Dad. Where's Tory?" she asked.

"She's tired and she decided to take a nap." Michael looked down at his daughter. Her wet skin glistened in the bright sun and he noticed suddenly that she'd grown. The pink ruffled swimsuit was almost too small. He squatted down in front of her. "How about you, honey? Aren't you getting a little tired? Maybe you ought to go take a nap, too."

"Oh, no, Dad!" Her voice rose in protest. "I'm not tired at all! Can't I stay and play with Shelly and Jennifer and Tim?"

Before Michael could answer, the children's mother called to him from the chaise where she sat next to the pool. "Oh, let her stay. They're all having so much fun. And I'm going to be here at least another hour, so I'll be glad to keep an eye on her. It's no trouble."

Michael stared at the woman with an unreadable look. Then he said, "Okay, thanks. I'll be in the bar."

As Michael walked away, he heard his daughter shout, "Watch me, Shelly," followed by a noisy splash as she jumped into the shallow water. Melissa is a nice little girl, he thought. Tory was right—killing a child like her would be the ultimate demonstration of his ideas, the crowning proof in his experimental design.

It was too bad that Tory wouldn't be around after he did it to see how her ideas had once again become reality. And after he'd published his journal articles, she wouldn't be there to join in the acclaim that was sure to follow—and to admit he'd been right all along.

After a quick detour to the desk in the lobby, Michael settled into a deep lounge chair in the dim, cool bar and permitted himself a small smile. In spite of his disappointment in Tory's rejection of his ideas, he couldn't help feeling that everything was going very well.

Zack pulled into a parking slot in front of the Wagon Wheel, got out, and walked through to the pool area. He glanced around but saw no sign of Tory. Backtracking to the front desk, he asked the switchboard operator to ring Ms. Ryan's room.

"I'm sorry, Captain. Mr. Canfield left specific orders not to disturb Ms. Ryan with any calls. She's not feeling well and she wants to get some rest." She saw Zack's frustrated expression and added, "I think he went into the bar, if you want to talk to him."

Zack thanked her. Inside the swinging doors he saw Michael relaxed in a chair, a glass of beer in front of him. Zack walked over. "Mind if I join you?"

On the walkway outside Tory's room, Billy Cassiday, age seven, was chasing his sister Carla, age nine. Suddenly Carla turned around. Her brother barreled into her, and she fell with a thud against Tory's door. "Billy, I'm telling on you," Carla shouted as she got to her feet and raced toward the stairs.

Inside, Tory was jarred almost awake by the children's noise. Why did she feel so groggy? Waking up was like trying to surface from deep water. She shook her head to clear it, but all she got was double vision. Her tongue felt furry, as if she'd taken a bunch of sleeping pills. But before she could pursue that thought, a nagging realization hanging on to the tag ends of her worries thrust itself into her thoughts. There *was* someone else who could have known what she planned to do about the stripper murder—Michael. She had left her notes about the new scene on the kitchen table at home. And he had gone back there to pick up his briefcase. He must have read the first draft.

Tory struggled to maintain consciousness. Michael? What did it matter if he had read her notes? Then she remembered the murders. He was the only person who could have known about the first one in the script and who had not been at the set when it was filmed. But Michael hadn't even arrived in Yuma until the next day, she reminded herself. Who says? her thoughts echoed back. Well, he was with Missy—or at least he brought her down with him. She tried hazily to keep this sequence in focus. Missy often stayed the night with her baby-sitter, Ellen. No one would have known if Michael had taken a plane down here and flown back that same night.

Reluctantly Tory accepted the certainty that was thrusting itself into her consciousness: Michael was the murderer; he'd killed them all.

"My God!" Tory croaked. She tried to get up and succeeded only in rolling with a thud onto the floor. Her arms and legs felt as if they were made of lead, and her body was drenched in icy sweat.

She looked toward the phone, so impossibly far away. She had to get to it. Inch by inch, she struggled toward the long, low table. If only she could grab the cord and pull the telephone to the floor. She reached out her hand. Almost. Next time. Adrenaline pumped through her system. She stretched her arm as far as it would go. Her fingers grasped air and then the cord. She had it! She yanked back with the last of her strength. Waves of nausea washed over her. But she'd done it. The phone slammed to the floor, its receiver falling off on the carpet. "Oh, please, someone answer." Her voice was barely audible. Swirling mists drew her down. She could not fight free of them anymore.

As Tory sank into unconsciousness, the monotonous dial tone of the phone continued to hum in the room.

Zack smiled as he sat down at Michael's table. Just because he was Tory's boyfriend wasn't any reason to be ungracious, Zack thought. "I came here looking for Tory, but the woman at the switchboard tells me she's asleep in her room and can't be disturbed."

Michael nodded seriously. "Yes. She's really depressed and upset about Debra, and I told her she ought to lie down and try to relax. I hope she's sound asleep by this time."

"It's a pretty upsetting case. And I've come up against a dead end, I'm afraid." Zack ordered iced coffee from the hovering waitress and went on, "As long as I'm here, maybe I can pick your brains a little and get the psychologist's slant on the whole business."

Michael laughed shortly. "I doubt if I can help you. We psychologists sometimes don't know as much as we wish we did," he responded, thinking how wrong he'd been about Tory. He'd been sure she was smart enough and open enough to understand. But he'd been mistaken.

"At any rate you know more about psychology than I do," Zack persisted. "You've had training. If you were in my position, what kind of person would you look for?''

Michael heaved a deep sigh. ''We're all looking for someone, something, but it's hard to know if you've really found it. Sometimes I wonder if what I'm looking for really exists.''

Zack's glance expressed both surprise and confusion. This guy seemed totally preoccupied with some problem of his own. Could he and Tory have had a fight? Michael certainly was acting a little off center. Zack tried to steer the conversation back into more practical channels. ''You know these movie types a lot better than I do. I mean, to me they all seem pretty peculiar, but they all seem perfectly sane at the same time. I can't work out which one of them might be crazy enough to kill people.''

Michael gazed at Zack, then looked away. ''What makes you think the person you're looking for is crazy?''

''Maybe that sounds rather simple-minded to a professional, but three murders in one week is crazy—or insane, psychopathic, whatever the right word is.''

Straightening in his chair, Michael stared at Zack, his green eyes boring into the other man's. ''You and Tory would have gotten along perfectly. You think the same way she did, but you're wrong. An individual who kills is as normal as you or me. He's only reacting to the stresses exerted upon him by society and its arbitrary rules. I've done studies that show this is true, but people are trapped in conventional outmoded ideas. They can't adapt to a strong, healthy way of looking at things; they can't accept a mind-set that negates their own. I tried to explain that to Tory, but she was too stubborn to open her mind to me.''

Zack looked at Michael—what was he talking about? He shook his head slightly, then set his half-finished coffee on the table and stood up. "Well, thanks for your help. I'm sorry to have bothered you. Please ask Tory to call me when she wakes up."

Michael stood, too. "Of course. I guess I'd better go and check on my daughter."

Both men left the bar, and as Michael turned toward the pool, Zack walked toward his car, his mind reeling. Michael Canfield's words seemed to have little connection with reality. He'd gotten on a soapbox, but no one was there to listen. If Zack was looking for a crazy person, maybe he'd found one in Canfield.

He opened the door to his car, running through the conversation again in his head. The guy was a fast talker, but some of his ideas were pretty weird. What was it he'd said about Tory? "She was too stubborn to open her mind to me." And before that: "You think the same way she did, but you're wrong." He'd made it clear that Tory hadn't changed her mind. But why had he talked about her in the past tense? Zack froze, one hand on the door, as the whole picture slid into place.

"Jesus Christ!"

He slammed the door and took off across the parking lot, bursting through the front doors. He raced into the lobby and yelled to the astonished desk clerk, "Call a squad car—it's an emergency! And which room is Tory Ryan's? Quick!"

After a moment's hesitation, the clerk blurted, "It's two-oh-seven. Up the stairs on the left, overlooking the pool."

Partway up the stairs, Michael was saying to his daughter, "I'm sorry, Missy, but I think you really do need a nap now.'' He reached for her hand. ''No arguments.''

Pounding footsteps echoed across the patio. Michael turned to look. Then, sweeping the little girl into his arms, he ran with her up the remaining stairs and along the walkway. With his back braced against Tory's door, he snarled, ''Leave her alone!''

''Move aside, Canfield!'' Zack's voice rang with authority.

Michael stood defiantly. ''Stay out of it! It's my experiment!''

Zack stopped a few feet from the other man. ''Don't make things worse than they already are,'' he said evenly. ''Just step away from the door.''

At first he thought it had worked—Michael moved out a little from the door into the middle of the narrow walkway. But before Zack could react, Michael put his hands under his daughter's armpits and held her out in front of him. Her legs dangled close to the railing. ''Back off or she goes over!'' His voice held an edge of hysteria.

Oh, God, Zack thought. Now what do I do? Forcing his voice to stay calm and reasonable, he said carefully, ''Mr. Canfield, there's no need to get a child involved in this. Why don't you just . . .''

As Zack kept talking, another level of his mind ran through the training course for hostage situations he'd taken: Keep them talking, give them time to reconsider, and all that. But he didn't have any time. Who knew what was happening to Tory behind that door? She could be bleeding to death while he stood here.

Michael's eyes never wavered from Zack's, and he still held his daughter out perilously near the railing high above the concrete patio. But Zack thought he detected a trembling in Michael's arms. The man couldn't continue holding a five-year-old child at arm's length forever. But what would he do when the strain became unbearable? He might just toss the child over the rail as a final act of mad defiance.

Zack's quiet voice went on. "I'm not quite clear about what you were telling me earlier, Mr. Canfield. Maybe we could go downstairs and you could explain it to me a little more—"

"Don't patronize me!" Michael spat out the words. He was stretched so tight he seemed ready to break.

"I'm sure we can talk this over and see what the problem is, and then . . ." As he continued to talk, Zack tensed his whole body. He would have only one chance.

With a pantherlike leap, Zack sprang toward the man and the child in front of him. His left arm swung toward Melissa, sweeping her small body out of Michael's grasp and in against the building's wall. She fell and immediately cried out in fear and pain, but neither man heard her.

Uttering an inarticulate scream of rage, Michael lowered his head and charged at Zack, catching him in the midsection. His hands scrambled for Zack's holstered gun. Off-balance, Zack shoved hard with his hip and shoulder. The force of the shove should merely have knocked Michael down, but in the narrow space, his own momentum was enough to topple him over the low railing to the concrete below.

Steadying himself with his hands on the railing, Zack glanced quickly at the patio. Michael lay motionless where he had fallen. People were gathering excitedly around him and someone was yelling for an ambulance.

Zack took a deep breath and stepped toward the door

of Tory's room. He slammed his heel into it below the knob. Once, twice, and it crashed open. He rushed inside. Where was she? The beds were empty. Then he spotted Tory's unconscious body sprawled on the floor between them.

"Tory!" He moved quickly to her side. Thank God she was still breathing. He gathered her up and lifted her gently in his arms. Outside, he could hear someone talking to Melissa and the sirens of an approaching ambulance.

Chapter 17

Zack opened the door of Tory's hospital room slowly and poked his head cautiously inside. But Tory wasn't asleep; she was sitting up in the bed, staring out the window. She glanced at him and clicked off the TV.

"Come on in—I'm awake."

He smiled, but as he walked toward the bed, he saw that her face looked wan and there were dark shadows under her eyes. Awkwardly he thrust a colorful bouquet of spring flowers into her hands. "I thought you might need a little cheering up."

"Oh, Zack, they're lovely. Thank you."

He glanced around the room, which looked like a florist's display. Julie had pulled out all the stops, and there were long-stemmed roses everywhere, along with a huge pot of flowering hyacinths. "I guess I'm carrying coals to Newcastle."

"Oh, no. I love these daisies and daffodils. They're real garden flowers. Let's see . . ." She looked around, then stood the cheerful yellow and white blooms in the water pitcher on her bedside stand.

Zack stood near the foot of the bed. "I'm glad you like them." He went on somewhat formally, "I'm happy to see you're doing okay. The doctor says he's letting you out of here today."

"Yes. I'm just waiting for them to come around and do their final round of blood tests or whatever they have in mind. After that I'm a free woman," she said with forced lightness.

"Well, that's good news."

There was a silence between them. Then Tory said quietly, "Michael's dead, isn't he?"

"Yes, he is. He died early this morning in the operating room." Zack stared at the floor. "I'm sorry, Tory."

"That's what you came here to tell me, isn't it?" She gazed unseeingly toward the brilliant blue sky outside. "At least he avoided what he feared most—being locked up in an asylum like his mother." She looked straight at Zack. "There's no doubt that he killed those people, is there?"

"No, I'm afraid not." He raised his eyes to meet hers. "We're still checking things out, but it looks as if he arranged the whole thing."

"And he tried to kill me, too, didn't he?" Tory asked. Zack nodded soberly. "But why?" Her voice was anguished.

"I don't know," Zack said slowly. "But when I talked to him, right before I found you, he seemed to feel that you didn't understand or accept his ideas. And he said something about an experiment."

Tory shook with horror. "That's what it was—an experiment," she whispered. Staring at Zack, she went on, "He wanted me to believe that killers are normal people, that they aren't crazy. He pointed out that I'm a normal person and yet I came up with the murders in my script. He was sure that he was normal, too, and so by enacting the murders in my script, he meant to show me that, since we were both normal, the killings must be the acts of a normal person and not someone who was insane.'' Her eyes were questioning. ''Does that make any sense?''

''Not really. But that's probably as much as we'll ever understand about it.''

Tears were sliding slowly down Tory's cheeks. ''Those poor people.. I feel responsible. How could I not have known?''

Taking her hand, Zack said firmly, ''Tory, listen to me. You can't blame yourself. There's no way you could have known. These charming psychopaths can fool everyone, including their own families and often their psychiatrists.'' He tilted her chin so that she was forced to meet his eyes. ''I know it's hard to find out that someone you cared for wasn't what you thought. But it wasn't you that was crazy—it was Michael.''

Tory wiped her eyes. Then suddenly she asked, ''What about Melissa? My God, what's going to happen to her?''

''That's one of the things I needed to ask you,'' Zack told her. ''I don't know who to get in touch with. For the time being she's at my house. We couldn't see putting her in foster care down here for just a few days. The poor kid will have enough to deal with without that. And my housekeeper Juanita is a warm, motherly person. I figured she'd do more for Melissa right now than anyone else I could think of.''

''That's the terrible thing—there isn't anyone else. Michael had no family and Melissa's mother died four years ago. Actually, she committed suicide.''

"Yes, I know," Zack said quietly.

Tory looked at him in dawning horror. "She dissolved some pills in her tea, didn't she? Oh, my God, it's the same . . ."

He nodded, grasping her hand more firmly in his. "I'm afraid it looks that way."

"Poor Missy," Tory whispered. "What an awful thing for her to grow up with." She paused, then said slowly, "Maybe I could . . ."

As her tears welled up again, Zack said, "Well, she's fine where she is for now. I'm sure something can be worked out—"

He broke off as a young doctor breezed into the room. "Well, Ms. Ryan, it looks like we won't be able to keep you here much longer. You'll have to give up that bed to someone else." His voice changed as he noticed her tearstained face. "Hey, you're not going to fall apart on me, are you?" He turned to Zack. "Captain, can't you help this young lady recuperate? She needs some relaxation in pleasant surroundings. A hospital room isn't quite the right atmosphere." Glancing at his chart, he said to Tory, "As far as I'm concerned, you can leave any time. Just take it easy for a while. You've been through a lot."

"Okay." Tory nodded, and the doctor hurried out. She looked at Zack. "Looks like they're kicking me out," she said with an attempt at a smile. "My God, I haven't even thanked you for saving my life. It's just . . . the whole thing is hard to deal with."

"I know," he said gently.

"Well." Tory sighed. "I guess I'd better pull myself together and get out of here."

He looked at her, his expression hard to decipher. "I

suppose you'll be heading back to L.A. as soon as you can?''

"I guess so." Tory sighed again. "But I've got my car here, and I don't really feel like driving back alone right now. Maybe I'll wait until they're finished shooting and see if Sally or somebody will drive back with me." She leaned back as the silent tears once again slid down her cheeks. "I don't know who I'm crying for," she said shakily. "Michael—or Debra and those other innocent people. Or maybe for myself."

Zack moved to her side and covered her hands with his. "Tory," he said impulsively, "come home and stay with me." He saw her wary look. "You can't go back to that motel room. I have a huge house, and you can stay as long as you like."

Tory gazed into his clear gray eyes. It sounded so safe. And he was right: She cringed at the thought of returning to the Wagon Wheel Inn and fending off everyone's well-meaning questions and comments. Maybe a little quiet solitude here in this seemingly endless desert was what she needed to begin to heal. But could she impose on the generosity of a virtual stranger and expect him to take care of her? Shouldn't she stand on her own two feet? And then there was Melissa.

Zack saw the confusion on Tory's face. "It'll be all right," he said gently. "We'll just take it one day at a time."

An hour later he drove up the winding driveway and drew to a stop in front of his house. The thick old adobe walls promised cool shelter from the blazing Arizona sun, and the casement windows stood open to the soft breeze that rustled the drooping mimosas. As she got out of Zack's car, Tory felt welcomed by the rustic Spanish charm of the rambling hacienda.